Is That An Aura of Wild Magic Engulfing You, Or Are You Just Pleased To See Me?

Michael Coolwood

Coolwood Books

Citation

The explanation of disabled time that Laceco gives to Rikolta in Chapter Eleven is adapted from Ellen Samuels article 'Six Ways of Looking at Crip Time', published in Disability Studies Quarterly.

Preface

In 2012, I played a game set in a school for disabled teens. I loved it. I lost myself in it. Feelings were felt. This was before I knew about any of my disabilities, so I didn't understand why I was so drawn to the game.

I never played a game like that again. Never read a book like it, or saw a film like it. Every time I found a game, or book, or film with disabled characters their disabilities were always *exceptional*. The disabled characters were always outnumbered by the not-disabled ten to one. The characters lived in an ablest world, rather than a world designed for them.

I longed for a book where disability was everywhere. Where disability was normal. Where disability was challenging, and everyone understood that it was challenging, but it didn't define every moment of every day for the characters. I longed for a book where disability wasn't the focus of the story, because whilst disability often impacts every aspect of our lives, it doesn't define our lives. We have a lot going on in our lives beyond our disabilities. This book is the result of that longing.

Chapter One

For everyone else I knew, it was simply the Telegram Flu. For me, it was a catalyst. It brought me everything I'd never known I'd wanted. Eventually.

The manifestation in front of me resolved, freeing me from the last of my obligations. I pulled myself together, stood in three or four halting, juddering motions, and staggered out into the crisp autumn air.

The circus was packing up, preparing to move on to the next town. I dropped down to the mud slick which might once have been a grassy field, and felt about under my caravan's deck for the sack I'd stashed there two days before, when I'd made my decision to run away from the circus. I couldn't have left back then because the manifestation hadn't resolved.

Burly men hauled on ropes whilst burly women chased children. The arbitrary divide still felt natural, despite my time away. The one reason I was glad to leave, getting away from the bizarre features of my homeland, that the circus had dragged with them to Akoma.

I walked with purpose, leaving the mud, then the grass, then the rising undergrowth behind. No-one tried to stop me. Everyone was too busy disassembling tents or trying to prevent children from being crushed by people disassembling tents. The undergrowth became a wood and then the wood became a forest.

The midday sun and the relative position of both moons gave me a heading. The walk was already burning through what little energy I had, but I settled in for the longest of long hauls. Maybe I could have stopped once I'd reached the deepest, darkest part of the forest, away from the animal sets and reality-warped knells where magic had taken a liking to some rock or stump, but I didn't stop. My circus... my old circus had pitched near to a farmstead, and we weren't far from the Ember Trail, so I couldn't be sure my curse wouldn't draw people from the farmstead in. I needed to get as far away from people, from civilisation as I could. I wouldn't let my curse strike anyone ever again.

They say that if you cross the Ember Trail—cross, rather than travel its winding length—you will be cursed. I, the first child of the newly free circus, crossed it seven times before I could even walk. My people were ignorant of Akoma's traditions and might well have sneered at the superstition. '*Something, something, curses aren't real, something, something*' they'd have said. Well, it might have taken a while to bite, but after twelve manifestations over eighteen months, I considered my curse pretty well established. It was time to get away from my victims and make sure I could live a life free of guilt.

I left the forest behind just as the sun was setting. Camping near a shimmering creek, I revelled in the birdsong, the wind in the willows and the total lack of human activity. The next day, I reached the lowest slopes of Mount Iwa. The day after that, I found a plateau overlooking the Ember Trail. The trail's eponymous embers glowed. Soft amber and gold winding away to the horizon.

My legs ached from scrambling up slopes, my lips were cracking from the dry air, and I was on the edge of falling apart again. And... I was alone on the plateau. I let myself go, watching the shimmering embers, my cheek resting on smooth shale.

I'd planned to make a home for myself on the summit of mount Iwa – the furthest point from civilisation I could reach. Given it had taken me two days to reach my plateau and I was barely a third of the way to the summit, that romantic idyll was something I'd have to let go. The plateau was surrounded by conifers, I'd found a stream whilst foraging, and I hadn't seen any recent bear droppings all day. I'd make this plateau my home, at least for now.

When explorers from Oro had blundered into some other country as if they owned the place, and then started planting flags to behave as though they *did* own the place, they often named plateaus such as this, as if such places didn't already have names. Maybe one day I'd learn what the plateau's name was, if I stayed. I pulled myself back together, and set about making camp.

It took me a week to decide that the plateau was, indeed, perfect, and another two for me to find and fell enough wood to build a shack. Fatigue nipped at my heels as I worked. I'd neglected to bring nails with me, so I had to fall back on years' old joinery lessons to get my shack into shape. Getting the pitched roof right took another full week – a sign I'd been far too enthusiastic with the size of my shack. I should probably have made something the size of a single caravan room, or a hospital bunk.

The night after I'd finished my roof was my first night of truly refreshing sleep since the manifestations had started. Not wanting to waste momentum, I built up stores, found more wood for the upcoming winter, and experimented with making moonshine. The experiments left me temporarily blind.

The next morning, a silken siren song tugged at me, the sensation cutting through my hangover. The terribly familiar silent tune must have been building for days. I hummed to myself and tried to perform whatever task I was involved in louder than before. I wouldn't give in. I wouldn't give in.

Six weeks after running away from the circus, an enormous cavalcade of caravans rumbled down the Ember Trail. Tiny figures pitched camp next to the farmstead my circus had visited. The magic tugged at me as it silently sang. I hid in my shack – a blanket wrapped around my head to keep the noise out.

The following morning, I woke up, finding my bed significantly less comfortable than I was used to. I'd been quite proud of the bed I'd built – a wooden frame with part of my old tent canvas stretched across to make a rudimentary mattress. The surface under me was biting cold. It felt as if I was lying on bare rock. I felt about blearily. The surface I was lying on was either smooth stone or rough ice. I opened my eyes. I was lying on the ground. I'd surely have woken up if I'd fallen out of bed? My bed was...

My bed was where I'd left it, in a corner of the shack opposite the door. It seemed to be occupied. I hadn't heard or seen any people near my plateau the entire time I'd been here, and I couldn't believe a brown bear would have been so polite as to lift me out of my bed and take my place, all without waking me.

The figure in my bed shifted, and then sat up, tugging her scraggly blonde hair from in front of her eyes. She stared about, blearily. Deep pits lurked under her eyes, and the right side of her neck burned a raw red. Eventually, her gaze came to rest on me.

She had to be a woodland spirit. That was the only explanation. Except... I could no longer feel the magic tugging at me. If it had given up on trying to get *me* to move...

I screamed. She screamed right back. I scrabbled away from her until the back of my head thunked into the wall of my shack. She, for her part, scrambled into a corner of the shack, dragging my bedroll with her, holding it up as if it were a protective screen.

I ran out of breath. The silence gave me a moment to think. I clenched my fists, and shouted, "Get out!" She shouted something at the same time, but her words were lost in mine. "You're in terrible danger! You have to get out!" Again, she shouted at the same time, but her words felt like echoes of mine.

She glanced from me to the door, and bolted past me. I heard her crashing through the trees beyond. I counted to a hundred before peering out after her. She'd gone – a trail of trampled bushes and snapped branches marking her passage. She'd thoughtfully thrown my bedroll aside at the tree line. Retrieving it, I returned to my shack and began to give some serious thought to panicking.

Having strange femmes wake up in my bed was entirely unprecedented, although my sleeping on the floor wasn't. I hadn't been drinking last night had I? I didn't think so but... I did a quick search of my camp for evidence of boozing. My moonshine still was pretty full. Besides, if I'd been drinking, my eyes would have crusted shut and I'd be experiencing serious bladder control issues.

Magic sinking into people and places was known fact – part of life. Magic sinking into people who then caused magical effects in others around them? That was more folklore. I personally knew it happened, and had happened twelve times before, but such magic is by definition sneaky and duplicitous and resists scientific study as a result. I was alone with this condition, although I shared my ignorance with the rest of the world.

My hands shook as I built my fire that evening. "It's the cold," I said from behind the knobbly wool of my scarf, "it's the Month of Veils, of course you're cold. You should be putting your gloves on rather than grumbling about it." My gloves were in my pack. I didn't put them on.

It turned out that worrying that your magical curse might have dragged a stranger into your mess can interfere with your sleep a little. I was awake long after sundown. Lying in bed, wrapped in every scrap of material I'd brought with me. Still shivering.

Sleep rose around me eventually, a tide whose rise I welcomed – although I tried not to think about it too hard, lest it notice my attention and get stage fright. What felt like minutes later, I shifted and found the surface under me uncomfortable. Unforgiving. I wriggled a hand out of my cloth cocoon. Stone. I was lying on the floor. I held my breath. Over the pounding of my heartbeat, ghost breaths whispered from the darkness.

My teeth ground together and my eyes reflexively clenched shut. I rose, bringing my bedclothes with me and slunk from my shack like an embarrassed lover. The first flutters of crimson were showing at the horizon so I collapsed onto the log I'd positioned next to my fire pit, and shivered, angrily.

Was it the same femme from yesterday in my bed? I'd worked hard on that bed. Pretty hard. As hard as I'd been able to work, given the circumstances. All I'd been focussed on when I'd seen her yesterday was making sure she got away from me with all possible speed. If it was indeed the same femme, then I might have been too late.

Closing my eyes, I breathed. The ground lay solid under my boots. I wriggled my toes, a delightful dullness ran through my feet. The first promise of a breeze brushed against my cheek. A little way into the woods, there was a curtailed squeak as something with claws met something without. My shirt was sticking to my back and my armpits felt revoltingly clammy – I'd need to bathe today. The sensation of magic tugging at me, attempting to draw me back to civilisation so the manifestations could continue, was notable by its absence.

I slumped, sighing. I caught my head as it fell forward and cradled it in my palms. I couldn't do this again. I was too tired. Medically exhausted. Post-Viral Fatigue they called it. The condition had ruined the back half of my teens and I'd spent most of my early twenties in hospital as I recovered. It should have just been the Telegram Flu. For most people it was. It left a little present behind inside me – along with maybe two percent of other infected.

As dawn rolled inevitably on, I drew water from the nearby stream, set a fire and hung my kettle over the flames. The intruder in my cabin snored. I wondered if I should wake her, but an oozing discharge from the wall of my shack caught my attention.

Mould had sprung from the logs overnight. A malignant yellow which bloomed into clusters here and there, oozing white pus. The stone under the logs was taking on the same hues – the grey shale infected with sickly yellow.

My eyes widened and I looked down at myself, convinced I was about to see pallid, yellow flesh where a healthy golden brown should have been. Hands fine. Forearms fine. I peered down the front of my shirt – seemed fine.

I tossed a fallen stick at the warped ground. The stick landed with a light *clack-a-lack*, before lying still. Unchanging. Still no movement from inside the shack. I breathed, scraping my energy back together.

Fifteen minutes later, I hauled myself to my feet, approached the yellowing, mould-ridden shale by my shack's wall, and squatted down to peer at it. The infection had spread a little way out to the surrounding stone since I'd last looked. Gingerly, I poked at it. The rough texture remained, but the surface gave under my touch as if It was a rotten tomato. I whipped my hand back reflexively, and dashed to the stream to wash the mould from my fingers.

The femme in my bed was still snoring when I returned. Was she okay? "Er," I called, a hairline crack breaking the sound, "are you all right in there?"

The lump of bedding stirred. An arm thrashed about, before finding the bare stone floor. An indistinct maelstrom of clothing and blonde haystack hair burst from the bed, before freezing, glancing about and then making a break for the door. She found me standing in the doorway. She was definitely the same femme from last time.

"You have to get away from me," she rasped.

"Why?" I pointed down at the rot. "Are you doing that?"

She bared her teeth, "Yes. And it'll happen to you too. Move."

"That's not how..."

"I said move!"

She said move, so I moved – stepping out of the doorway. She sprinted past me, making for the tree line.

It would have been nice to be able to run after her – to explain that she couldn't outrun what we were both caught up in, but my legs could barely move as it was. My muscles felt as if some sadist had coated them in iron during the night – heavy, dragging me down. "Wait!" I called after the rapidly disappearing thatched hurricane. "You're caught up in a magical manifestation! It's going to keep dragging you back here until we find a way to fix it!"

Thrashing foliage and cracking branches answered, then a hissss. I whirled round – the kettle was boiling over into my fire. I rescued one, thus rescuing the other, and made tea. I felt an itch deep within me for the rest of the day. The can I'd been using to transport water from the stream sprung a leak. When I set out to bathe, I managed to drop half of my soap in some animal droppings. The air felt heavy with the magic's silent song.

I struggled to sleep that night. My bushcraft bed had never been comfortable, exactly, but that night I could feel every gnarled knot where I'd been sloppy pruning twigs. Every lump and slight curve in the wood dug into my back, then my side, then my front, and then my back again.

Long after sundown, having failed to sleep for hours, an idea struck me. The femme always showed up as I slept. What if I didn't sleep? Would she still appear? It wasn't a strategy that could work in the long-term but it was worth an experiment or two.

I lit a small fire by the entrance to my shack and huddled by it, re-reading one of the two novels I'd brought with me by the flickering firelight. Focusing on the words was hard. The light jumped and danced, twisted, and tumbled. I turned page after page as the book grew heavier in my hands.

My eyes fluttered for one brief moment... and then the air was freezing cold – my fire had gone out. Grey light crept through the doorway, illuminating the figure sleeping in my bed. I sighed and knocked my head against the shack wall a few times.

The intruder didn't stir as the light outside brightened. I closed my eyes and counted to ten, trying to block out the jealousy rising within me. Finally, when I found myself drifting off to sleep again, I shook my head, stood, cracked my knuckles, and prodded the femme in my bed.

She opened her eyes, and stared up at me in alarm.

"Get up," I said. "We need to talk."

Chapter Two

She scrambled to the corner of the bed, but I was already heading outside to get a fire started. The sky was milky blue, rolling clouds bore the last of yesterday's rain over the horizon. I set to work with my tinderbox.

Footsteps – light and hesitant. "Do you know what's going on?" Her voice had blades – as many facing in as out.

"Not exactly," I said, as my kindling caught. "Broad strokes only. What do I call you?"

"You... but... there's terrible... Ven. Call me Ven. Look, you're in serious danger. The world around me turns toxic – you've seen it, right? Your cabin... even the ground underneath. It's spreading to you too."

It was? Crap. I turned to see where she was looking – not meeting my eyes. Lower. Greasy mould had spread up the cloth covering my right leg – the side I'd slept on closest to her. "Ah. How long's that been going on?"

Ven glared at me. I poked at the fire. It crackled and spat, the flames dancing to their own music – a repeating pattern I couldn't follow.

Emerald cores shimmered above the wood before rising, blending into amber flames and then spinning off into the world as vapour and smoke.

"You're going to die if you don't get away from here," said Ven. The blades in her voice grinding inwards.

"Well, that's a problem," I said, hanging the kettle above the delighted flames. "I can't leave. No way I'll be in a fit state to travel for another week or so."

Her accent was Akoman. She probably knew what I was saying – yes, her lips had pulled back a little. Her gaze scanned for signs of missing limbs or other obvious malady. "Ah," she said, wrenching her gaze to meet mine before it skittered away.

"Post-Viral Fatigue," I said, collapsing down onto a log and wincing as the sodden wood immediately soaked through the seat of my trousers. "Can't move about much – getting up here damn near killed me."

"If you stay, you'll die."

"If I leave, I'll die." The lie felt hollow and obvious, but she didn't seem to notice.

She turned and stared down at the cavalcade on the Trail below. "Fuck."

I shrugged. "I've got some rabbit left over that we can have for breakfast if you're hungry."

She grimaced, but didn't say anything.

"Chestnuts and buttercress? I haven't been able to lay down any crops. Might not be able to until spring now. Left coming up here a bit late. Delays, you know how it is."

"Chestnuts?"

"Very nice if you cook them right."

"Who the fuck are you?" The blades in her voice unfurled.

I set some chestnuts cooking before bowing to my companion. "My name is Laceco. You know they say people who cross the Ember Trail are cursed?"

"Folklore."

"Maybe. My people didn't know about the curse, or they didn't believe it. Since the Telegram Flu, wild magic manifestations have struck people I meet. I came up here to keep people safe from the magic swirling around me. Then you came – I'm guessing you didn't intend to wake up in my cabin."

"Last three nights I've gone to sleep in my caravan."

"Which Cavalcade?"

"Ember Shrine. That one down there."

I puffed out my cheeks and let my breath flicker the flames of my fire. "That's why the cavalcade is so big. I've never seen it before – nice place?"

"No idea – might have been nice before I arrived. Place is currently a mire of rot and decay – all of it centred on my caravan."

"Death count?"

"Only illness so far – none fallen."

I poked at the chestnuts before retrieving a couple and handing them over. "That's good then."

She threw up her hands. "Why is *everyone* like this?"

That jerked me out of my... well, it might have been a sulk. "No-one's taking this effect you're creating seriously?"

"No! They don't even seem to understand what I'm saying. Half of the cavalcade is being drawn into a sickly green morass and no-one's doing anything about it – they don't even see it! Do you see it?"

The walls of my cabin looked as if the mould and its oozing white pus had consumed all its structural integrity – it looked as if it could collapse in a stiff breeze. "I see it."

"And yet you're still as fucking calm as my fucking boyfriend's fucking mother."

I scratched my head. "Who's your fucking boyfriend's fucking mother?"

"Priestess of the Ember Shrine."

"Can *she* see the... whatever you're calling this effect?"

"No!"

"Interesting..." I pulled the kettle down from its hook and set about making tea. "Look, I don't particularly want to die up here, and I'm sure you'd rather your cavalcade wasn't being drawn into a toxic morass, so what have you tried to resolve the effect?"

"What... how..."

"You're right, sorry, I was getting ahead of myself. How long has this effect been happening around you?"

"Couple of weeks? Not sure – it took me a while to notice."

"The Cavalcade must have been a hundred kilometres or so away from me two weeks ago. Did you ever cross the Ember Trail, Ven?"

Her shoulders jerked upwards before settling back.

"Well I know my curse has been acting up since I started hiding up here. Still... I might have misunderstood..." A golden trail spun out before me – questions leading to further questions, and so on and on.

Sages spent their entire lives trying to understand why magic settled into the people and places it chose – trying to understand the motivation behind seemingly random effects. I shook my head. My fatigue was sucking the marrow out of my bones and that was making me feel woozy. I'd got distracted. "Sorry, Ven. Did you say something?"

"I asked if you were all right."

I looked at her. She'd stepped closer and was staring at me. Her expression seemed familiar but I couldn't place it. An eyebrow raised. She was standing... there was something... "Yes, I'm fine. You okay?"

Ven rolled her eyes. "No. That's the point."

I made the tea whilst Ven stomped into the woods for reasons she refused to elaborate on. When she returned, she accepted a mug of tea before pinning me to the spot with a glare. "So. Can you sleep somewhere else tonight? Even if it's a few meters away – not in your cabin."

"Nope."

"Why not, you unhelpful twat?"

"The tent I used on the way up here is currently an integral part of the cabin's roof. Besides, it's only a one person tent. If the magic is bringing you to me, rather than that point specifically, it might bump me out of the tent."

"And you don't like the idea of being shoved outside into the undergrowth, rain, and furious territorial wild boars?"

"I do not."

She frowned. "You can tell you're not a local – an Akoman would have jumped at such a proposition."

I frowned. That didn't match with... oh. Belatedly, I laughed. She rolled her eyes. "All right, I'll get back down to my cavalcade and see if I can borrow a good sized tent from someone. If I go to sleep with it hopefully it'll come with me if I get zooshed to your cabin again."

"Zooshed?"

She waved this away. "Why *you* anyway? Oh yes, you're cursed. I forgot. But surely hundreds of people crossed the Ember Trail, why you specifically?"

That wasn't a question I'd considered before. Deep within my brain, a tired octogenarian stumbled towards the massive crank which she needed to turn in order to get my thoughts into gear. She heaved at the crank, which only moved a quarter turn, then a half turn before stopping. The octogenarian rested against the immobile crank, panting. I blinked a few times – maybe I was hoping doing so would clear the fatigue.

"Don't worry," Ven said, a hint of warmth in her tone, "invisible disabilities are the worst."

She had... I mean obviously... there was gossip about the Ember Shrine's Cavalcade. How could I pull that sentence together... there must...

Hands on my shoulders. The world swam into focus. Yawning nothingness in my head. Stopping me thinking. Ven gently guided me to a log – eased me back. Dry – the log was dry. I looked down. Ven had spread a jumper across the log for me to sit on. A tsunami of gratitude roared through me but I still couldn't line any words up to offer thanks.

"Will you be okay if I get going? I'm getting pretty good at falling down this mountain but it takes a while, and if I'm going to get us another tent..."

Single word answers – I could do a single word. "Yes," I said. Inadequate. Barely an answer.

"I'll try and bring some food, too."

What was she saying about my cooking? Might be an objection to my supplies I suppose.

"We'll get this figured out," she said. "Maybe get some sleep whilst you can. Need a hand?"

She helped me into my bed. I didn't even hear her leave. I was in pieces for hours after she left. It wasn't just the fatigue. My body was a mess of knotting innards and contracting bones. My head... swirled. Few coherent thoughts longer than a few sentences were able to rip free from the clinging web of fatigue.

I should have stayed at the circus. But then, if Ven had joined me there the entire place would be sinking into toxicity. The air in my shack was thick with the scent of decay, but I only noticed after stumbling outside to attend to some business behind a tree. On my return, bleary eyed and still on the verge of collapse, I felt the ground sink underneath me, the solid rock feeling spongy and slick.

At least I wasn't coughing – whatever mould spores or toxins that must have been saturating the air didn't interfere as I wolfed down what little remained in my dry store before returning to bed.

I was going to die on this mountain. I might have been able to make it through the winter if the damned wild magic hadn't intruded. Even if I could climb back down the mountain to the Ember Cavalcade and seek sanctuary there, that would mean the manifestations would restart... but they'd restarted anyway. Ah well, a moot point.

The next morning, I woke up with dawn already long past. I shifted – something was wrong. No, not wrong. Different. I was in my bed, rather than on the ground. Had the magic relented? Realised it had pushed me far too far? About time.

My limbs were too heavy to move. It felt as if my blood was syrup, sluggishly crawling through my circulatory system. Weighing me down. I was amazed the slats of my makeshift bed hadn't collapsed.

Outside, something moved. It was hard to tell exactly what – the view through my doorway was obscured by the Morning sun's glare. Nevertheless, through that glare something moved – gentle and slow. Flowing as if following internal music. Almost certainly not a bear, unless Mount Iwa's bears were significantly more contemplative and balletic than I'd hitherto given them credit for.

Part of me was being lulled by the gentle motion – a silent lullaby. If I could sleep for a week my fatigue would fade enough for me to reset and restart. Of course, I'd starve before that, which was inconvenient but there was little that I could do about that. Annoyingly, other parts of me were needling me, keeping me awake. There could be danger outside. Bandits or something. An odd notion given that Akoma didn't really have bandits. It had occasional bands of guerrillas sponsored by Oro or another neighbour but if they'd found me I was dead anyway, if Ven's toxin didn't get me first.

That thought made me squint down at the bits of me currently visible. I was covered in cloying white mould. My throat clenched tight, a gagging sensation which only relented when my lungs started to burn and I realised I'd been holding my breath. I coughed, expecting flurries of spores to fly into the morning air – thankfully only air emerged.

"Laceco? Are you awake?" Ven's voice. But I hadn't woken on the floor. What?

I coughed again, less of a wretch this time. "Yeah. You okay Ven?"

"Woke up on your floor. The toxicity has spread to the forest around your cabin. You gotta get out of there."

Groaning, I pulled myself together, rose shakily from my bed and stumbled outside. Ven stepped back as I emerged from my chrysalis. I half expected her to take my elbow and support me on my long, winding path to the logs lurking at the periphery of the fireplace. She maintained a respectful distance, which prompted a frown.

"Are you a doctor?" I asked, once spots stopped swirling in my vision.

"What? No."

I squinted at her but couldn't quite work out what was strange about the way she was acting. Shrugging, I warmed my hands at the fire, only mildly surprised to see the kettle hanging over the flames.

Ven sat on the next log, leant back, and glared up at the crumpling clouds. "You said you'd seen manifestations like this before?"

"Twelve at the last count."

She sighed, closed her eyes and seemed to relax – or maybe she was giving up in the face of the will of the wild magic. "How can I stop it?"

Onus the Dyad had tried to stop it. Wile the Disappearing had tried to stop it. We'd nearly been too late. I opened my mouth and surprised myself when I didn't start talking. Instead of a quick, insightful and very slightly spikey explanation of how to deal with manifestations there was only void.

I needed to go back to bed. Not my bushcraft bed in my drafty, leaky cabin. A proper bed on a cavalcade. This was the longest I'd ever been in one place if you didn't count hospital. Personally, I didn't. That had been statis. Dead time.

Ven shifted on her log, "You don't have to tell me if things are too hard right now."

That jerked me to life. "Look, what's going on? How are... why are you talking like a doctor?"

She frowned, an adorable v appearing between her eyes, "I'm n ot... Ah." She nodded, her expression clearing. "Sorry, I forgot. The Ember Cavalcade... it's mostly for people like us. We don't have many not-yet-disabled people in the place. I haven't been there long but the habits have sunk in. We all have days like the one you're having now. I get it, that's why I don't need an answer right now, but I'd like one soon."

I tried to fit the words she'd used into my head but I felt like a toddler trying to jam a green square into the hole meant for a red triangle. Still, if she did understand... I slumped sideways, and then onto my back so I was lying on my log, staring up at the clouds. "Okay," I said, closing my eyes and enjoying the heat of the fire on my left cheek. "Right. So. You can't stop your manifestation."

"I'm going to be like this forever?"

"Sorry, I said the wrong thing. You can't set out to stop your manifestation – tackle it head on. The magic seeks out people who want to make some sort of change, conscious or not. The manifestation isn't something you stop, it's something you resolve."

"Okay... how do I *resolve* the fact that I make the world around me toxic?"

I rubbed my palms into my eyes – dark flares burst like fireworks. The Curse of the Ember Trail couldn't have let me know any clearer if it had sent a signed telegram along with a basket of apology snacks. The manifestations weren't going anywhere. Neither was my post-viral fatigue. I could end things right now – roll off the ledge on which I'd built my cabin and crack my head on the rocks a few hundred meters below. It'd be preferable to a creeping death thanks to the poison Ven was creating. Or I could accept life as it was, not as I wanted it to be. Didn't mean I couldn't try and change things here and there...

"All right," I said. "There are proper ways of doing this but I can't think straight. Okay. Simple way to start – can you let the rot or whatever it is flow out of you and into something else? A rock or something. Toxic rock."

A breeze tickled my cheek and tossed my hair across my face. Fallen leaves rustled whilst a few danced and tumbled, their two-step shuffle a playful whisper across the stone plateau. I cracked an eye open – Ven had pulled her coat tight around her. She also had a bundle at her feet – no, a pack. She was staring down at her cavalcade.

I closed my eyes again. "You don't want to make a toxic rock?"

The log creaked under her as she shifted. "Is there anything else we can try?"

"Probably, but that's a good place to start. Try to drain whatever it is out of you and into something else which won't harm anyone. I assume that's why you keep being whisked away up here – you don't like this effect being visited on the Ember Cavalcade."

"Yeah, sure, yeah but... The world has been... I really don't like the idea of taking all this and just thoroughly ruining spirits-know how large an area of pristine forest. I've only visited you three times and the entire plateau is already in decay. It wouldn't just be a toxic rock. It'd be an entire toxic forest. A fucking mire. A toxic wasteland which would slaughter animals and fell trees which had grown unhindered for hundreds of years. Fuck that."

The gears which had been ever-so-slowly turning in my head ground together before locking up. That had been my one idea. Still, a smile played across my lips. No idea why – not enough brains. "All right," I said, stretching. "I'll have a think. What's in your pack?"

"Mm? Oh this. Yeah – remember I said I was going to bring a tent? I fell asleep with this pack strapped to my chest."

"Bet your boyfriend loved that."

"Oh he was staying over with his triad."

"His who-how-where-what?"

"Triad. Stable triad."

"Stop saying 'triad', I don't know what 'triad' means."

"You're from Oro, aren't you? Accent should have been a clue. Rikolta's dating me, and he's also dating two other people, who are also dating each other. Three people dating each other. Triad."

The gears in my head continued grinding together, the noise blotting out any reaction I might have otherwise had. "Right. Gotcha," I said, hoping what Ven had said would make more sense to me later. "Well, thanks – the tent is for me?"

"No, it's for another fucking hermit I know. She's two plateaus down, you'd like her, only speaks in riddles and cries when she sees the colour blue. Makes looking at the sky tricky. She has special goggles."

I cracked an eye open and took in her expression – knotted brow, tight jaw. She was either furious or... "That comeback got away from you didn't it?"

Her frown cracked, revealing the grin beneath. "Yeah, there was more than I expected and then I kept thinking of problems with it and..."

I laughed, rolled over on my log, coughed and laughed again, only to have the whistling kettle interrupt me. Ven shot to her feet but I waved for her to sit back down. "I've got it," I said, the tell-tale creak of fatigue at the periphery of my voice fainter than before. "Well, thank you for bringing a tent."

"And supplies."

"Amazing."

She accepted a mug, blew on the tea and took at tentative sip. She winced, then held out her mug to me. I clanked mine against it. She sighed. "I meant - do you have any cold water?"

"Oh," I said. I grabbed a canteen from the cabin – the leather straps had all but rotted away. I unscrewed the cap and sniffed gingerly at the liquid inside. It didn't seem to have turned. I held it out. "Might be drinkable?"

Ven's lips drew back from her teeth – she inhaled through her grimace. "Best not chance it. Will you be okay to move soon? Would be good to get you out of the pestilence zone as soon as possible."

I began packing some essentials but Ven glared at me until I sat back down. She scraped the mould off the few items I needed and packed them in a separate bag. Before I could properly frame any objections, we set off up the mountain, looking for a non-toxic place to camp.

Chapter Three

Having grown up in a cavalcade, I never quite appreciated hiking before that particular Thursday. It turned out that hiking is a bit like those ink blot tests psychiatrists used to wave at people during the 600s. Hiking, like ink blot tests, revealed information about the people involved. I learned that Ven, for example, was a femme of great character and good humour. She also had a prodigious imagination when it came to the gory and the grotesque.

For her part, Ven learned that when I'm tired I can be what my father always used to call a grumpy-boots. I had a great many things to grumble about on our hike up Mount Iwa. Looking back on it, for Ven it must have been akin to being stuck on a trans-continental rail ride with a stroppy toddler. "Are we nearly there yet - My leg hurts - I need the toilet - Why are we going this way - Watch out for that hole, I nearly fell in it - Where are we going anyway - Spirits, I'm knackered - Fuck me it's hot – This path is too steep – I can feel blisters coming on – If this drizzle turns to rain I'm going to get soaked – Why are you doing this to me – I hate you – I wish you'd never married mum – I wish I'd never been born."

Ven kept up a smile throughout. Possibly she simply enjoyed bearing her teeth. I needed regular rests, and she would fill the time by pointing out interesting features of the surrounding woodland and how she could murder me in any one of them and then be back at the Ember Cavalcade by dusk, with time to wash the blood off her hands on the way down if she felt so inclined.

"See there?" she said as I held my head in my hands, my vision swimming, my lungs heaving. "If I rolled your corpse down that little incline, gravity would do all the hard work for me, and you'd wind up crashing into that thicket between the suggestively shaped boulders. This far up, I don't think your earthly remains would ever be found. By people. All sorts of wildlife would probably you. If a bear found you first she'd probably snack on you for a little and then take a shit in the remains of your chest cavity."

I coughed, trying to suppress a laugh. "Why would a bear do that?"

"Bears are very good judges of character."

My natural inclination was to snark right back at her, but with my brain being smothered by fatigue, the only snark which came to mind in the moment was 'fuck off', which lacked a certain elegance. I settled for groaning piteously.

"Do you actually know where we're going?" I asked, during our fifth rest of the day.

"Why?" Ven asked, stretching her calves out. "Worried I'm trying to lead you unsuspectingly into a trap? Worried that there's an unremembered sect of blood-spirit worshiping fanatics on this mountain? Worried that all they need is the sacrifice of one masc with a bastard of a disability and a bit of a martyr complex, and they'll be able to give their grand blood-leech spirit corporeal form at last? Don't be. They're on a different mountain."

I glowered at her, or at least tried to. Her expression didn't appreciably change.

Ven shrugged. "Please yourself. I asked around about this moumanifestation's toxicity. I smiled. Putting the lack of toxicity together ntain in general, and the area around your camp in specific. No-one from the Ember Shrine knew much, but they pointed me at some nerd in the Obsid University Cavalcade who found a map for me. This stream we're following splits off from a larger source. The spot where it splits sounds like a good place to camp, not least because it has a natural hot spring."

I swayed, my vision blurring as the thought struggled to find a way to settle into my head. "Holy crap, seriously?"

"Yeah."

"I haven't had a warm bath in months."

Ven glared at me. "Hermits are weird." The glare appeared to freeze, though I initially thought it was merely persisting. Her brow furrowed. "I should say, since you brought it up, your cabin smelled strangely... fine. For someone who's been camping on a mountain for... however long you've been up here."

"Two months, one week and... three days? Maybe four. I started losing count when I met you."

"I have that effect on people."

"You make people lose count of things?"

"Shut up. So, why doesn't your cabin smell like my school friend Banna's laundry basket?"

My gaze darted from point to point, completely outside of my control. I wasn't looking at anything, it felt as if my brain was trying to communicate that it was holding up a finger and saying 'hold on, I'll be with you in a second'. "Er," I said, when my mental wheels had done nothing but spin for what felt like several minutes. "I don't know if I understand the question."

Ven smiled at that. She had a nice smile, which is probably why she was loathed to show it. "Why don't you stink?"

I pinched the bridge of my nose. I couldn't work out where the trap in the question was. "Washing?" I said, giving up and blundering into the trap, much as my countrymen had during their numerous attempts to steal land from other people.

"You didn't have a fucking shower in that cabin. I'm sure I would have noticed."

"I had a bucket and a stream. I brought some soap with me and I was trying to work out how to render animal fat but that wasn't going super well. Still have a sliver of soap left thankfully. If you'd showed up a month later I might have let things go a little. Why the interrogation, Ven? Setting me up for something?"

"What?" Ven looked as if she'd been slapped. "No. Fuck off."

She spun and strode up the bank of the stream, pebbles grinding under her boots. "You coming?"

I was no-where near ready but I could borrow some more energy from my future. If Ven could find a hot spring that would make my seclusion vastly more bearable. I pulled myself together and only paused for a moment – the ground near Ven had been standing had grown pale and sallow – the whiff of rotting plant matter soured the air. "Fucksocks," I said, before setting off after Ven.

A faint tinge of sulphur hung in the air when we took our sixth rest. Some sort of aneurism might have been sneaking up on me, but more likely we were downwind of the hot spring. If I asked nicely, Ven would probably help me set up the tent, but then she'd likely bolt for fear of infecting my new spot.

I stretched and yawned. “So, Ven, tell me. When did this whole mess begin for you?”

“What mess?”

“What do you mean ‘what mess?’”

“I can’t think of a better way to phrase the question.”

I bit down on the urge to snap at her. “The toxicity,” I said. “You know. The thing where the area starts to decay if you spend too long in it.”

“Oh,” Ven said. “That.”

I blinked at her. I nodded encouragingly. I waited. I sighed. “Yes. That.”

“Why do you want to know?”

“It might,” I said, “be helpful,” I continued, trying not to sound as if she was getting to me, “in trying to work out what’s causing the issue.”

She stared at me. Her eyes were blue, flecks of gold dancing at the edges of her irises. Wait... I was missing something. Her gaze was steady, the dancing gold the only movement. Was she looking past me rather than maintaining eye contact? Maybe, but there was somethi ng...

“Oh, fine,” she said, throwing up her hands and finally breaking away. "It started around the time Rikolta asked me to move in with him.”

“Doesn’t he live with his two other... people?”

“Sometimes but not always. He’s got a spot by himself, which he lives in for about half the week. He asked me to move in there.”

“And you said... yes?”

Ven nodded. No eye contact now. She was making a close examination of a nearby tree.

“Do you think that has anything to do with your manifestation?”

Ven's eyes flashed, she appeared to be trying to bore a hole in the trunk of her tree using the power of her glare alone. "How the fuck should I know? Yes? You tell me, you're the expert."

I couldn't stop myself – the laugh rose up my throat and out before I could think. Ven rounded on me. I held up my hands. "Sorry, I'm sorry. I just... I love how you're handling it. You're *furious*. Most people who work through a manifestation just want to give up. You're still fighting, and you don't want to sink your manifestation into the world around you. Your boyfriend's a lucky guy. Rikolta was his name?"

Ven shifted from foot to foot, still glaring at me but her intensity wavering. "Yes," she spat, eventually.

"Ok, so. Your manifestation started around the time Rikolta asked you to move in with him. Before he asked you or after?"

Ven folded her arms before breaking her gaze from mine. "After. Pretty much immediately after."

Ah. "Right. Right. Ok. Let me think about this one."

"You ready to move?"

My legs felt weak, and a weight in my chest was dragging me down. "Sure."

The forest thinned as we ascended, which meant more light. I asked Ven if we could stop a few times so I could gather mushrooms, some of which were edible, and one which wasn't *technically* poisonous but you still wouldn't want to eat it unless you had no other option.

I returned to the bank of the stream, where Ven was staring up the mountain. She pointed. "I think that's the spring up there."

"Good," I said, "between you and me I'm close to falling apart."

"Hold together a little longer," she said. "let's get to the spring and then find a spot to set up your tent."

"Your tent."

"I'm lending it to you."

The sulphur smell grew as we climbed, but not to choking levels. Scrambling up a steep incline, we emerged onto a ridge. The stream gushed from a fissure in the rock. It split as it reached the ridge, around half of it continuing down as the stream we'd been following. The other half diverted off to the right in a new channel, following the ridge along before flowing into a natural pool. A broad dalliance of water, nearly perfectly clear. Steam rose from the surface. I dipped a finger in cautiously. Warm but not scalding.

"Is it drinkable?" Ven asked.

"Best not given the stream's there," I said. "Sometimes springs like this are fine but sometimes they can be breeding grounds for bacteria and such. Anyway. Thanks, Ven, this place is amazing. I'll pitch there, if that works?" I took a step, and a wave of fatigue crashed over me. I couldn't hold myself together.

Ven turned to look where I pointed, then turned back and... she *saw* me. Her expression cracked. "Are you okay?"

I'd tried so hard to hold myself together. People always worried if they saw the toll the fatigue had taken on me. I smiled, doing my absolute fucking best to make it seem warm and disarming. "Yes, sorry. Long day."

"You don't need any... help?"

"No, I'll be fine in a minute."

"Sit down, Laceco. I'll pitch the tent." She unslung her pack and unrolled the canvas. She kept her eyes on her work, not staring as I pulled myself back together. She found three long metal poles and started screwing them together. "Did I ever tell you I'm on the autistic spectrum?"

She was trying so, so hard to sound casual. I had to force a reply past the lump in my throat. "No, I don't think so."

"Yeah. Slipped my mind I suppose."

"None of my business, Ven, unless you wanted to tell me."

"Look, I don't know. You're among the first people I've told."

"No-one else knew?"

"Oh, *everyone* where I grew up knew. I just didn't tell them. I told one friend – first friend I made at school. Banna. Not a bad friend in some ways. We liked a lot of the same stuff. Books. Puzzles. Games. Banna introduced me to his friends. '*Hey guys*,' he'd say, '*this is my autistic friend Ven*.'"

"Ah."

"Eh, it wasn't a big deal at first. I worked out quick I could make people laugh. Blunt humour. Shock value. But they never let the autism thing drop, you know? Anything I didn't understand, or any time I didn't like one of their jokes it was always because of the autism." She started hammering tent pegs into the earth at her feet with precise swings of the mallet. "Every new person I met, I was Autistic Ven. I started doing it myself. Took me until moving to a university cavalcade to wake up a little."

"I thought the Ember Cavalcade was supposed to be—"

"I didn't grow up in Ember. Shitty little town just off the trail. Not a drop-kerb in the place, if you follow me."

"How did you wind up at Ember then?"

"Got a placement studying with a choralist there after graduation. Hated the idea of going to... what did Banna call the place... the Disability Ghetto. *Hated* the idea. But I found a place, and I worked on my craft, and I never told anyone about the Autism Spectrum Condition. Turned out I didn't need to. Everyone there got it. They might not know exactly *what* I was being quiet about, but they got it. I met Rikolta. You know what happened there. So, believe me, Laceco, I get it too. I'm really sorry things are so rough for you right now."

I exhaled, some of the fatigue flowed away with my breath. "Thanks, Ven."

"Yeah," she said, driving another tent peg into the ground with a single swing. "No problem."

"Do you think that's what your manifestation is doing?" I asked.

"Mm?"

"It might be... wait..." I frowned.

"What?"

"Sorry, I was about to say that your manifestation could be making Banna's way of seeing you true, sort of. He introduced you to people as this broken person. This... I don't like to speculate about what he thought ASC even *was,* but I bet he indulged in a certain amount of stereotyping."

"Maybe. So what?"

"So I thought your manifestation could have been showing you the world which Banna created when he did what he did. Maybe your manifestation wanted you to see how ridiculous it was that *you* were the source of this toxicity and decay."

"But you don't think that now?"

"No, I've missed something. Unless you think I'm right?"

Ven had her back to me. She fiddled with a guide rope which already seemed perfectly well adjusted. "No, I don't think that's it."

"Damn. Sorry. I'll think about it."

"Get some damn sleep, Laceco. I can work the toxicity stuff out myself. I don't want to make anything worse for you."

"Thanks, Ven. Stay for dinner?"

Ven stood and stretched, still not turning to face me. "Thanks, but I gotta go if I'm going to get back to the Cavalcade by sundown."

"It's a hell of a trek, Ven..."

"Ah, but I won't have you slowing me down. Don't worry, I'll be fine. Get some fucking sleep."

She gave a half wave without turning to face me, and scrambled down the slope. She was lost in the forest within seconds.

When I first snagged the curse of the Ember Trail, I'd thought it was a gift. Those who underwent manifestations emerged stronger. Then, I'd felt the first true bite of post-viral fatigue, and with that came the knowledge of the dark side of the manifestations. The knowledge that something needed to be done, but with a head filled with churning fog, I lacked the faculties to understand *what.*

I stripped, found a route down to the stream, and washed myself, fervently wishing I'd found a route down before taking my clothes off. With the grime of the day sluiced away, I was clean enough for the hot spring. I wanted to fall forwards into the thing, but I was in Akoma and disrespecting Akoman traditions hadn't gone well for me thus far. I stepped in, sat back and closed my eyes.

The water only burned for a few moments. My skin adjusted and I could breathe. Fumes in, fatigue out. Fumes in, fatigue out. My steel-tense muscles began to relax. The weight in my chest lightened ever so slightly with each breath.

Thunder rumbled in the distance. No, that was wrong. The rain was far closer than the thunder. Water splashing intermittently. Not rain at all. Something familiar. Even with the spring draining the fatigue away, my head was still too foggy to wonder about it too much.

Footsteps. Wet slapping of soles against stone. Without thinking, I opened my eyes and turned. Ven was approaching the spring – she'd cleaned herself in preparation just as I had. I froze and had to resist the urge to cover myself. Akomans didn't share my homeland's neurotic approach to being unclothed in certain settings, such as a hot spring.

She stepped into the spring opposite me. She looked as tired as I felt. She swirled a hand across the surface of the water. "I didn't think it was fair that I did all the work and you got to enjoy the spring by yourself. You okay with me being here?"

I smiled, or at least I *hope* I smiled. It might have been more of a grimace. "I'm still getting used to some Akoman customs."

She sighed. "In no way does that answer my question."

"Sorry, sorry. I'm fine with you being here."

She sighed again but this time a smile shone on her face, and she closed her eyes. "Good. I needed this."

I opened my mouth to ask a question, but bit down on it so fast I nearly caught the tip of my tongue between my teeth. I breathed. I relaxed, and I tried to keep my gaze on the water and rocks *around* Ven without keeping an eye on Ven herself.

The distant sounds of thunder dissipated as the sun loped towards the horizon. We must have soaked for well over an hour in companionable silence before Ven rose from the spring and began towelling herself dry.

I steadfastly looked in any other direction but Ven's. The customs around hot springs in Akoma were, honestly, a little confusing. As far as I understood it, nudity was seen as perfectly normal whilst actually bathing but the cleansing beforehand and afterward, as well as the dressing and undressing were seen as far more personal.

Normally it would have been deeply tempting – a beautiful woman in a state of undress nearby. Thankfully, I felt only a flicker of a temptation to peek. Partly because I didn't want to disrespect her, partly because she was in a relationship, so it wasn't as if she'd be sending me signals that she was interested in me or anything, and partly because it gave me the chance to make a closer inspection of the part of the spring Ven had been sitting in.

Both the water and the rocks were perfect, just as they were on my side of the spring. Not a hint of the manifestation's toxicity. I smiled. Putting the lack of toxicity together with the details about herself that Ven had disclosed earlier, I had the beginnings of a theory.

"I'm changed," Ven called. "I left some food for you – rice balls and some pickled vegetables. I'm having some, is that okay?"

"Hell yes, go for it!" I said, my exuberance taking her aback for only a moment.

I climbed out of the spring, washed off under the stream again, dried myself and changed before returning to the campsite, where Ven was staring at the setting sun. She didn't seem to be in a hurry to move. The rock she was sitting on was beginning to turn black, however.

"It's too late for you to climb back down the mountain tonight," I said. "Sleep in the tent with me. I'll be fine."

Ven nodded. A femme from Oro might never have taken such an offer in the spirit in which I meant it. Too many mascs in Oro had hurt too many femmes over too many centuries. The Telegram Flu had been a disease, but the ongoing monstrosity that was Oro's treatment of femmes was an epidemic. A virus handed down from generation to generation. I'd only lived in Oro for a few months but I'd grown up with those who carried the virus – carriers both symptomatic and asymptomatic. That night, as I bedded down next to that magnificent femme, I breathed. I worried about the virus, I came close to panic – what if I did something awful? What if...

I breathed. I rode the wave. Ven trusted me. I had to trust myself too. That said, I would have to fray that trust a little tomorrow, if my theory was correct. If Ven was to resolve her manifestation, she would need to shift her thinking a little. The best way I could think of to do that, was to *epically* piss her off.

Chapter Four

Waking up next to a woman in a tent felt a little surprising. I'd only woken up next to someone in my adult life a few times. Before I caught the Telegram Flu I'd been dating Tiri. He'd stayed over a few times, which had been wonderful until it wasn't. When he'd slept, he'd sprawled on his back, his mouth open and sloughing out a near-constant stream of cute rasping and hiccupping noises.

Ven lay facing me, and I felt unable to actually look at her because it felt like creeping on a femme in her sleep. I squeezed my eyes tight shut and wished that I could remove Oro's viral attitude to femmes from my head with a drill.

Momentary panic fading, I re-opened my eyes. I could be a real child sometimes. Who was I panicking for? Ven? Hardly. Still, I felt *intensely* awkward. Ven's proximity wasn't due to intimacy, only necessity. Her shuffling around during the night had kept waking me, and I'd be willing to bet the quality of her sleep had been crap as well. The canvas shrouding us let through the light of early dawn. Getting back to sleep would have been nice but the tent had been pitched inexpertly – the ground under us uneven. A particularly troublesome rock had been digging into my back for most of the night. I needed to get out.

Only when I pulled back the flap of the tent did the full morning's light stream through. Dawn had long past, so... My head turned with creaking slowness. The walls of the tent were slathered in thick, grey mould which oozed white pus. So thick it had kept the dawn light at bay. I retched, and scrambled outside. The effects of Ven's toxicity were accelerating. I had to help her on her way to resolving her manifestation. I stretched, cracked my neck, and scrambled down the slope next to the stream. It was time to look for some mushrooms.

I hadn't been able to fully appreciate this part of the forest during our hike yesterday. The emerald trees that had engulfed the slopes by my plateau had given way to thinner trees – dark knotted trunks and mint-green needle leaves. A carpet of brown needles softened my footsteps, leaving the ka-ka-kaaaaws of Yunin Birds the only disturbances in the still morning.

Ven had seen my stores previously. I didn't know if she knew much about mushrooms, but I needed to gather a variety with specific properties, just in case she was secretly a mycologist. *'No mushrooms with white gills, no red mushrooms, no ridged stems. You listening to me, Laceco?'* my dad's voice echoed in my head. One of the memories of that strange time that still made me smile.

It took me nearly an hour of stalking the forest, keeping my eyes low so I could spot my fungal prey, before I found what I was looking for. Their caps were red with white spots, which as a general rule was a bad sign, *but*, these particular fungi had a tell-tale pattern on the stem – hazy stripes. I picked three, not wanting to overdo it and started back to the camp.

I'd been damn near inactive yesterday evening, so I was feeling very nearly awake. Fortunate for me, and hopefully for Ven as well. I found her clothes lying splayed on a rock by the stream down the slope from our camp. Not wanting to surprise her whilst disrobed, I called out "I'm back, Ven!"

"Good for you!" she shouted back. Her voice was jovial but there was a definite note of tension.

"Am I okay to come up?"

Ven groaned like a teenager being asked to clean their room. "Yes! I'm in the spring."

Again? Well she'd woken up in a plague-tent. I scrambled up the slope, less gracefully than I might have liked due to having one of my hands occupied with magical mushrooms.

Ven lay in the spring, her bare shoulders out of the water, her arms spread back on the stone rim of the pool. She raised her head as I climbed into view and peered at my prizes. "What are those?"

"Ah." What I had planned wouldn't really work with her in the spring. "Well, I had an idea about your manifestation. Are you going to be bathing long?"

"Probably," she said, a smile quirking her lips before vanishing as quickly as it had come. "I might well need to bathe for a week or so to get the feeling of waking up in that tent off me."

My idiot brain instantly began to panic – *she'd hated sleeping next to me, it had made her feel unclean.* No. I thumped the palm of my free hand against the side of my head. She meant the mould on the canvas. Obviously. "Fair enough," I said. "Do you want some breakfast and then you can carry on soaking?"

Ven cocked her head and swept her hands through her hair as if she were a classical courtesan. "Does the raw power of my nudity make you uncomfortable, Laceco? I'm really sorry. So very sorry. Wait." Her eyes widened and she sat bolt upright. "Fuck, does it actually? I'm sorry, I'll—"

I waved my hands, "No, no no! Sorry, it was... never mind. You're good. Please carry on soaking."

She visibly relaxed. "You need to chill out, Laceco."

"Says the one who just panicked that she was shocking me with her nudity."

Ven narrowed her eyes. "I was being considerate. I shall know that such efforts are unwarranted in future." She flicked a spatter of spring water at me.

I set the magical mushrooms down, and prepared them as best I could. I then wolfed down some of the supplies Ven had brought with her, to try and settle my growling stomach. I checked behind me. Ven was still soaking. I could wait until she was done, but if this didn't work I'd need time to think of a new plan for her to free herself, and the effect of her toxicity was accelerating... Fuck it.

"Mind if I join you?" I called.

"Go for it, dude. Water's warm. You know to wash off before you get in, right?"

"Yes, yes." I scrambled down to the stream, stripped, shivered at the cold of the stream, and then hurried back up to the camp. The morning air bit me as I moved. I grabbed my magical mushrooms, dashed to the spring, and slipped into the water, yelping at the sudden change in temperature. "Hot-hot-hot-hot."

"Yes," Ven said. "The hot spring is hot." She slapped her forehead. "Oh! That's why they named it a hot spring. I only just got that."

I laughed, nearly dropped my mushrooms and... I breathed. Focussed. I opened my eyes and looked at Ven, who was grinning at me. "I have an idea for how you might be able to resolve your manifestation."

"Goody."

And, like a blessing from the spirits, Ven dispensed my first opportunity to aggravate her. I shrugged, irritatingly. "I mean I can always *not* tell you if you don't want to hear it?"

The glare she shot at me was probably supposed to be withering. It was mostly eyebrows with the addition of a slight snarl which turned a mere expression into something approaching art. "No," she said. "Please do enlighten me. I'd rather not pollute the world any more than I already have. Besides, if I have another night like the one we just shared I'm pretty sure you won't survive." She jerked her chin, permitting me to continue. Then, a spark flashed in her eyes—

"Oh, lovely," I said, cutting off '*not that I'd mind you not surviving*', or whatever she was about to say, in the hope that'd wind her up still further. "Well, I was just out for a bit of a stroll, you know how much I enjoy a stroll about these parts. Anyway, I came across these!"

I flourished my mushrooms at her. She looked from me to the mushrooms and then to the sky before muttering something under her breath. From the movement of her lips, she either said 'spirits, give me patience', or 'some grated parmesan'.

"These..." I said, flourishing the mushrooms once again when she looked back at me, "are..."

"Mushrooms." Her tone was dead, flat, and dangerous. It distracted me from what I was saying but I wasn't immediately sure why.

I shook my head and pressed on. "Not just any mushrooms, Ven. Mushrooms of a particular genus, Ven. These particular mushrooms are well known in Oro for absorbing natural background magic, Ven. They're known for producing a number of different effects, one of the most potent of which is to kick-start a healing response in anyone who eats them, Ven. Eat two of these mushrooms, Ven, and the magic contained therein will expunge the toxic effects you're experiencing, at least in the short term."

I held out the mushrooms. She hesitated for about half the length of time I'd expected before taking them. She lay two on the rim of the spring by her bare left shoulder whilst she peered at the remaining fungus. She frowned. She sniffed the cap and the stem. Finally, she broke off a small piece of the cap and chewed it, thoughtfully. She grimaced and turned, spitting the mangled mushroom off into a nearby bush.

"You don't want to be cured?" I asked, innocently.

She folded her arms. "Laceco... do you think I'm a fucking idiot?"

"Well I'm not really sure intelligence is a real thing," I said, airily. "it seems to be used as a catch-all term for a bunch of abstract ideas which—"

"Hey!" she snapped. "I'm talking."

"You asked me a question, actually."

"Shut the fuck up. I want to understand exactly what flavour of bullshit you just tried to pull. Placebo effect? Because there was absolutely nothing magical about those mushrooms."

"Er..."

"Not placebo effect?"

"Well..."

Ven grabbed her hair and yanked her own head back, howling, through rage, or pain. "No! No, no, no! Tell me you didn't just try to convince me that the cure was within me all along – '*they were perfectly ordinary mushrooms, Ven! I just gave you the confidence to cure yourself, Ven! The real cure was the mushrooms we ate along the way!*' It was that, wasn't it?"

"Not exactly," I said. I could feel an awful *space* opening at the back of my head and my concentration was leaking out. Ven had gone from irritated to furious in seconds. I might have made a mistake.

"Fuck this," Ven said, standing. "I'm going home." She started climbing out of the spring.

"Ven, stop!" I said, standing too, water cascading from me. I couldn't reach out a hand to stop her because there currently weren't many safe places I could touch her, so I had to hope my sudden switch in attitude would be enough to distract her.

My change in tone made her look around – when she saw me standing, she looked down for a moment before frowning at me. "What? What is it?"

I'd fucked this up. We'd have to start again tomorrow. Damn. Ah, well, may as well be honest now. "Ven – do you know *why* you're making the world around you toxic?"

She held her hands to her temples and clenched her fingers as if crushing imaginary fuzzy animals. "I'm not doing this, it's the thrice-damned manifestation!"

"No..." The word sounded weak and hollow after her broadside. She started turning away again. "No!" I shouted, trying to match her tone, her volume, and overshooting massively. "The manifestations are... fucking... they're giving your subconscious the ability to express itself! It's trying to tell you something!"

"What? Like your brilliant idea that my subconscious was showing me the world how Banna told all my friends it was? Why don't you tell me your next theory, Lacecο? Come on, I'm fucking agog."

The shouts, the freezing cold air on my back, my shoulders – all at the same time as I was trying to *think*, trying to find a way to express the idea I'd had – it was too much. I was fighting my way through a mental bank of fog and getting lost. "Ven, I know *you* know that you're not actually fucking toxic – you don't turn the world around you toxic, that's not you, that's not who you are. You went really seriously out of your way to help me. Got me a tent. Supplies. A new camping spot.

You don't fucking know me. You're practically an outreach worker given the amount you've helped me!"

"Only because my fucking manifestation is killing you!"

"It's not!" I yelled – my voice was growing hoarse. "It's not killing me! I'm not ill! No more than usual – look, Ven, you're not turning the world toxic. This isn't a literalisation of autism or anything like that. You're pushing people away!"

Ven halved the distance between us in one step. Steam from the spring gushed up between us. Her hair was plastered to her shoulders. "I'm *what*?"

"Think, Ven! You had a bunch of deeply shitty friends when you were growing up, who always treated you autism first. That's what you were to them. Not Ven. Not a person. Not the funny, caring person I've spent the last few days with. You weren't Ven, you were '*my autistic friend Ven*'. And then you went to live in the Ember Cavalcade, and you didn't tell anyone about the ASC, and you went on dates, and no-one knew. But then Rikolta asked you to move in with him, and I bet, I *bet* you thought about telling him about your autism, didn't you?"

Ven drew in a sharp breath. She was staring, her gaze unsteady. Her lips parted but no sound emerged.

I tried to drag my voice back down to a manageable volume. "You thought about telling him, and your subconscious panicked. '*What if I tell him and he starts treating me the way Banna did?*'. Faced with that question, your subconscious tried to do the only thing it could think of: push Rikolta away, push *everyone* away before they can hurt you, and de-fucking-humanise you in the same way your awful 'friends' did when you were younger. I'm sorry, Ven, I'm really sorry that happened to you, if I can..." I faltered – I'd wanted to lay out a plan but my head was too foggy. I had nothing.

Ven's breathing was quick and sharp. Her eyes glittered. A suggestion of tears one moment which turned to diamonds in the morning sun. Her cheeks flushed. A blooming carnation, a crimson petal on each cheek. "I..." she said. Her gaze skittered away from me. She looked down at where she was standing, water sloshing around her waist. Off to the distance. the forest and the cavalcade. "I've been..." Her eyes snapped back to me. She reached up and clamped her hands on my shoulders. "Laceco," she growled. "I really want you to kiss me."

"Er..." Wheels spun in my head. I hadn't expected... Fuck. Was Ven vulnerable in this moment? Would I be taking advantage of her if I said yes? She was beautiful, of that there was no doubt. The Oro Virus had been screaming at me to peek at her changing, to stare at her when we shared the spring. Did I even want to kiss her? Because the worst thing I would do would be to reject her – I knew about her ASC. If she opened herself up like this to someone who knew and they turned her down... but I could do that. I knew I could do it if I did it the right way... but why was I... Ven was...

"Laceco..." she said. "Come back. You're standing here with me."

I looked up, into her diamond eyes. I was there with her. Everything else melted away. She drew me a step closer towards her. Her grip on my shoulders was immovable, but her touch was light. For *days* now, I'd felt as if trying to carry any extra weight would make me collapse. Ven's touch carried no weight. I reached out, and encircled her waist. We closed the distance and our lips met.

She kissed me as if she had a grudge against me, fast and firm. Her hands moved to the back of my neck, she stepped forward, pressing into me. I felt her heart hammering before I lost my balance and fell back into the water. She didn't let go as we fell – she crashed into the water on top of me.

When we broke the surface, we were laughing. She stroked my cheek. I brushed some hair from her eyes. Then a thunderbolt struck me. "What about Rikolta, Ven?"

"What..." Light dawned. She rolled her eyes and patted my cheek, gently. "Rikolta currently has two other partners. Don't worry about that now, there's a whole process. Now, I'd like to move somewhere less windy for a moment, if you'd be interested in picking up where we just left off?"

Chapter Five

When Ven and I emerged from the tent an hour later, it was to a brisk autumn afternoon. The tent was pristine, as were the rocks and bushes around it. The clothes I'd worn, which had been decaying prior to our heart-to-heart were returned to simple cloth and stitching.

We cooked a simple lunch together, before we started taking down the tent. We'd done some talking whilst in the tent, as well as other wholesome activities. The wild magic which surged in my wake was clearly going to continue causing manifestations. My attempt to live as a hermit had solved nothing. If anything, my ability to cope with manifestations was reduced when I was secluded – I was spending so much time taking care of myself that I didn't have much spare capacity for dealing with magical phenomena, and not every manifested would be as understanding as Ven.

Ven... Ven talked as if she had been suffering under an enormous weight that I'd lifted from her shoulders. We'd lain facing each other in the tent, my fingers tracing the curve of her side, her hip, her leg... and she'd just *smiled*. Her eyelids drifted shut and she let out a contented sigh.

"Thank you," she said.

"Mm? For what?"

She opened her eyes and scowled at me. "For wiping away the manifestation."

My hand froze on her leg. "What? You did that."

"I very much did not."

"I rambled on at a high volume. I might have given you the idea to wipe aside the manifestation, the... the way of looking at what was happening which enabled you to deal with it, but you set it aside. You were the one who stood there whilst a relative stranger ranted about toxicity, and took the biggest chance I've seen anyone take. You set the toxicity aside, not me."

"You were so surprised when I asked you to kiss me."

"I was, yes."

"Would you like to continue being surprised by me?"

It was my turn to smile, to close my eyes. "I would very much like to, yes."

She drew me into a warm, warm hug, and we made plans.

With the tent packed away, we'd begun the hike back down the mountain. We could see movement around the Ember Cavalcade, even from up here. Caravans were moving, shuffling into a rough order – procession formation. They'd be on the move tomorrow, or maybe the day after.

I needed breaks. Too many breaks. Ven was understanding to a fault, but after my sixth, I suggested that she go on ahead so she could make sure someone stayed behind to pick us up if the Ember Cavalcade left without us.

That had been the decision which had surprised me the most. Ven had asked me to join her at the Ember Cavalcade, at least for a little while, and I'd said yes. I'd always assumed that if I were to leave the mountain I'd return to my old circus cavalcade... but I wanted to be free of the Oro Virus, and I wanted to make a fresh start and...

Word of the Ember Cavalcade had reached my circus. Only rumours, and it depended on who you talked to. Some of the elders referred to it in the same... unflattering terms Ven's school friend had. They'd called it a disability ghetto. Others had been closer to the truth as Ven described it.

The Ember Cavalcade was named such because it was a cavalcade that travelled with the Ember Shrine. So far, so straight-forward. The Ember Shrine was all that remained of a temple to the local spirits which was nearly burned to the ground when my countrymen invaded Akoma around two hundred years ago. The temple had been a haven for the sick and a home for the disabled because the local spirits had taken particular care of those who had been neglected elsewhere.

Only three people had survived the attack – a priestess and two friends who had managed to hide from the invaders. Together, they'd rescued the shrine from the burning temple, and then collected its ashes as the flames died. They'd found the embers in the ash never faded, so they scattered the ashes in their path as they set off to find a new home for the Ember Shrine. They started and never stopped, traveling Akoma and taking care of the sick and disabled as they went – honouring the spirits who had helped them at the temple, and who helped themWe camped that night in the lee of a cluster of again on their journey. They scattered the ashes as they travelled, and just as the embers never faded, the ash never ran out. They scattered ash for kilometre after kilometre.

A year after they'd set out, they found themselves in a familiar spot. "Is this the spot where we camped by the Lightning Falls?" the priestess asked. "No, it's got to be the place where we found the paper town," said one of the two survivors. The other survivor groaned.

"Look at the ground, you two." Her friends turned their gazes down, and saw the place where the Ember trail had begun. They laughed and cried with joy – the cry running back as the story ran through the cavalcade which had formed around them. They honoured the spirits before setting off on their second circuit of the Ember Trail.

That had been two hundred years ago, and much has changed since then. The salient point is that the Ember Cavalcade has a reputation for taking care of people with disabilities. This reputation became self-reinforcing as people with mobility needs, visual impairments, deafness, invisible conditions, conditions of invisibility and so on made their way to the cavalcade. These days, supposedly, there aren't *that* many not-yet-disabled people traveling with the cavalcade at all.

When I'd first heard of the place, I'd thought it sounded like a hospice, or a place society shoved inconvenient people to get them out of the way. I was keen to learn the truth of the matter. I finally made it to the bottom of the mountain to find Ven waiting with a caravan. She was waiting there with a masc about my age with bags under his eyes – maybe not bags. Luggage. He wore a check shirt and battered cotton trousers – nothing too unusual, apart from the white necktie which hung limply from his collar.

Ven was resting her head on his shoulder when I struggled out of the undergrowth at the edge of the forest. She raised her head, kissed him and then said something I couldn't hear before waving to me. This, my genius brain deduced, was Rikolta.

I didn't quite know where to look when I finally reached the couple, but Rikolta shattered my awkwardness. He beamed at me. "Ven told me what happened," he said. "Thank you."

"She told you what happened?"

Ven rolled her eyes. "Yes, Laceco. I told him what happened."

Rikolta grinned. "I'm delighted, Laceco, I really am. The more people who make Ven happy the better."

Ven growled at him before walking towards me, wrapping her arms around me and kissing me. I'd half-wondered on my way down the mountain if I'd misunderstood something about Ven and about me. Were we a *thing*? It seemed we were. Her lips were soft, the kiss slow. We drew back. I rested my forehead against hers and she smiled.

"Welcome home," she said.

"Thank you."

We piled into the caravan which turned out to be Rikolta's. He cranked the motor into life and as I collapsed onto one of the battered couches, we rolled off in pursuit of the Ember Cavalcade.

"If the manifestations had stopped," said Ven, sitting next to me, "would you have just stayed on the mountain forever?"

"That was the plan, yes."

Ven sat back on the couch and glared at the ceiling. "Bloody hell."

"What? That doesn't sound nice to you? Quiet?"

"Extremely boring."

I thought back to the first exciting weeks on the plateau, building my cabin and stores. I thought about the weeks following that blissful frenzy of activity. "You might be right about that."

"So what I'm learning is that you're not someone who thinks long-term."

I winced. "Yeah. I used to, but then my world shrank and shrank because of the post-viral fatigue. I find it hard to conceive of what the future will hold, now."

Ven shifted to face me. "Do you want me in it?"

Her smile was warm. Her fingers, when they brushed my cheek, were soft and playful. I smiled. "Yes, I do."

"You my boyfriend, Laceco?"

"Yeah. You my girlfriend, Ven?"

"Yeah."

"How does that work with Rikolta?"

"We'll talk about it. Rikolta wants me to be happy, and he's not going to demand I don't see anyone else because that's not how these relationships work. It'll be fine, we just have to talk."

I could feel the fatigue dragging at me. Rather than hold myself together, I let myself slump. My hands fell to the cushions of the couch and my head drooped until it was resting on Ven's shoulder.

"You okay, L?" Ven asked, a note of... tension sang at the back of her voice. Maybe it was sadness.

"Yeah," I said. "Can I rest like this for a while?"

Ven shifted, turning so that my head rested easier on her shoulder. She rested a hand on mine. Our fingers interlaced. "Rest as long as you want, L," she said. Her words blurred slightly – she must be damned tired too. "We're in no hurry."

Through the caravan's windows, the world rolled past. The farmstead gave way to grassland which gave way to arid earth. All the way, the ash trail we were following glowed, its embers inextinguishable.

We camped that night in the lee of a cluster of trees, each weeping crimson sap. Rikolta offered to drive through the night so we could catch up with the cavalcade but neither Ven nor I even considered it. Fatigue was nothing to play with. Rikolta didn't necessarily need to worry about the deep, deep tiredness that came with fatigue. If he was disabled (and, from what Ven had said, it was likely he was), his condition wasn't obvious. From my own experience, I knew that those are the sorts of conditions which can sneak up on a person.

There was a double-width bunk in Rikolta's caravan, which he graciously offered to us for our first night – he'd sleep on cushions on the floor. Feeling a little awkward, I said "No, no, you two have been a couple far longer. I should sleep on the cushions." We went backwards and forwards on this for a good ten minutes, as Ven grew increasingly annoyed.

Finding the veins twitching on the side of Ven's head amusing, I grew more reasonable the more frustrated she was. Rikolta matched me, compromise for compromise. This led to me bedding down in the double-width bunk next to Rikolta, with Ven lying in a nest of cushions, muttering about how she was going to murder both of us in our sleep.

Interlude: The Soulmate Tether

We caught up with the Ember Cavalcade the next day. Weary from travel, none of us were in any fit state to find our own beds, so we had another protracted negotiation about who should sleep in the bed. With the inevitability of a joke that has really got rolling, the only two people not attracted to each other slept in the bed whilst Ven grumbled from a nest of cushions.

The mystery, if you could call it that, of Rikolta's disability had been solved on our first night, when he'd been changing. He'd removed his trousers, revealing a wood prosthetic leg below his left knee. This, he'd unstrapped and stood in a corner. I hadn't known whether I was allowed to look, so I'd done my best to avoid staring.

The next morning, fed up with being left out, Ven clambered into bed between me and Rikolta and wiggled until we made room for her. "Rik," she said, her voice blurry with sleep, "do you know about wild magic manifestations?"

"Can't say that I do..."

"Fill him in, would you Laceco?" Ven opened her eyes, saw my surprised expression, and chuckled. She leaned towards me and kissed me before pulling back. The warmth of her breath played across my skin. "Please?"

I grinned, "Since you asked nicely."

"Good!" Ven's eyes half closed. "Now, I'm going to snuggle Rikolta. He's less bony than you. Are you going to get jealous?"

"Don't let her bait you, Laceco," said Rikolta.

"Snuggle away," I said. The Oro Virus was throwing a tantrum inside me, which was all the motivation to relax that I needed. "You want to know anything particular about the manifestations, Rikolta?"

"Mm," Ven said, turning and wrapping an arm around Rikolta's chest. She shoved her free hand back and zmoozhed it into my face. "Fewer questions, more explaining."

"Yes ma-am. So, Rikolta, you've probably heard rumours about wild magic manifestations. Stories about them made the rounds of my home Cavalcade every once in a while, although more among my friends when I was still a teenager than the adults. Urban Legends. Modern folklore. Stories of the girl who everyone started forgetting or the one who kept looping time to cope with social anxiety."

"Sure, I've heard a few stories like that," said Rikolta.

"Shhh," said Ven, sleepily, "Laceco is weaving a narrative."

"Ah, well if he's weaving it would be rude to interrupt."

I stretched and shifted to be a little closer to Ven before continuing. "Manifestations like that are just supposed to be stories. Magic sinks into places and people, but it's unusual for it to create one temporary effect and then move on. So yeah, you can imagine my surprise when I was running errands between caravans and I saw this femme with a red string emerging from her chest and looping away into the distance."

"Who was the femme?" Rikolta asked.

"I didn't know at the time. Found out later her name was Talin. Anyway, no-one else was staring or whatever, so I did the smart thing. The reasonable thing. I pretended I didn't see the red string thing in case having red string come out of your chest was perfectly normal and I was being the weird one for noticing."

"Ven," whispered Rikolta, "I think Laceco's going to fit in quite well."

Ven, for her part, smacked her palm into her forehead. "Stop this relationship, I want to get off."

"I saw her a couple more times over the next few days, each day she had the same red string, each day no-one else noticed. Eventually I worked up enough courage to ask one of my friends about it. They looked at me as if I were a complete moron, thus confirming my worst fears, *but* they said I was weird for noticing things that weren't there. You can imagine the relief, right? I was being weird because there was some arcane fuckery going on, not because everyone else had been living life with a full spectrum of colour vision whilst I'd been stuck with only buttercup yellow and mud brown.

"So the next time I saw Talin I introduced myself and asked about the string. She was pretty chill about it – far more so than I would have been. She explained it was a soulmate tether."

"That's not a thing," said Ven.

"Oh, Ven, honey," said Rikolta.

"Fuck off, it's not."

Rikolta pantomimed heartbreak. "I'm hurt you can't sense it."

Ven huffed. "If that's how you're going to be about it, I'm gonna tell Indi and Jans that I'm your soulmate and I imagine they're going to be rather upset."

"That's a fair point, please don't do that. I apologise for teasing you," said Rikolta.

I couldn't help but laugh at the ridiculous pair. "I'd never heard of such a thing anyway, so when Talin said, calmly and confidently that it was a soulmate tether, I returned to my fall-back: assume my lived experience was the weird one and try to accept this bizarre new knowledge into my worldview as best I could."

"And you're sure you don't have ASC?" Ven asked.

"*Anyway*, after that, Talin and I got to talking every once in a while. She said I was the only other person who could see the tether, which was something of a relief. She seemed happy carrying on her daily life, knowing that her soulmate was out there. She felt as if every action she took caused the tether to tighten a little, drawing her closer to her soulmate.

"Talin started to look stressed after the third week. She was losing her intuition for the actions that would made the tether tighten or loosen. When I saw her, she was at an intersection turning one way and walking a few steps, then returning to the intersection. She tried a different direction, and then another, and then another, trying to make the tether tighten."

"Try saying that six times fast," muttered Ven.

"So being an essentially helpful sort of person, I tried to work things through with her. What had she tried? What had worked? That sort of thing. Scientific principles, insofar as they apply to magic.

"As an approach, it lacked... humanity? I ended up upsetting Talin quite badly. Or maybe agitating her is more accurate. She couldn't work out any patterns and the more she tried to focus on exactly what was happening, the more elusive and arbitrary the tether felt. She started losing herself in the problem. Analysis paralysis it's called."

"Oooh," said Ven, rolling over and resting an arm on my chest. "someone's read a book."

"Damn it, Laceco, stop wowing Ven with your intellectual prowess," said Rikolta, "it's not fair on the rest of us."

"Tell me," Ven whispered, her breath raising the hairs on my neck, "was the book you read a hardback? Was it words all the way through, no illustrations? Talk academically to me, you big brained bastard." She traced a finger down my chest, the tip of her fingernail digging in just enough to make me shiver.

"Soooo," I said, not knowing how I should be feeling about enjoying whatever the hell was currently happening, "after another week or so Talin wasn't going to work. She was barely eating. Her self care was minimal. Every action she took felt as if it weakened the connection with her future soulmate. Her family were worried. *I* was worried, I had no idea what to do. Eventually I pretty much gave up. Stopped trying to work the problem out and I just talked to her."

"Damn, that's hot," said Rikolta.

"I talked to her," I said, trying not to blush, "and that was it for... hours. Eventually, I hit upon the bright idea to check, just *check*, because I was sure I'd checked but I might not have. I asked her how she knew the tether was to her soulmate."

"Huh," said Ven.

"I know, took me a while. She said it was a feeling. And *I* said I didn't know what that meant, what sort of feeling? Because like... as far as I know... Okay, at the risk of developing a bit of a reputation for myself, I once read a thing about soulmates."

Ven's eyes snapped wide. She boosted herself up to a sitting position, threw a leg over me and, before I could react, she was straddling me, her hands pressed flat on my chest. She bit her lip. "What sort of thing?" she asked. "Tell me it was a book."

"Er..." I said, glancing at Rikolta, who appeared to be trying hard not to laugh. "It was a book, yes."

Ven leant down and kissed me, her hair cascading around our faces. "Sorry," she said, dismounting and collapsing back into her spot between me and Rikolta, "continue, but keep the erotic material to a minimum please, there's only so much I can take."

"The book..." I said. Ven moaned as if in ecstasy. "The research..." I tried. Ven's moans were more dramatic the second time. Rikolta burst out laughing. I frowned, before giving up and laughing with the pair of story-ruining bastards.

"Apologies," said Ven, once she could maintain a straight face. "Continue."

"The thing what I read," I said, "essentially said that if your soulmate is randomly assigned then we each have something like a 0.008% chance of ever actually meeting the person, and that's if you meet a *lot* of people. And what that essentially means is, if soulmates *did* exist, we'd never find out that they did because anyone actually meeting their soulmate would be so rare as for it to be basically impossible. Anyway, I said this to Talin, who looked as if she didn't know whether she wanted to burst into tears or thump me."

"For the record," Ven said, "if I'm ever in crisis, I'd appreciate it if you didn't give me a lecture on statistics."

"Right," I said, "yeah. I should definitely have intuited that with Talin as well. Anyway, her expression definitely communicated that I wasn't being as helpful as I thought I was, so I... I just tried to talk to her about what she thought a soulmate was and why she wanted one. Turned out she wanted to feel as if there was a future for her in the world. To her, that meant moving into the future with someone. The problem was she was neglecting herself to focus on finding the person she wanted to move into the future with.

"When I pointed that out she sat *bolt* upright. Her tether, which had been limp this whole time suddenly *snapped* tight. She frowned, and concentrated. She looked at me, and then looked to the door to her room – the tether ran through the crack under the door, band-saw tight. She plucked the tether with a finger – it let out a high note as if it were the string for a massive viola. She looked back at me, and I could see something different in her eyes.

"The door to her room opened. Talin walked in. She was sitting in the chair and walking into the room at the same time. She was tethered to herself. She walked forward until she was standing over herself, then she turned and sat down. Then, it was just her. No tether."

"Huh," said Rikolta.

"Next day she said goodbye to her family and left the cavalcade. I heard she's studying at a university in Shai now."

Rikolta lay back, wiggling the back of his head against his pillow. "And that's what these manifestations are like?"

"Well no two are exactly alike."

"And you're the only one who can see them?"

I shook my head. "Plenty of people can see them, especially if they've experienced a manifestation before. It sort of gets your eye in. Besides, I'm far from the first. I once met... no, sorry, that's a whole other story and we've got stuff to do."

"Yeah we do," said Ven. She held out a hand to Rikolta, who high-fived it.

"Oh," I said, "sorry, shall I give you two some alone time."

"I was joking," said Ven, "*but* we should probably have the boring conversation about how you, Laceco, and me and you, Rikolta and me are going to work now we've had a bit of a switch-up."

"Goody," said Rikolta, "admin. Best part of a relationship."

"And once we've done that, can I get someone to show me round the cavalcade?" I asked.

"I volunteer Rikolta," said Ven. "It's literally his vocation to do that."

Rikolta winced. "Being a settlement officer is a little more complicated than..."

"He's basically a tour-guide," Ven stage-whispered.

"All right, Ven, all right," Rikolta said, rolling his eyes. "If it makes you happy, I'll show your new boyfriend around the cavalcade."

Chapter Six

The Ember Cavalcade was truly enormous – forty individual caravans of varying sizes at Rikolta's count. The vehicles were mostly steam-powered although a few were still drawn by horses or bison – these travelled at the front of the cavalcade so as not to clog the poor creatures' lungs.

Each caravan was superficially similar to the ones from the circus – between four and twelve wheels with tyres so knobbly they could travel the Ember Trail without getting bogged down in the ash during the rainy season or the Month of Veils. A flat bed sat atop a simple chassis, and on the bed was the fun bit of each caravan. Some looked like traditional Akoman houses – wood walls with windows on all sides and a sweeping tile roof.

Other caravans were more adventurous. Rikolta was keen to show off the Ember Library – a rickety looking two story construction with six doors – three on the bed level and three on the first floor – accessible via ladders. The Ember Shrine itself was a simple alter inside a room-sized shelter, with the rest of its caravan being taken up by prayer mats for the faithful, food stores and a small lodging for the Ember Priestess, Rikolta's mum.

Other than the size and occasional delights such as the library, the purpose of the caravans weren't too different to the circus cavalcade. Lodging caravans, hydroponics caravans which grew crops all year round, rainwater collectors, storehouses and hygiene facilities. What really made the Ember Cavalcade stand out were the ramps, the signs and the people.

Back home, no caravans bore signs identifying them – we all lived in the cavalcade. By the time I was ten I knew every caravan like the back of my hand. Here, each caravan was clearly marked with bold words or sigils. At first I thought they looked a little ugly – no patterned backgrounds or subtle colours. Everything had apparently been designed for maximum contrast and readability. Once I'd grown used to them, I was able to see the beauty. Form from function.

The people, the few who were out in the open air at least, were not what I expected. Only around a third of them had obvious impairments, and I only saw a few wheelchairs. Everyone wore goggles – tinted or clear. Rikolta had lent me a pair as well, and the reason why had been immediately obvious. The cavalcade's wheels threw up ash and cinders from the Ember Trail, which would have been blinding without eye protection. Other than this unifying aspect, no two residents of the cavalcade appeared to dress alike. I saw suits, overalls, robes and what were almost certainly pyjamas. An odd formality was lent to most outfits thanks to the neckties most of them wore.

The ramps I found curious. Rikolta was leading me along the gangway of a hydroponics caravan as the Cavalcade was slowing. In the near distance, buildings sat in neat rows. Some sort of town? To my left was the glasshouse of the hydroponics farm – hundreds of climbing plants, their roots dangling in a nutritious mix of water and bio-fuel waste products. Ahead was a gangway which led to the next caravan in the cavalcade, as well as another which we could use to get across to the next caravan over – a two-storey residential model which rumbled along stolidly, its tyres barely kicking up any ash at our slowing pace. The path to the caravan ahead was a steel ramp, which rattled softly to itself whilst to the right was more of a rope bridge.

"Rikolta!" I called – the chuffing of steam engines nearly drowned my voice, along with shouts from four people a little older than me who were sitting on the roof of the adjacent residential caravan. One, a femme wearing a white suit with a lime green tie and maybe six different necklaces was waving a bottle and came damned close to falling off the roof.

Rikolta turned, "what?"

I pointed at the ramp, "For wheelchair users?"

"Right!"

I pointed at the rope bridge to my right and raised a questioning eyebrow.

Rikolta looked puzzled for a moment and then light dawned, "Right! We don't have ramps leading between every caravan. There are specific routes people who use wheelchairs tend to take – connectors like that bridge are more for quickly scurrying across or for people undergoing physiotherapy. We have a bunch of spare ramps we can set up if someone wants to wheel from one caravan to another."

"Okay..." The quartet on the adjacent roof all cheered, which made me wince. One of them slipped a buttercup yellow tie from their neck and wound it around their bicep instead. I turned back to Rikolta, "What's going on with the ties? You all formal or something?"

"Oh yeah, right," said Rikolta. "Let's walk and talk. Down this ramp, that's right. Okay, so you know about the history of our cavalcade?"

The next caravan was a sprawling, single-storey residential joint with gangways I might have thought were excessively wide, until I had to squeeze past two chaps in wheelchairs, who were pointing animatedly at some spot on the horizon and yelling good-naturedly at each other. Rikolta slipped through the gap between the handles on the backs of their chairs and their kitchen window effortlessly. I bounced off first the kitchen window and then one of the chairs. "Damn!" I said, "Sorry. Sorry, Rikolta, yes I know some of the history."

"Right. Careful with this next caravan transition, it's a bit tricky – needs a repair. So yeah, the thing about having a cavalcade which acts as a home for people who struggle when their needs aren't met is... well. There's an issue with self-identification."

"Right." A couple of hundred years ago in Oro, our democracy had fallen apart for the Nth time, resulting in a fascist dictatorship. They'd made multiple groups wear markers to identify themselves - Q.A.P.I.T. people[1] , adherents of the Kipina faith and, of course, people with disabilities. Things had deteriorated sharply after that.

Rikolta held out a hand for me to grab as I navigated the transition from a hydroponics caravan to a coach with solid wooden walls behind which rang the sound of metal striking metal – likely a workshop or repair-house. Rikolta waited for me to find my feet past the transition before continuing: "So at first no-one in the Ember Cavalcade self-identified but that led to problems as we grew. Certain disabilities aren't obvious. For example, you've seen what mine is?"

"Missing part of your leg, so you need a prosthetic."

---

1. Queer, Asexual/aromantic/aroace/demi/grey, Polyamorous, Intersex, and Transgender

Rikolta nodded. "Right, but let's say you hadn't seen me minus my clothes. See my tie?" he turned and flicked his white tie at me before stepping lightly onto the transition to an enormous, rattling storehouse caravan.

"I see it."

"White means I have reduced mobility."

"Doesn't feel too reduced," I said. I was having to work damned hard to keep up.

"You'd be surprised," Rikolta said, pausing at the next transition. "You alright, Laceco? Need a break?"

I squinted into the distance – we were nearly at the head of the cavalcade. "Let's press on."

Rikolta's cheek bulged – he might have been grinding his teeth. "Alright," he said. "So, check this out." He lifted his left trouser leg revealing his prosthetic leg I'd first seen two nights before. "This thing can be an absolute bastard sometimes if I don't stay on top of my self-care. There's also some nerve pain stuff I don't intend to bore you with. Point is, today is a good day, but not every day is like this. Wearing my tie means that people know that if I'm moving slowly, or having trouble getting out of a chair, there's a specific reason why."

He led the way down the next gangway, past a caravan whose walls were canvas, rather than wood, strapped down to keep out the ash. Inside were clusters of people, chatting or playing games at a motley of tables. I was hit by a dose of deja-vu – evenings around campfires with my friends before the Telegram Flu had hit. Not all the people in the hall wore ties, and those that did weren't all wearing them around their necks. One wore a black tie around her forehead, another had a yellow tie wound around his forearm.

Rikolta joined me at the mesh window, "Nightingale Hall. One of our communal spaces. Nice, but a bit noisy."

"Ay. I'm not great at places like that. For now, at least."

"No problem. Everyone will understand. There's plenty of communal space to choose from anyway. Ven doesn't like being around too many people."

"Right," I stood back and crossed the transition to the lead caravan. "Ven doesn't wear a tie, though."

"Strictly optional for most people," Rikolta said, catching up in only a few strides. "With one exception – people who aren't yet disabled have to wear a red tie. Not for discrimination purposes, but... if people choose *not* to wear a tie, it has to be because they choose not to for their own reasons, not because they might not have needed one."

I'd seen a few red ties in Nightingale Hall... "You have many not-yet-disabled people here?"

Rikolta grinned. "A fair few. Plenty of stories behind them if you're of a mind to ask them. Anyway..." Rikolta rattled through the various colours of tie and what they meant as we swayed along the leading caravan – a long, many-wheeled vehicle with towering brass tanks bolted to its boards. Three had pressure locks – probably contained pressurised steam. The others gave off the tell-tale pong of fermenting biofuel.

"Rikolta," I said, as I swayed past two overall-clad engineers, both wearing green ties - identifying them as having auditory impairments. "What does everyone *do* around here?"

"What do you mean?"

"Well, my home cavalcade was a circus. People lived there, worked there, some studied... but everything was centred around the circus. The Ember Cavalcade isn't like that."

"That's right. It's probably better to think of us as more of a mobile town. We're named for the Ember Shrine but that's more of a philosophical whatsit than a practical one. People do a bit of everything here

– studying, research, we've got a few inventors, plenty of fuel distillers, farmers, entertainers, you name it. And that's without counting the Obsid University Cavalcade which is traveling with us for the next two seasons."

"All right," I said, closing my eyes and driving my thumb into my right temple. "All right. Thanks for the tour, Rikolta."

"No problem. We're at the best bit! Round this corner..."

Round the gangway's corner was... empty road. At the head of the cavalcade, the Ember Trail wound through wild grasslands, off past a small town, through a forest in the middle distance and the mountains beyond that. We were slowing, however. Rikolta took hold of the gangway's rail. I followed his lead just as our caravan shifted course off the Ember Trail and towards the cluster of pale houses.

I pointed at our apparent destination. "Next stop?"

Rikolta nodded. "The Town of Lonely Windows. Completely empty If you don't count spirits. We drop in there whenever we're passing. Good to keep the place in good repair and free of general crap for the spirits, you know?"

I didn't, but I didn't want to advertise my ignorance. "Right."

Rikolta grinned. "Right! Anyway, get ready for the sight of the Ember Cavalcade parking up at a stop. It's like a really slow ballet. As beautiful as it is boring."

With the elegance and attention to detail of a funeral procession, the Ember Cavalcade turned from the trail, caravan by caravan. Rather than gathering around a central point, as my home cavalcade had – gathering around the big top like flies around manure – they formed dozens of small groups, each moving according to some shared consensus. After spending five minutes marvelling at the sight, I surrendered to boredom. Rikolta offered to show me to the caravan where I'd be staying, a repurposed model from an animal cargo cavalcade. It sounded as if I'd be living in a stable, but I was too tired and too well mannered to wonder about that out loud.

The Ember and Obsid University cavalcades had burst into life during the parking ceremony. I stuck close to Rikolta as we navigated through the throng. The sedate pace of travel had been swept away, and an electric atmosphere had taken its place. The chuffing of steam engines replaced by excited chatter. My gaze still snapped to sights I wasn't used to – wheelchairs and long white canes and missing limbs and blacked-out goggles. The ashen dust was settling, the embers drifting back to the ground. Soon we'd be able to slip free of our goggles. Most of us would, anyway.

My new home turned out to be a wooden shack perched carefully atop the flat bed of what might once have been a refuse truck. It had been parked in a rough semicircle of similar caravans, with Rikolta and Ven's nearby. I caught Rikolta's gaze and nodded to his home. "We neighbours?"

Rikolta shrugged. "Good for people to have someone they know nearby. We can absolutely move if that's a problem."

I waved my hands in a flurry of flustered awkwardness. "No, no! I appreciate the thought!"

"Good!" Rikolta thumped on the side of my caravan. A florid face topped by a stovepipe hat stuck out of an upper window. "This is Tabitha, she's on the upper floor. You're on the cav floor. Tabitha, this is Laceco."

Tabitha nodded to me, scowled at Rikolta, and then withdrew without saying a word.

"Charming," I grinned.

Rikolta blinked at me. "Did you see the silver tie she was wearing?"

I winced. Silver meant problems communicating generally – through injury, mental health, or any other reason. "Ah, yes. I was forgetting."

Rikolta patted me on the shoulder, his touch leaving ice in its wake. "Try not to forget too often, eh? We're also parked up next to a journalist who's writing some puff piece about how inspiring we all are, and Graco's home."

"Who's Graco?"

"A researcher at Obsid University. I thought you two should meet, she's interested in the interactions between magic and 'mundane existence'."

Rikolta clambered up to the door of a two-storey residential caravan and knocked on the door. A frazzled looking femme poked her head out. She was a researcher from head to toe – the bleary expression, the pallid skin, the...

Rikolta asked if Graco was home. The femme retreated. Ah, not Graco. I was not having a good day for observation. After a mere moment, a tall person wearing a grey trouser suit, a black shirt and a blue tie (signifying vision problems) opened the door.

"Graco!" Rikolta chirped, "it's Rikolta. I've got someone you should meet. Tall masc, grey shirt, black trousers, cascade of brown hair. Looks scruffy but he's been living up a mountain for three months. Name's Laceco, he's dating Ven and has more experience of wild magic than anyone else I've met."

Graco frowned, and turned on the spot before facing in my direction. "Laceco? Laceco was a weary soul, and a weary soul was he. He carved us a pipe, and he carved us a bowl,and he trained up fiddlers three. Do you know the second half, Laceco?"

I winced. "The second half of what?"

Graco drummed her fingers on the railing of her caravan. "Traditional rhyme. The second half gets really recursive and reflexive. I thought you might know. It comes up a lot in texts about wild magic. Well, never mind, seems you're an alumnus of the university of life. Come see me at the Obsid University labs tomorrow if you have time. Can't spare a moment now. Birds are ill and poor Kay is struggling a bit. Thanks for the introduction, Rikolta."

The door clicked shut. Rikolta jumped back down to my level. "That's everyone," he said. "Why don't you rest up, you're looking a bit..."

I was swaying. How long had I been swaying? I nodded, clambered up onto my caravan, slipped inside and collapsed onto the bed. The sheets smelled fresh. I'd have to find out who to thank about that. Perhaps later. I fell apart to the muffled sounds of bustling industry outside.

The main thing I've found about lying in bed being unable to move is it's *extremely* boring. The room allocated to me... my room was blanketed by fog. It covered the battered carpet – the only thing which kept drafts from sneaking through the joints where the floor of the building met the chassis of the caravan. It covered the bare shelves. It covered the bed. It covered me – its smothering warmth making me comfortable, at least, if unable to break free enough to think in a straight line.

The fog chained me to the bed, but it couldn't keep the outside world out. Snatches of strangers' conversation were rendered unintelligible by the walls. Laughter, scampering feet, pots clanking together and the sounds of someone industriously starting a campfire intruded into my fog-bound prison.

My fatigue was holding me at a precisely calculated distance – unable to get out of bed and engage with the world outside, but not so far that I could tune the world out. Unwelcome thoughts welled up inside me. It had been quiet on Mt Iwa. No-one had intruded on my sleep there. I was putting people at risk by being here. The bustle outside was making me more ill, and the more ill I got, the less able I'd be to deal with manifestations.

I hated Ven for bringing me here. I hated myself for thinking that. I hated the world outside. I hated the tightness in my chest, the weight in my limbs, the curse which hounded me, the fog, the virus, the *other* virus and on and on and on my brain went. I was a splinter in the world – a shard of seething hatred, polluting the Ember Cavalcade. My resentment flowed out of me, into the home which had been provided to me without my needing to ask, out into the throng of caravans outside, out into Ven who had trusted me, into Rikolta who was innocent in all this, into Graco who I'd only just met and beyond into the rest of the Ember Cavalcade, into the Ember Trail, into Akoma and Oro beyond. That last bit cheered me up a little.

When I'd been stuck in hospital, I'd felt similarly bleak. The doctors had encouraged me to revel in the hatred. One in particular, a fussy seraphim who kept losing her glasses, had explained in exhausting detail that it was better to let the hatred flow out than stuff it down inside me into a nice little box where it would fester. I'd retorted that I liked putting it in the nice little box where it would never bother anyone ever again. She'd laughed, which I'd resented, thereby conceding the point to her. It felt as if I were a festering wound in the world – that anyone could be capable of such endless oozing hatred seemed perverse. But I also knew that it would pass. Maybe not quickly, but it would pass.

Breathing came easier as the shadows shifted from the floor of my room to a wall. The hatred had fled, leaving emptiness in its wake. I was extremely hungry, which I welcomed because it meant I'd have to move sooner rather than later. I also didn't know where the cavalcade conveniences were, but those were usually pretty easy to find; all I needed to do was follow the smell.

The hunger eventually overcame my fatigue as the battle for control of my body, and I was just pulling my energy together when someone knocked at my door. “C...” I doubled over and coughed a couple of centuries worth of dust from my lungs. “Come in?”

Sitting as upright as I could manage, I pawed at my hair to try and lose that classic ‘bed-bound invalid’ look. Ven opened the door, a steam of golden light trailing in her wake like a cloak.

I frowned. “Isn’t today a Rikolta day?” She was carrying something... a tray. Crap, had she brought me food?

Ven strode forward and flumped down on the bed next to me. She had brought food – two plates. Bread, jam and... tomatoes? She started loading up tomatoes onto the bread, but didn’t touch the jam. “It’s a Rikolta day, yes, but I hadn’t seen you about. New cavalcade, still in recovery after a journey, you know how it is.” She folded her slice of bread around the tomatoes and bit it in half.

I pointed at the other plate. “Is that for...”

Ven sighed, paused in her industrious chewing to give me an indecipherable look and pushed the second plate towards me. I took the hint and started making my own sandwich.

“It’s a lot, isn’t it?” Ven said, through the final bites of her sandwich. She was staring off into a corner of the room, her posture relaxed.

“The Ember Cavalcade?”

“Mhm.”

“It’s *enormous*.” I said, around my sandwich, sour bread mingling with the sharpness of the tomatoes.

Ven shifted, her shoulder brushed against mine and rested there. “What do you think of Rikolta?”

I swallowed, the gulping noise echoing in the sudden stillness. "He seems nice?"

Ven sighed. "Is that an actual answer or are you trying to answer the question without answering it?"

"Not sure, sorry."

"Mm. He likes you well enough. I think he's a little intimidated by you, to be honest."

I coughed as a piece of sandwich went down the wrong way. "What? Why?"

Ven shifted away, leaving a conspicuous space between us. "Don't do that."

"Er..." I said, suddenly unsure of what it was that I just did. "Sorry?"

"Mm." Ven stood, taking her plate but leaving the tray. "Well, I gotta get back. It's Rikolta's day and we're gonna check out the dancing statues. I'll see you tomorrow, okay?"

"Yeah, sounds good," I said, my tone wavering.

Ven turned as she reached the door. "Privy is just past that caravan there," she pointed out into the glimmering glow outside. "There's a washing up station nearby. You can't miss it. See you tomorrow!"

She closed the door in her wake, the light leaving with her. I finished the bread Ven had brought, along with the tomatoes and a third of the Jam. I forced myself out into the golden light of dusk, managing to wash up my dinnerware, find a home for the remains of the jam and use the privy all whilst managing to avoid talking to anyone. With that minor miracle accomplished, I returned to my caravan and was asleep within moments.

Chapter Seven

My sleep was thankfully dreamless, apart from one strange occurrence. I found myself stirring long after nightfall. A skull-white shadow stalked past my window. My heart pounded and I scrambled away from the window in one flurry of gasping motion. The skull-white shadow passed, slowly. Unhurried. Unstopping. I stared at the door to my room, my breath coming quick and sharp. A vulnerable call that the shadow would surely answer.

Silence reigned. When I was finally able to move, I padded to my door and peeked out. The cavalcade was still, other than the sound of some distant festivity. No shadows, other than the mundane ones I was used to. It must have taken an hour to get back to sleep, but I woke with the dawn to find myself alive and unconsumed by shadow creatures, which was a relief.

Not wanting to be trapped inside by fatigue for a second day I scraped together what energy I could and forced myself out into the day. Green shoots were beginning to poke through the wood chips our little thicket of caravans had clustered on. The wind was biting, and last night's fire had long-since died. Ven and Rikolta's caravan was still and I didn't see either of them around. The sickly disappointment that rose as I realised I couldn't glom onto them this morning as if I were a social limpet was another prod in the small of my back. I could leave Ven and this new cavalcade or I could try *living* here.

I sighed, used the privy, stumbled across a hastily thrown-up structure of pipes and a water barrel which my fellow dawn-birds were using as a shower, borrowed someone's towel, cleaned myself to an acceptable level, returned the towel and wandered blearily off to find breakfast.

In Oro I would have needed to pay for breakfast. My homeland chose to starve people unless they could perform arbitrary tasks during the day. Not for the first time, I was glad my parents had fled the cursed place.

I joined a line of people who were all waiting for cinnamon porridge. Thankfully, no-one tried to talk to me in the queue. I could get out and about, finding my place in this new cavalcade, or I could talk to people. Both would have been pushing my limits. A nice chap with a brown tie and a kind eye ladled steaming oaty goodness into a wooden bowl, winked at me and then turned to the next person in line. Wooden tables were arranged in rows nearby but there weren't any empty ones so I found the closest tree stump and sat on that to eat my breakfast.

The steaming porridge immediately burned the roof of my mouth but it was the most delicious thing I'd tasted after months of subsisting on whatever I could forage. Again, no-one came up to introduce themselves. I frowned and checked my surroundings as I blew on my next spoonful of porridge. The rows of tables were filling up but no-one was paying any particular attention to me. Every once in a while someone would glance over. I met one curious femme's gaze and she waved before turning back to her meal. It seemed as if I was allowed to be solitary.

I sighed, feeling tension flood free from my core. I slipped my spoon into my mouth. Tangy cinnamon, smooth porridge. I closed my eyes and listened to the low chatter of the cavalcade, the clunk and thump of wooden bowls landing on wooden tables, the distant shrieks of children playing and beyond that the breeze tussling needlebare branches.

Back in my old cavalcade, everyone had been expected to pull their weight, which was fine but there was this general assumption that everyone carried more or less the same weight. All mascs should be working eight to twelve hours a day to either make sure the circus went well or support the circus' work through farming or foraging. The femmes looked after the childer, cooked, and cleaned – which usually took more than twelve hours a day..

When I'd returned from my stay in hospital they'd understood that I couldn't work the same amount I'd used to, but there'd been this... unspoken question in the air around me. Was I ready to work full hours yet? When would I be properly recovered? Here... I'd have to find out if that same unspoken question would dog my steps.

Grinning, I finished what little else I needed to take care of that morning before striding around the cavalcade looking for people who might be able to give me tasks. Before I knew what was happening, I was walking the dead streets of The Town of Lonely Windows with a fabric sack and a metal claw device that could pick things up from the ground without needing to bend down.

The Town of Lonely Windows' streets were wide – vast tracts of ochre dirt spanned the ground between buildings. Caravans could have driven down the streets two abreast if they didn't mind the occasional scratch to their paintwork. The streets were also straight. Ruler straight – javelin straight. Rather than twist and turn as people or the environment desired, the buildings stood in an ordinary, militaristic line for five or six buildings and then stopped to allow a cross-street to cut it at a right angle.

The town gave me the impression that some enormous creature had grasped an ordinary town and untwisted it until every building was in a precise location according to some perverse internal logic. Leaves, twigs, paper, and other detritus blew into the headache-inducing order, but couldn't escape. The group I'd joined were walking the strange, identical streets gathering the crap up, bagging it and removing it.

I'd been partnered with Sol – a femme who hadn't quite shed the cascading energy of her teens. She looked around my age, possibly a little older, but she seemed to have been living for all of it. She wore white, which was a bad choice for stalking the ochre dirt-caked streets, but though our steps caused plumes of mustard dust to fountain around our shoes, it never seemed to stick to us. She also wore necklaces – too many necklaces. I tried to count them but lost track after five. The wooden beads clacked against each other gently when she moved suddenly, though not as she moved at her seemingly typical sedate pace. She walked with the shaft of her metal litter-picker across the back of her shoulders. She seemed content for me to pick up the majority of the crap which was gunking up the town.

"Why, exactly," I said, grabbing a crackle of dry leaves that had snagged between a lamppost and an anonymous shop window, "are we doing this?"

Sol clicked her tongue in her mouth. She wore a green tie wrapped around her left hand, meaning she had hearing issues as well as, I suspected, a hangover. "Ffffucking... spirits like it. I think."

A breeze caught the scrap of paper I'd been closing in on and teased it out of range of my grabber. I leaped forward, stamped on it, and slipped it into my bag. "The spirits like it?"

"Ha. I like that."

Her answer made my foot pause in mid-step. I was already feeling a little displaced – now I felt as if I'd stepped through to a mirror universe. Slightly different, just enough to leave me wrong-footed. I turned to face Sol, trying not to look aggravated. "What do you like, Sol?"

"People repeating my wisdom – an echo for the world."

I nodded, wondering if it was too late to find a new litter-picking partner. I wanted to ask why we cared what the spirits liked or didn't like, but that would mean engaging with Sol. Five leaves pattered down the street like a procession of ducklings. I stepped in front of them, catching them between my legs. As I placed them in their new home, I caught a glimpse of movement in the nearest shop window – little more than a glassy pool, a juniper mirror imprisoning the street around me. Three figures. Me, Sol and...

I turned. A few other litter pickers were strolling across a distant intersection but... I turned back to the murky mirror. Just me and my irritating partner. "Sol?" she didn't reply. I turned and waved at her. "Sol?"

Her gaze snapped to mine. She sighed, "did you say something?" She pointed at her ears before rolling her eyes. She seemed to snap into focus – the bags under her eyes, her listless stance. Then she cracked and Sol was standing in front of me once again – bored and not afraid to show it. Too good for this duty but doing it anyway because what else would she do with her morning? That felt judgy. Was the Oro Virus flaring up?

I shivered myself back to the present. "Sorry, yeah. The spirits in this town, can they be seen?"

She sighed, the tortured breath of a steam engine venting excess vapour. "Yes. Which one is it?"

"Er... don't know. I only saw a flash of movement."

Sol nodded, swinging her litter claw from her shoulders, and listlessly grabbing a passing leaf. "Ok. Well if you see a femme with blood-slick hair, pallid skin and nails which could tear the flesh from your bones let me know. She can be a bit tetchy. Doesn't like me much for some reason. We got a bit previous last time I was here."

I was an only child, but I was starting to think of Sol as the little sister I'd never had. I focussed on picking detritus from the streets whilst keeping half an eye on the Lonely Windows for blood-spattered spirits. Whenever I blinked I had to force my eyes back open once they'd closed. I was trapping myself in a cycle. Sol was winding me up, which was making me bad tempered. Ruminating on how much I disliked feeling irritable only made things worse. I hated that I couldn't tell if this was just a mood or if it was a sign that the fatigue inside me had built to dangerous levels. Was I on the verge of falling apart?

What was I doing in the Ember Cavalcade? Was I just dating Ven? I did *want* to be dating Ven, didn't I? Had I just got caught up in a moment? I stopped, closed my eyes, and pictured her – blonde haystack hair, piercing eyes, that wicked smile, her hand in mine, that first kiss that had felt eruptive. Burning. She'd seen me at my worst and she'd still seen me as a person rather than a burden. A person she'd wanted to *be* with. Utterly incomprehensible, but those were the facts. I wanted to be with Ven, and if Ven was with the Ember Cavalcade then there must be something to the place I wasn't seeing.

Sol and I reached an intersection where three litter pickers were waiting. One took my bag (almost full) and Sol's bag (barely rustling) and strode off in the direction of the cavalcade. The other two asked how we were and loaded us up with snacks. The snacks made Sol come to life for the first time since I'd met her. I munched on a rice ball whilst Sol batted away attempts at conversation from the others. That was when I saw a figure in the window across the street. A femme in white who definitely wasn't part of our group. She was behind me by a fair way, standing stalagmite still. Our eyes met.

"You alright?" asked Sol, her tone stating that there was only one correct answer to the question.

"Yeah," I said, "yeah. Saw a spirit. No blood, no fangs."

"Ah," Sol nodded wisely. "Probably nothing to worry about. Come on, people will get all mopey if we don't get this place sorted before sundown."

My litter picker trembled as it missed the next leaf I aimed it at. "So," I said, trying not to look at the windows. "what's being deaf like?"

Internally I slapped my forehead. We were having a verbal conversation. She clearly wasn't completely deaf. Hearing loss maybe?

Sol glanced over her shoulder, the bags under her eyes visibly deeper than a few moments ago. "You're not wearing a red tie."

I glanced down, as if checking to see if she was right. "yes?"

"So you know what it's like."

Ah. I held up my hands "I'm not..."

She sighed. "Every time I meet a not-yet-disabled person I wonder if they're going to patronise me, ignore the difficulties I have or treat me like some sort of magnificent inspiration. I need certain things to get through life that people outside the Ember Cavalcade rarely get. Some days it's fucking awful but most days it's just what life is. You might as well ask me what it's like being left handed. Any of this sounding familiar?"

I nodded, slowly, suddenly feeling as if I was standing on quicksand "Some of it. I'm only fairly recently..."

Her expression softened. "Right. And it's your first day in the cavalcade?"

I held up two fingers.

She nodded. "Second. Okay, so you're going through the unicorn stage. It's perfectly normal for people who haven't grown up here. It's gonna be painful and embarrassing for everyone but try not to worry about it. A good third of us go through it."

The quicksand had risen to my waist. "what's the uni—"

"The unicorn stage is where you're wandering around the cavalcade and your brain is screaming 'look over there! That person has only got one arm! That's weird! They're a unicorn! And look! Another unicorn! That one's in a wheelchair!'" Sol grimaced. "it's worse to be on the receiving end if your disability is visible. My mate Sash has burns covering the left side of her face. When not-yet-disabled people meet her for the first time they often freeze for a few seconds whilst they get over the shock of someone who looks different." She waved weary jazz hands.

"That sounds depressing."

"She was pretty cut up about it when we were in our early teens. Eventually we hit on a game. Whenever the cavalcade set up near a town we hadn't visited for a while, every time one of the Reds gave Sash *the look*, she was allowed to find one of us and punch us with no repercussions allowed."

I scratched the whorl at the crown of my head. "Did that help?"

"It made her feel a bit better, so... yeah, why not?"

I nodded, trying to remember how in the thousand names of the thousand spirits we'd wound up talking about Sash. I bore no particular ill will against Sash, Sash sounded perfectly fine, she could punch

Sol all day if it pleased the both of them. Nevertheless, I'd lost track of how she figured in the conversation.

Movement flickered – a shop window, deep and green as the Kháryb vortex. Eyes. The spirit of the femme was back. She was standing behind me, her lips moving. She was whispering something into my ear. Her name... her name as Antigia.

A hand snatched mine. "Okay!" said Sol, "just got to move you away from whoever's trying to chat to you I think..." her voice sounded cheerful, it was uncanny, like a wolf in gingham dungarees.

"What..." she was dragging me away from my friend. Down the street – the narrowing street. "What's happening?"

"Spirit's taken a liking to you, don't worry mate, it happens all the time. It's why we co-ordinate clean up detail in pairs minimum. Spirit probably doesn't want to harm you... probably. But the spirits are supposed to communicate through the shrines – we gotta go there. You with me?"

"Mm." My vision swam. I found myself staring at Sol's ears. They looked as if they worked perfectly well. They weren't weirdly shaped, except in the way ears usually are. She had a crimson pearl stud set into her earlobe, and that seemed a little out of step with the rest of her vibe. "You wear earrings, Sol?"

"Can I get a hand over here?" Sol yelled, trying to hurry someone along whose hand she was holding. They didn't seem to be helping much. "I got someone a touch spirit-struck!"

"Sol," I whispered.

Her gaze flashed to me only for a moment. "What?" she whispered right back.

"Earrings?" I pointed at the nearest shimmering crimson pearl, wondering if they were edible. I could feel Sol's hand gripping mine, and Antigia's hand gripping my other. She was whispering quietly, urgently, but I couldn't understand her. Too many people were rushing around.

Antigia pointed – there was a shrine at the end of the street. A slender wood building with an alter at its core that seemed to drink light and then release it back in waves – an ocean of light over which Antigia and Sol were sailing me.

"Oh, these?" Sol grinned, before going back to dragging whoever it was she was dragging. "They're not earrings, they're parts of my hearing aids. They capture sound and route it through this metal plate I have in my mouth – it's a bit like a retainer. It vibrates, transmitting the sound through the bones in my skull. Lets me hear even though I have two busted eardrums. Neat, huh?"

"It looks like a tasty pearl," I said, wisely.

"Well it's not. Stop looking at it like that."

"But how does it do... all... that?"

"Blood magic. This little place in Shai makes them for us. We have to sacrifice a bunch of blood to get the magic to work – linking the bead to the bone-conductor and suchlike. Difficult work and the bone-conductor can seriously make my jaw hurt so I don't wear it every day but yeah, I'll take it."

"Neat."

"It is, Laceco. It is neat. How you doing? Spirit still with you?"

"Antigia is here, yes."

"Crap."

"Mm?"

"Nothing, nothing. Okay, here we are. Wash your hands, will you?"

A font of water rose in front of me, a shimmering pool, concentric circular ripples pulsing across its surface. The stone in which the water sat was grey and pock marked. Tiny cracks split the surface here and there, but otherwise it wore its centuries well. I lowered my hands into the shimmering water as it hung above me, the glass-like liquid tingling against the skin of my hands. Antigia released me as I reached for the water. I felt for her once my hands were clean, but I found a warm hand. Familiar. Safe. I turned.

"Hey," said Ven, smiling at me. "You're having a busy day."

She was still – unmoving at the core of a street that swirled and sworled, tumbled and turned. Antigia moved behind Ven, staring at her all the way before she returned to my side. Her expression never changed from her stern glare, but I was sure a hint of a smile played in her eyes.

I grinned at Ven. "There's a... Antigia wants..." My mouth felt as if it was filled with cotton wool.

"It's okay," said Ven, grasping my shoulders and turning me towards the shrine's alter. Her solidity transferred momentarily to me. We stood, one still point in the vortex. Then, I lost focus. I was walking to the alter. Had I meant to? I clapped twice, and bowed.

Colour flooded the world, trees were everywhere - pear blossom and shuffling banana trees. People sat and stood about, chatting. Hundreds of them. An enormous picnic? They didn't seem to mind me joining them... but a hand in mine kept me still. I squeezed the hand and the hand squeezed back. That was right. Everything was going to be okay.

Antigia stepped lightly in front of me, her skin cala-lilly rich, her eyes twinkling stars. Her lips moved – I could barely hear her. I frowned – she took a step closer. She tried again and I heard her this time, although her voice was little more than a whisper. "She'll be counting and you might not notice. Look for the birds. Look for the silver and gold. Remember the rhyme - she'll stop before seven. She won't be able to say seven out loud. You can."

I kneaded my forehead with the palm of my hand. "Did you expect me to understand any of that?"

Antigia's expression never cracked, and yet I was sure she desperately wanted to roll her eyes. Her lips moved again – silence, or maybe the hint of a whisper on the breeze.

"Sorry, what?" I said, frowning. Something was tugging at me.

She slapped her palm against her forehead before she drew herself back to her full height. "Let it be for now. Your Expression just wanted me to tell you that you're likely to struggle with an Expression down the line. You'll know when you see the birds."

"What birds?"

Antigia stepped forward, her face grave, her eyes no longer sparkling – now burning. The world around us began to crack. Rumbling, roaring, crashing, and through it all only a hint of a whisper. "Contextually significant motherfucking birds."

The world around me focussed as the spirits faded – it was as if one world stepped forward as the other stepped back. Ven caught me as I fell.

Chapter Eight

I must have slept. I woke briefly, catching a glimpse of a cowled wraith stalking past my window again. This time, the jolt of fear was fleeting, quelled by Ven lying next to me in the bed, snoring like a malfunctioning steam engine. I was asleep again within seconds.

The next day, Ven stuck around to make sure I was okay, but it was her day off – No Rikolta, no Laceco, just Ven doing Ven things. She left me with a couple of books, as well as an off-handed mention that she'd be singing at the Dancing Statues that evening, along with a few other performers.

"I didn't know you sang..." I said, still struggling to focus.

"Very well, as it turns out," she said, the door clicking shut on her satisfied grin.

The tide of my fatigue was ebbing, which after yesterday's chaos was surprising. I was able to wash, breakfast and find a place to wash my soiled clothing all whilst the morning was still fresh. Then, I set out to find the wild magic researcher Rikolta had mentioned – Graco.

Graco's caravan sat just over the fire pit from mine. The caravans on either side of Graco's had been parked closer to hers than their other neighbours – they were also smaller which made them look as if they were sheltering under Graco's home. My footsteps fell softly on the steps as I climbed up to the doorstep. My knock was drawn inwards, barely any sound echoing out.

Twenty seconds later the door hadn't opened and I was looking about for any green signals – indicators of deafness. There was also the possibility that Graco was simply out. I was just wondering if I should come back later when the door opened, revealing a femme wearing an apron. Her face was streaked with white warpaint – or possibly flour. She introduced herself as Graco's wife Kay and pointed me in the direction of the Obsid University Cavalcade, where Graco was working on her research.

Finding my way out of the riot of colours and idiosyncratic approaches to parking that characterised the Ember Cavalcade took longer than I might have liked. Still, at least the shift when I crossed from Ember to the Obsid University Cavalcade was obvious. Two-storey caravans arranged in two meandering rows, each more sombre and serious than the last. Following Kay's directions, I examined the brass plaque set into each of the doors – I was looking for the cluster of caravans with helixes bordering their plaques.

People, students and teachers presumably, bustled around me as I searched. There were fewer obvious signs of disability here. I'd come from Ember where a good third of people were visibly disabled and another third were wearing a non-red tie, but here those numbers were around a quarter each, and there were far more red ties. Dozens of people passed me in both directions every minute, far more than I'd seen since my stay in hospital. I kept having to pause to stand in the lee of a caravan and squeeze my eyes shut to clear out the calamity of randomly moving students.

I gave up and asked someone wearing a black tie after I'd failed to locate the helix caravans. She refined the directions I'd received from Kay and, apparently noticing my distress, pointed me to a shortcut between the rows of caravans that would take me away from the stream of students.

Graco's research room was supposed to be on the top floor of a sprawling duplex with four rooms on each floor. I needed to catch my breath after climbing the stairs, and used the time to look back the way I'd come. Not being in the thick of the calamity below let me appreciate it slightly more. The drab caravans no longer seemed regimented, more like a line of academics dryly sauntering to the nearest pub.

With my breath finally coming easier, I checked the doors on the top floor and found Graco's room on the third try. The door was dark ash, either badly burned or deliberately stained the colour of a mortician's coat. The brass nameplate set into the door invited me to knock any time, so knock I did.

"Come in," said a chilly voice from within, so come in I did.

Graco's research room turned out to be more of a laboratory. A hulking slab of a table sat at its centre, whilst racks of books, storage tins and alchemical miscellanea lined the walls. The scientist herself was standing at the far end of the slab, looming over a beaker that was bubbling over a Bunsen burner. She'd tied her hair back and wore a pristine white coat over her battered linin shirt and trousers beneath. Her blue tie (signifying visual disability) was clipped to her shirt with a gold clip. The tie was so tightly knotted I was honestly surprised it was letting the blood flow to her head. She looked up and smiled in my direction. "Who's this?"

"Er... hi!" I said, waving and then feeling stupid for doing so. "I'm Laceco, Rikolta introduced us a couple of days ago."

"Ah," she said. She adjusted the flame on the Bunsen.

I rubbed my hands together – my fingers felt as if I'd been plunging them into midnight snow. "I wondered if I could ask you about your research into wild magic?"

The corners of her mouth twitched, "Oh, *that* Laceco. Very well, let us trade questions." She turned and brushed her fingers along a rack of metal tins before selecting one. She set it down next to the Bunsen with barely a sound. "What is your interest in Wild Magic?"

"Er..." The beaker of boiling water being so close to her was making me nervous. She had trouble with her vision – how much exactly? I might need to be ready in case she tried to pick up the tin but ended up putting her fingers in the flame. Her fingers... one of them was tapping the tabletop. Right, yes. She'd asked a question. "I was cursed when crossing the Ember Trail as a child. Wild magic causes manifestations around me. I want to know how it works."

She nodded, slowly, before reaching under the table and rummaging around until her expression cleared and she drew out a set of metal tongs, which she pointed at me.

My turn? "So can you tell me how it works?"

She twirled her tongs. "What? All of it? Hark, hark the young dogs bark, curiosity's come into town."

"All of what? And what have dogs got to do with it?"

"Never mind the dogs, I was being expressive. I initially referred to Wild magic. It's not really a *thing* by itself. More a series of effects to which we've given a fancy name. Personally, I don't think it actually exists."

Good to know I'd completely wasted my time by coming to see her... "You're studying something you don't think exists?"

She shrugged. "How will I know if it exists or not unless I find out. Anyway, my turn. What form have these manifestations taken?"

I rattled off the bullet-point version of each manifestation I'd witnessed so far, although I changed the names. Graco listened intently, showing no obvious sign of disbelief. She reached behind her and grabbed a mug from a rack. There was a sour tang in the air... what was she making? I was getting distracted and she didn't appear to have any follow-up questions. "So, wild magic?"

"Oh yes, that. Okay, I'll give you the short version." Graco cracked her neck. "Magic is the umbrella term we give to the energy that sinks into places and people. The people become witches, demons, and that sort of thing. The places become magical hotspots, or places such as the lovely town we've parked up next to, where worlds brush up against each other. Wild magic is different because it's not permanent. It manifests for a short period of time. Usually a few days or weeks. Up to a few years in exceptional circumstances. Afterwards, it dissipates, with few after-effects. Because of that, it's damn near impossible to study because by the time someone finds a manifestation to study, it's usually already ended, thus preventing us from establishing If it was a genuine magical manifestation or something else."

"What sort of something else?"

Graco shrugged. "Delusion, performance art, or some other kind of magical manifestation caused by a pre-existing source."

"A witch did it and ran away?"

Graco nodded. "Will you come get me if you're able to demonstrate a manifestation for me?"

I paused for just a second too long. She turned her head and seemed to be looking at me out of the corner of her eye. Sighing, I gave in and told the truth. "Probably not."

"Interesting..."

"So," I said, trying to hustle the conversation on. "I was in the Town of Lonely Windows yesterday and a spirit spoke to me. Do I need to be worried about that? I've had plenty of experience with magic but never met a spirit."

Graco smiled. "As far as I know you should be fine. You came out the other side of the experience and seem reasonably coherent. If there were any lingering effects you'd probably know about them by now. Did the spirit say anything in particular?"

"A prophecy, of sorts. Mostly a jumble of words." I rattled off the prophecy.

Graco nodded. "Right. Vague statements that the prophecy recipient can insert their own meaning into. Like that general from hundreds of years back who consulted the spirits. The spirits told her a great army would be defeated in the battle ahead, but the general didn't realise that meant *her* army!" Graco put her mug down and clapped her hands to her cheeks. "What a twist! Almost certainly apocryphal. I doubt anyone would be naïve enough to miss the very obvious loophole built into that prophecy but that's generally what we've come to expect from such things. Occasionally they match up very well with future events but it's maddeningly difficult to work out which communications from spirits are prescient and which are garbled nonsense until long after the fact."

"But how... I was picking up litter and then I was in the spirit world but also ours, I don't understand how..." I flapped an arm uselessly in the general direction of the town.

"Right," Graco said. She started spooning brown granules from her tin into her mug. "Imagine... hold on a second." She grabbed the bubbling beaker with her tongs and held it away from the flame for a moment before pouring it into the mug. The sour smell intensified, along with notes of cedar and maple syrup. Coffee? Graco turned off the Bunsen without even turning in its direction before grabbing a glass jar filled with clumps of white crystal. She twisted open the lid, and felt about inside until she drew out two lumps of white crystal.

"Sugar!" she said, before dropping the lumps into her mug and returning the jar. "Imagine the first lump, wherever it is, is our world. The second lump is whatever plane of existence that spirit's world exists in. The two worlds are separate but if certain forces are applied..." She grabbed a glass rod and stirred the coffee, causing the sugar lumps to smack into each other. "The worlds might touch for a brief while. However you notice," she stopped stirring, "that they don't stay together for long. Maybe a couple of granules of sugar were able to pass between the two. Of course we don't understand what such forces are, or where they come from, so this is all theory."

I pinched the bridge of my nose. "So I'm not about to explode or anything?"

Graco thought about this for longer than I would have liked. "Come and see me if you do."

"Right. And you're saying I should ignore the prophecy?"

"Ah!" She grabbed her metal tongs, flourished them, and then started wiping them down with a cloth. "No. So... your prophecy is almost certainly bunk. Prophecies are bunk nine times out of ten, but yours might be the tenth. What I'd suggest is not getting bogged down in the details. For example, look out of that window and tell me how many birds you see out there."

I scanned the cavalcade's rooftops as well as the treeline. "Two blackbirds, a raven, a crow and two starlings."

Graco stared in my direction. "Why do you know so much about birds?"

I frowned. "I don't understand the question."

She sighed and sipped her coffee. "Never mind. So, is six birds a contextually significant number of motherfucking birds? Who can say. What you definitely shouldn't do is start looking for birds all over the place because you'll start seeing patterns out of chaos. Humans are very good at that, I hear."

"So I just carry on as normal but keep the prophecy in mind?"

She shrugged. "It's your life. Did you want anything else?"

"If wild magic *is* manifesting and, hypothetically, if I keep seeing a cowled wraith stalking past my window at night, what could be a scientific explanation for that?"

"Costume," she said. She took a triumphant sip of her coffee.

I wanted to glower but had to admit that was the most likely explanation. Then I remembered she might not be able to see my sour pus expression, so I went ahead and glowered anyway.

If I wound up staying with Ember I should probably get myself one of those ties. It meant people wouldn't necessarily ask about my fatigue. I'd grown weary of giving the same explanation over and over and over again in my home cavalcade. I still wanted to ask Graco about her visual problems – she seemed to have little trouble navigating her laboratory. She was clearly tactile – to pick up her coffee cup she brushed the worksurface edge, then moved in to where she'd placed it before tracing her fingertips around to the handle. She tended to look in my direction rather than *at* me, but she still might have *some* vision. Every once in a while I got the impression she was looking at me out of the corner of her eye but I might be just so very off about that. Ah, well, if I didn't want people asking me about my fatigue I should probably extend people the same courtesy.

"Thanks for the consult," I said, and moved to leave.

"Come back anytime," said Graco. "I need research subjects."

Chapter Nine

I lounged about until Ven's performance in the evening. No, that was an unkind way of phrasing it. The Oro way. I rested. I badly needed to recharge, like one of those automata they have in the cities. I had books and a quiet place to exist in, so I gave some serious time to turning the pages of *Blood on the Staircase*. It turned out the murderer was Old Mister Winshaw's long-lost nephew and this was relevant because of the blackmail and the stolen carbon copies of Mirimine Anning's final wishes.

That evening I returned to the clearing where meals seemed as if they were being served and managed to finish my meal without talking to anyone again. The peace of the glade was really making my heart warm towards the Ember Cavalcade. The residents were friendly enough, but if you needed your space they let you have your space.

When I'd fled to mount Iwa I'd felt as if I could breathe for the first time. The feeling hadn't dissipated since reaching Ember. Maybe the place could be home for me after all. This idea spread through me throughout the evening. People started leaving the clearing in ones and twos, then in a flood. Not knowing where the dancing statues were, I followed. No-one talked to me on the way. They respected my space. It made me wonder how they'd react if I were merely being shy. Still, not having to make small talk gave me space to enjoy the walk.

Around half of the caravans were illuminated, either with bio-fuel lanterns, glow globes or old-fashioned wax candles. The smells of autumn leaves and carved pumpkins mingled with the warm lights to give the cavalcade a festival feeling. Off in the distance, someone whistled a few bars – a melody that skipped and jumped, repeating enough to make it damned catchy. The tune was taken up here and there and, relenting to the atmosphere, I joined in.

I'd been strolling along with the rest of the cavalcade for maybe ten minutes before I realised something was off. Trees lined our route. Had they been here earlier? Their bark was silver and black, whilst bulbous crimson apples hung from their branches. It was the month of veils, far too late for fruit. No-one paid any attention to the trees or reached to pluck their fruit. I glared at the trees. This, thankfully, did not prompt any sort of response

As we left the cavalcade behind, The Town of Lonely Windows rose on our right. We kept walking for maybe another five minutes before the ground rose to a slight crest before sloping into a majestic basin. Braziers had been lit on all sides, illuminating the hundred or so people sitting and standing, all facing the base of the basin. Twenty figures stood below, contorted and spindly at this distance. One had arms encircling their head, another flung their chest forward whilst their arms splayed back. My approach to dancing had always defaulted to the old 'flail your arms around, twist your feet, and hope' technique. By my standards, the statues were the model of choreographed elegance.

I found a spot about half way down the slope to the statues where I could sit near enough my fellow Embers that I wasn't being antisocial, but not so close I was at risk of someone talking to me. I sighed, let my head roll back and listened to the excited chatter of those around me. Snatches of conversation, occasional fragments of context flowed past me, and I bobbed along on the surface. I breathed, filling myself with the odour of earth, and fresh leaves.

A distant peel of laughter made me crack an eye open. Sol was on the other side of the basin with a cluster of friends. They'd spread out a picnic blanket and appeared to have found booze from somewhere. Good for them. People were still finding spots to sit around me, including one I recognised.

Spite seethed within me, its unexpected speed making me feel as if I'd been punched. I screwed my eyes tight, tight shut and shook my head. Where had that reaction come from? He wasn't a rival. I was being ridiculous.

I opened my eyes again and waved. "Rikolta!"

He looked, he saw me, he froze for only a moment before walking over and collapsing next to me. "You made it okay," he said, grinning at me.

"It was this or crash out in bed for a third night in a row."

Rikolta's grin grew a little wider, a hint of the shark glinting at the edges. "Might have been a better choice but I know Ven will be happy you came."

"Yeah... Er... Look, I hope I haven't caused any..."

Rikolta waved my half-apology away. "Jealousy is the domain of amatonormativity."

"You can say that again," I said, wondering if I should know what that cluster of syllables meant. "So Ven's going to sing for everyone?"

"Not just Ven, it's a whole... well, you'll see. Ah, you'll see now I think."

Down in the basin, the statues moved. First one, then two... four... eight... eight figures that had been perfectly still were now swirling around the others, peerless elegance, flowing curves, feather-light trails of fabric marking their passage. I slapped my forehead. They hadn't all been statues down there. I watched them move, trying to spot if one of the dancers was Ven.

Seven figures twirled as one was drawn to the eye of the circle of statues. They turned on the spot. A low, humming note rose, slow and certain. I hadn't heard its beginning but now I felt as if it was suddenly everywhere, filling the spaces between me and my fellow Embers.

The other twirling figures slowed and joined the song, adding resonance. Layers. A melody emerging voice by voice. The final two to join did so as one, laying lyrics atop the surging song. One of the two lyricists was unmistakably Ven. I was used to her voice sounding annoyed, tired, aggravated, amused, irritated and, occasionally, filled with desire. On that night, her voice soared over us, lifting us up with her.

Voice-by-voice, the singers dropped away, leaving only Ven holding her final note. A delighted hush sat around us as the song faded away. Only once silence had finally, finally fallen did someone begin to clap. The hush broken, the Embers joined. Cheers and whoops rose, vocal fireworks illuminating the crowd.

"Damn, they're good!" I called to Rikolta.

"Right?"

"I had no idea Ven could sing that well!"

Rikolta clapped on, but didn't answer.

An hour later, after announcing their final song, the singers began to disperse. They moved out past the dancing statues and out through the crowd, each making their own way, the song fading part by part. Ven, possibly by co-incidence, sauntered in my direction. Her voice danced ahead of her, and Embers shuffled aside to make room for her.

She moved step by unhurried step, and it was only when her face was illuminated by a nearby brazier that I realised she was looking at me.

Fire danced in her eyes as she approached. To my left, Rikolta shifted. To my right, an Ember shuffled out of Ven's way. The melody was slowing, and Ven's voice grew quieter as she walked. Her silken steps approached. As she reached me, she held out a hand. The wind teased her hair as it passed. I took her hand, and scrambled to stand as Ven resumed her coda.

Her voice was the only one I heard as we reached the crest of the basin. The crowd of Embers thinned. As we descended towards the cavalcade, we passed the last of Ven's audience. She let her last note fade. Ahead of us, the lights of Ember and Obsid University cavalcades glittered.

Without warning, Ven spun to face me. "Did you enjoy our performance?"

"I..." I had to swallow. She was smiling, her face framed by a sea of glittering lights. "I did, yes."

She leaned forward, traced my cheek with the tip of her finger, drew me to her and kissed me, her lips parted slowly before she pulled back. "Show me how much you enjoyed my performance."

She led me back to my caravan, my heart pounding the whole way. The last thing I saw before we slipped inside my caravan was the window through which I'd seen the cowled wraith. I only realised why it had snagged my attention an hour later, as I began drifting off to sleep in Ven's arms.

The window was around chest height in the caravan wall, and because my accommodation was mounted on a flat-bed truck base, that meant the distance from the ground to the window was around two and a half meters. Twice, I'd seen the wraith's cowled head through that window as it walked past. I had to hope the wraith wasn't another manifestation.

Crunch... crunch... crunch... Shifting movement – *my* movement. I rolled over, my head flumping down onto something soft. A pillow. An unclothed wonder in the bed next to me. I was awake. Why was... The window. A head shrouded in cloth stalking past, its footsteps wounding the ground as it passed. Three nights, three times the creature had passed. I hadn't heard about any mysterious deaths or illnesses sweeping through the cavalcade. Then again, I'd been very deliberately avoiding conversation. I sighed, wriggled free of the bedclothes, and packed them back in around Ven to keep the heat in.

I pulled on shoes and a jacket, before pausing at my door. My curse had completely thrown my sense of danger. It was entirely possible I was about to put myself into the path of a creature. Tall, and terrible. Remorseless, and rampaging through the cavalcade. Or, it might be a manifestation that was causing some poor Ember distress. I had no idea how likely either possibility was. Still, I could be sure I wouldn't find out by staying frozen still, my hand resting immobile on the doorknob. I opened the door and stepped outside.

The wraith had its back to me, a hunching figure enveloped in a grey-white cloak, ragged and pock-marked. Only bleached bone fingers emerged from the sleeves of its cloak, five-jointed digits that disappeared into the sleeves without a hint of a palm. Footprints gouged into the ground in its wake, the grass around the scars in the ground grey and lifeless.

The night was still, and the moons were full. The bats had fled. Not even insect life wanted to go near the thing. I took three deep breaths, stepped down to the wilting grass, and followed the Wraith.

At first, I kept well behind the creature, but as it stalked through the cavalcade without noticing me, I grew bolder. I slipped through gaps between slumbering caravans, keeping an eye on the wraith to my left. Dark crumpled shapes shifted around my peripheral vision, and I couldn't clear a sickly knot in my throat. I dearly wished I'd stop and just let the wraith go, but the cowled figure was lodged in my mind like an ice-pick. The wraith was either some malignant creature only I could see, in which case I needed to learn its purpose, or it was a manifestation. Either way, I couldn't let it go, and my reluctant determination was only compounded when I saw the creature was carrying a wicker basket.

The basket was half my size, and hung from the wraith's skeletal fingers with the weight of centuries. I couldn't see what was inside without getting closer, but I'd only ever seen such baskets in domestic settings up until now. The wraith looked as if it were on its way to an otherworldly picnic.

I managed to get ahead of the wraith and peered through the gap between two caravans. Its cowl was pulled low over its face, but a skeletal jaw was still visible, grinning in the moonlight. I was just wondering if I should be trying to stop the wraith or merely observe, when the wraith stopped by one of the silver trees the cavalcade had parked up next to. The wraith reached up and plucked one of the crimson apples, which it placed delicately into its basket.

I stared, unable to move, as the wraith approached the next tree and plucked an apple, before moving on. I sighed, the weight in my legs and chest suddenly obvious. Still, I'd come this far. I scrambled under the caravan I'd been sheltering behind and re-joined the main trail in the wraiths wake. It stopped at another nine trees and plucked another nine apples, never turning, never moving from the winding boulevard formed by the cavalcade.

It picked the next apple, its twelfth, and finally stopped. It hefted the basket in its hand, an executioner checking if she had sufficient heads in her basket that she could get away with knocking off early. It turned from the path towards a little family of caravans and stalked towards them. A yelp of alarm forced its way between my clenched teeth. Diving under the caravan that had been sheltering me from the wraith's purpose, my vision blurred and refused to clear. I wiped at my eyes as I stood, turned, and ran towards the wraith, only managing to focus when I was mere meters away.

The wraith was making for a caravan I didn't recognise. It had an artfully tiled roof, amber curtains and roses round the door. The executioner still walked with deliberate slowness, allowing me to sprint past it and reach the foot of the mystery caravan before the wraith. That was when I made the mistake of thinking.

Manifestations were harmless, nine times out of ten. I suspected this wraith was another manifestation, but I didn't know. I *suspected* I'd be fine if I tried to stop the wraith from entering the red roofed home. I *suspected* it meant no harm by approaching the caravan – maybe it wanted to offer the residents its blood apples. There was, however, the possibility that this was not a manifestation, a tricky yet ultimately benevolent expression of wild magic. There were creatures in the world who could boil my blood or make the world forget me entirely.

The wraith took another two steps forward — two steps before I was shamed into acting. No one wanted to live forever, after all. I stepped into the wraith's path and held up my hands. "Please," I said, amazed at how steady my voice sounded. "stop."

The wraith stalked closer – only a few steps away from me now. The bones in my neck cracked as I looked up into its empty eye sockets. A human skull but twice the size. Its cowl was pulled low, edges flapping even in the windless night. Crunching and cracking accompanied its footsteps. Those cracks would be my bones in a second if this didn't work.

"Please," I said, my voice finally cracking, "stop." The wraith didn't slow, its right foot cracking down into the ground mere millimetres from where I stood. I sighed. I'd left it too late to flee. It was already stepping forward. One more try. "Stop!" I yelled.

And... the wraith stopped halfway through its next step, the one that would have caused its indefatigable gait to send me sprawling. Its foot hovered above pristine grass before descending. It changed as it dropped, from a scraggle of bones in place of a foot, to something more flesh toned. A gust of wind rose behind me, flowed over my shoulders and into the wraith's face. The wind caught the wraith's cowl and cloak, which it tossed back. As the wind flowed around the wraith, the creature changed, morphing in shape and colour, discharging crackles of wild magic danced around the wraith's shrinking body. In less than a minute, the wind dropped and Rikolta fell forward into my arms.

Too heavy to hold, he hit the ground with a *flump*. Grey, greasy plumes of dust puffed up, showering him for barely a moment. My heart heaved in my chest, my breath feeling ragged. I was alive. It was just a manifestation. Rikolta's...

The door to Rikolta's caravan burst open and a femme wearing fluffy slippers and a pink dressing gown scampered down the stairs to Rikolta's side. "Riki!" Fluffy Slippers was followed by a dour figure wearing a simple black nightshirt – their nails painted with midnight.

"It's okay!" I said, hovering as Fluffy Slippers poked at Rikolta. "He was... he was..."

"He was coming to see us," said Midnight Nails. "Who are you?"

"I'm new to the Cavalcade, my name's Laceco."

Pink Slippers and Midnight exchanged meaningful glances.

"Are you Rikolta's partners?"

Midnight nodded. "Jans."

Fluffy slippers smiled. "I'm Indi."

I smiled, although the fatigue was coming at me in waves, leaving me feeling numb and displaced. I couldn't be sure I'd smiled properly. "Good to meet you both. Come on, let's get him inside."

The triad's caravan was cluttered wall to wall with curios, knick-knacks, and esoterica. Shelves lined every wall, only skipping over windows and the tiny stove in one corner, and every shelf was littered with pink statuettes, black candles, pink-jacketed books, black spiky ornaments... there was a definite theme. Most of the floorspace was taken up by an enormous bed, which Indi, Jans and I heaved Rikolta onto.

Janes peered at him, owlishly. "He's still breathing. Will he be okay?"

"Absolutely," I said, "there's a bit of wild magic hanging around, it's snagged Rikolta. He needs to sleep and I'll have a chat with him in the morning."

Jans nodded, mournfully. Indi's gaze twitched to meet mine. "*You'll* take care of... whatever this is?"

I found myself shifting my weight from foot to foot. "I'll do what I can."

Jans stood before bowing to me, their nightshirt rustling like bat wings. "Thank you."

"Yes, let me see you out," said Indi.

"Oh, there's really no need," I said, already finding myself being bustled towards the door. "I'll come and chat to Rikolta after breakfast, if that's okay..."

Indi opened the door and saw me safe down the stairs, before closing the caravan's door... but she closed it from the outside. She stood on the top step looking down at me on the ground. "I saw you," she said.

"Er..."

"You dropped Rikolta."

Crap. "I caught him but he was too heavy... I'm really sorry."

Indi's gaze flashed, fuchsia fire burning deep within. "You don't have a red tie. You know about the red ties right?"

I couldn't look at her. "I know about the red ties and no, I don't have one, I'm really s-"

"Save it. I'm going to assume that if you chose to wear a tie it'd be white. Unless you want to tell me otherwise?"

My skin cracked, blistered. Flames consumed me. I couldn't answer her.

"You're not wearing a red tie, which means you have some leeway," Indi said, her voice softening from diamond to granite. "but a thing to bear in mind is... just because you're disabled that doesn't give you license to be a prick to people."

She slipped back into her caravan before I could even begin to think about replying. I turned, trying to remember the way I'd come. I walked, unable to shake one particular idea.

Ven shifted as I slipped into bed next to her. "Mmsm?"

"Only me," I said, "sorry for waking you."

"Any... what?" she said.

The idea burned in my head. "Well," I said. *This was a bad idea.* "the thing is..." *This was a very bad idea.* "Rikolta..." *This was a very bad idea but I'd already started and I didn't know how to stop.* "Rikolta's working through a manifestation. He collapsed when the effect passed. Fell into my arms. He was too heavy, I couldn't hold him and I had to lower him to the floor. Just in case, you know. I don't know if you'll hear about this from someone else..."

"Is he okay?" Ven asked, sleep still dragging at her.

"Oh yeah, he's fine." I said. I was ablaze, my lies burning Ven along with me.

"Good," said Ven. She turned over and immediately started to snore.

Chapter Ten

Wood thumped against wood. Someone thumping a staff against decking? No, a door closing. I turned over. The bed next to me was cold.

"I have... breakfast!" announced Ven.

I sat up, finding a fully dressed and lively Ven holding a plate of mashed potato and assorted seasonal vegetables.

I groaned and sat up. "You're a life saver."

"This is true." She sat down on the bed next to me. "You were saying things last night but I didn't really understand what you were saying. Can you summarise?"

I swallowed. "Ah. So yeah, Rikolta's experiencing a manifestation. He's transforming into an enormous creature and walking about the cavalcade picking apples."

Ven stuck a finger in her ear and wiggled it, thoughtfully. "Huh."

"Yeah. Needs further study."

"Okay. Did you say anything else? I thought there was something..."

Crap. My cheeks were burning. "Ah, yes. Well when he transformed back from the creature I tried to catch him but he was too heavy."

Ven squinted at me. "You said that quite quickly, Laceco."

"Mm?"

Ven leaned in a little and poked at me.

"Er..."

Ven poked at me again. "Hmm. Something's going on... I think. You're sitting differently, you're not looking at me... Okay, this is really important. I'm not a subtext person. It feels as if you're trying to say something without saying it. Or maybe... what you just said was true, wasn't it? Because if it was, we'll be fine. If it wasn't true... Laceco... the words people use matter. If you say one thing and mean another, I won't necessarily notice. I can't be in a relationship with someone who lies to me. I need to be able to trust what you say. I'm sorry if I'm way off about this, but I've had... experience with people treating me like a child because I'm different to them."

Do I double down or... "Sorry," I said, shaking my head. The world was close around me, and it burned. I couldn't think straight – my thoughts felt as if they were drifting up from the bottom of a haunted well. Fuck it. The truth hurt but I couldn't hurt Ven further. "Yeah, I was lying. I caught Rikolta after he transformed back but when I saw it was him I... just... I didn't want to hold him up. I dropped him onto the ground – grass, it was only grass, he was fine. He was probably fine."

"Mm." Ven stared at me. "That everything?"

"Indi saw me drop him."

"Ah. So you panicked and thought you'd cover your tracks, is that it?"

I couldn't look at her. "Something like that."

Ven nodded, thoughtfully. "Interesting. All right. Thanks for telling me." She sat back, leant against the wall of the caravan, and closed her eyes.

"Are you angry with me?" I asked, confused.

"Mm?"

"You don't seem to mind that I did something spiteful."

"Mm. Still working on that one. You said you're sorry. You seem pretty cut up about it. At least, I think you are. Assuming what you just said was true... hm. I don't know. I'll see if an emotional reaction comes along to change things up some. Currently I'm feeling... what's that... not sure. Sort of fuzzy feeling. Crackly hazard fence sort of feeling. Not bad exactly... no idea."

"And... do you want to keep seeing me?"

Ven opened her eyes and smiled, "As long as what you said was true, sure. It was, wasn't it?"

I sighed, put my half-eaten breakfast on the floor and turned to face Ven. "Yes, it was. I didn't realise how much... I won't lie to you again, Ven. I'm sorry."

Ven grimaced and closed her eyes again. "Good. Eat your breakfast."

I did as instructed, alternately counting my blessings, and berating myself for trying to cover up my actions. Not least because I had attempted a coverup with the amount of forethought and attention to detail I might have expected from a toddler trying to explain herself with her hand in the biscuit jar.

"So, Laceco," Ven said. "It's a Ven day! Everyone applaud!" We both clapped and cheered, "so, I could give you a bit of a tour. I know you had a time in the Town of Lonely Windows but now the spirit has passed on its message she might be less fractious. I could introduce you to an Ember vocation specialist who might get you settled. Alternately, we could look into this Rikolta thing."

A hollow, draining sensation shivered down from my forehead to my stomach. Still, I owed him. "Let's look into what's going on with Rikolta."

"Ah, now *that* I recognised as the tone of someone who really doesn't want to do something."

"N..." I started, before remembering I'd *just* promised not to lie to Ven. "Alright, not really but it's the right thing to do."

"Oh, good," said Ven, "I'm dating a martyr." She then kissed me, hopefully to indicate she didn't mean it.

I washed and shaved before returning to the caravan, where Ven was still in bed. I asked if she wanted to get going. She removed the covers. Twenty-five minutes later, we left the caravan and set off for Indi and Jans' abode.

"Tell me about Rikolta," I said, Ven's proximity warming me to my core.

"Grew up in Ember, mother is the head priestess. Nice guy. One of us. You know about the leg – mostly it's fine but he's had trouble with it. Nerve pain and if he doesn't keep clean the spot where his prosthetic meets flimsy human flesh things can get real bad real quick."

"Any reason he'd start manifesting now?"

"I believe I mentioned a reason a while back. You did the thing I hate."

I looked down and realised I'd stepped on a land mine. "What thing?"

Ven sighed. "You waved away the idea that someone might be intimidated by you. People do that all the time – dismiss who they are, their accomplishments and how they might affect other people. 'Oh,

I'm nothing special'. Get fucked, Wendil, you're a fucking legend and we both know it."

The land mine stopped beeping, so I scampered to catch up with Ven. "Who's Wendil?"

"School friend. Terrible taste in partners. Good with her hands."

I swerved to avoid a chattering pair in wheelchairs. "Right. So... what were you saying before I indulged in self-destructive self-dismissal?"

Ven grinned at me. "I merely said that, if you were Rikolta, you might find a girlfriend of yours fleeing the cavalcade and then returning in the company of a short, handsome stranger who unravelled a complex manifestation of wild magic, who has seen and done more than he has, who is older and who your aforementioned girlfriend is clearly extremely into... you might find that a little intimidating."

"Ah..." Did that make sense? Deep within my brain, the five or six brain cells that had been able to break through the fog of fatigue took one look at what Ven had just said, decided they didn't want to have anything to do with it and gave up, letting the fog reclaim them. "Okay, well let's work with that as a starting point. How does Rikolta feeling intimidated by..." Fraud. Hypocrite. Braggart. The Oro Virus drove spikes out from where it lived deep within me. I needed to joke about how I couldn't really be intimidating. Something like 'intimidated by someone amazing and wonderful and brilliant' just to hammer home that I don't actually believe I'm amazing... but Ven had *just* said she hated people doing that... "Intimidated by me...." I said, the words flopping limply out of my mouth. "lead to him turning into a Wraith and harvesting crimson apples?"

"No idea," Ven clasped her hands on top of her head and stared ahead as she walked. "then again I still don't exactly get how my feeling deeply shitty about my autism because of how people treated me led to my teleporting to a mountain."

I paused at the next part of the trail, partly because my legs were feeling heavy and partly because I couldn't remember what turning led to Indi and Jans' place. This part of the cavalcade was pretty quiet – some Embers had strung laundry lines between caravans, but never crossing the trail itself. Down one trail the Town of Lonely Windows lurked, its houses teeny at this distance. Plenty of Embers seemed to be working there still. Ven caught up and guided me to the step of a caravan no-one seemed to be immediately using.

"Wild magic," I said once I'd gathered some energy. "Yeah, it's... I don't know. I *think* the manifestations are given shape by our subconscious. And sometimes the subconscious wants to show us how we're feeling deep down. Sometimes it wants to take our pain and literalise it to make us deal with it. It could be doing any one of a hundred things. Either the subconscious doesn't know how to communicate with us or we've forgot how to listen. Anyway – turning into a wraith and harvesting crimson apples is doing *something* and we have to work out what."

Talking to Rikolta was less illuminating than I might have liked. Indi was perfectly welcoming, which made me nervous but I tried to focus on the point of our visit. Rikolta had left the dancing statues after the performance and returned home where Indi and Jans were making food. They'd played a card game until the small hours when they'd gone to bed.

He didn't remember anything after that until waking up the next morning. He was deeply sceptical of my account of his movements. Neither Ven nor I pressed him about whether he felt intimidated by me or not, but I asked if he could think of a reason why a manifestation might have started three days ago – any changes other than my arrival? None of the triad could think of any.

That left Ven and me tracking down lunch none the wiser. "I think," I said, once we'd found a queue for rations, "we should talk to Graco. A scientist might be able to see patterns that aren't obvious to mortals. Plus I promised I'd tell her if I encountered another manifestation."

Ven didn't know the way to Graco's caravan, so I talked expansively about the history of the Obsid University Cavalcade as we made our way there. I was half way through an explanation of why one particular caravan I didn't recognise was a crucial part of the second Obsid University Schism between the liberal faction and the leftist faction when I realised the elaborate, entirely fictional story I was telling could easily be seen as an elaborate lie. "Er..." I said, suddenly stopping.

Ven turned and blinked owlishly at me. "Problem?"

"What's the difference between lying and making up a silly story for the purposes of a joke?" I asked, fidgeting my fingers in tense, spider-like contortions.

Ven frowned. She then grabbed me by the elbow and dragged me out of the thoroughfare, stashing me between two caravans. "That's an excellent question," she said. "and I don't think it has an answer. One time when I was little I went with some friends and whoever was babysitting us to pick up some fruit from a local farm. Being about eight years old, I didn't understand the principles of communal living. All I knew is we were going to go to this farm and do some duties – tidy the place up, do some washing up or whatever – as a thank you for the fruit.

"The babysitter said that one of the other kids, Yat, would do all the duties for us. Clearly a joke – we'd all shirk our responsibilities and get Yat to do everything. Eight year old Ven didn't understand that, so when the farmer's husband asked what I'd be able to help with, I said Yat was going to do my share of the helping."

"That's so damned cute," I said.

"Mm, sure. Anyway, I'm sure you've noticed that I'm no longer eight years old."

"That was an important factor in my dating you, yes."

"So I like to think I've learned enough about social whatevers to be able to tell the difference between a joke and an actual story, but I can't be sure."

"Ah."

Ven sighed, "But telling silly stories is fun so... I don't know, Laceco. Maybe try not to worry about it? Just don't lie about something which matters."

"Right," I said. "Sorry again about that."

"Yes, yes, you're a monster," said Ven. "Are we nearly there?"

"Just up there, I think."

Our route to Graco's caravan took us past one of the silver trees. I snagged an apple as we passed. Ven could see both the tree and the apples, which confused me. Maybe I was wrong about the other Embers not being able to see them. We reached Graco's lab only to find she wasn't there, which after we'd made our way across the cavalcade put me in a less than clement mood. We asked around the other labs and were pointed to a nearby community spot.

After making two mis-starts and blundering into a caravan that seemed to contain nothing but a bed and hundreds of intricately carved wooden statues of the same land mammal over and over again, we finally located a caravan with an enormous cast-iron pipe sticking out of the roof, through which steam vented industriously.

Knocking on the door resulted in it being opened by a slight masc wearing a painter's apron – the only part of him that didn't appear spattered with paint. Gold flecks covered his left cheek, his fingers were smeared with merging colours... if I weren't already in a relationship and if I had more energy I might have tried some flirting. As things stood, I asked after Graco and was pointed down a rickety corridor, past a hulking, churning engine with a steadily draining water tank on its top, to a door at the remote end of the caravan, where a blackboard set onto the door read 'Graco – booked room 10:00 – 19:00'.

I pointed to the sign. "What if someone with difficulty seeing comes along and wants to use the room?"

Ven blinked at me but said nothing.

"Isn't there a system?"

Ven blinked again, then closed her eyes and left them closed for a pointed length of time before opening them once again.

"There's a system, isn't there?" I asked, feeling my cheeks burn.

Ven fluttered her eyelashes.

I turned back to the sign and... yes, there was a little slot just under the sign that had a card in it. On the card were raised lumps and lines. Tracing my finger across it felt like touching one of those textured drums the machine-smiths use to program automata. "A second language?"

Ven blinked before shaking her head and laughing to herself. "Yeah. I forget what it's called but it's one of two things you'll see around the place. One is purely tactile, the other is based on the alphabet we use with tactile elements. It tries to mix the two forms. People are split over which one they prefer."

"Right." I frowned, trying to remember why we'd come to this particular caravan, before spotting Graco's name. I knocked on the door.

The studio was the same flavour of precision chaos as Graco's lab, albeit with a certain amount of condensation shimmering on one wall.

"Hi Graco," I said, "It's Laceco. Can you spare a minute?"

"Hello, Laceco." Graco was sitting at a table with a raised edge running around the outside. On the table, she had a sheet of metal mesh. She was bending the mesh into shapes, before cutting the shape free from the larger sheet with a pair of pliers, and setting it in a pile on the corner of the table. She cocked her head to the side. "And who's that with you?"

"Hi Graco, it's Ven. I'm dating this hunk and also Rikolta. I'm not sure we've been... formally introduced? If that's how it works. I don't know the rules, sorry. Wait, I remember... I'm a pale skinned woman in her early 20s with fabulous blond hair and I'm wearing a... what the fuck is this? Black and green dress sort of thing."

Graco nodded. "Hi Ven, nice to meet you. What can I do for you?"

"You asked me to come and see you if a manifestation was occurring?"

Graco nodded, "And you said you probably wouldn't."

Ven frowned at me. "Why not?"

"Exactly!" Graco said, flourishing her pliers at Ven. "Georgie Porgie over there ruins my fun. Georgie Porgie, pudding and pie. Blocks my research and makes me cry."

I was starting to feel ganged-up-on. "Look, I wanted to consult you about a manifestation and I have a physical expression of wild magic here." I placed the apple on her table.

Graco tapped a finger on the table. "When you say 'here'... what do you mean, exactly?"

"Yes, right, sorry. I placed it on your table just in front of you, maybe... fifty centimetres?"

Graco reached forward, her hand passing straight through the apple. She felt about for a moment before glaring in my direction. "Is this a prank? Because I hate pranks."

"It's there, I swear!" I said, taking a step back.

"It is, Graco," said Ven. "Your hand passed through it as if it was insubstantial."

Graco's eyebrows rose to her hairline. "Really?" She turned her head and seemed to be trying to look at the apple out of the corner of her eye.

It wasn't the first time I'd seen her do that. Which... fuck it, I hoped it wasn't entirely rude to ask. "Sorry, Graco, can I ask about your visual disability?"

"Smooth," said Ven.

Graco winked at Ven before turning to me. "Mm. Sure. It's called Corona Blindness. I used to be fully sighted, then the centre of my vision started to fade. Now it's as if there's a big ol' black hole at the centre of my vision. My peripheral vision works okay but that's going to go sooner or later. I'm in the habit of only using what little sight I have occasionally. I don't want to rely on something which is on its way out."

I pointed. "So, you don't see anything there?"

Graco shook her head. "But both of you do. Hold on..." She strode around her table, running her fingertips along the edge just ahead of her next step. She reached down into a cubby and emerged with two sheets of paper, which she flicked towards us. Ven caught them out of the air, then I caught the two pencils which Graco tossed in our general direction. "Write down what you see, don't discuss it between you, don't let each other see what you're writing." We did as we were told. "Now, swap papers and read what the other has written. Out loud, please."

"Blood apple," I read.

"A shimmering crimson orb, appearing similarly to an apple. It catches the light and reflects it in places. It's stalk is slightly curved, and there's no fuzz or burrs from where it was plucked," said Ven, before giving me an odd look.

"Mm," said Graco. "All right. Pidril next door has a set of scales, go ask if we can borrow them please."

Ven nudged me. I went and asked a greying femme whose arms were caked with clay for their scales. Returning with my prize, I set them on the table and weighed the apple. "Huh." A click-clack sound filled the silence.

"What do you mean, huh?" Graco snapped.

"Now that's interesting..." said Ven.

"Spirits claim both of you, tell me what you find so fascinating."

I turned, "Sorry, Graco. The scale... the needle is... the scale can't seem to decide if the apple weighs anything or not. The needle is swinging between zero grams and around three hundred. That's the clacking noise – the scale's mechanism must be struggling to keep up."

"Huh," said Graco. "Okay."

What followed was a series of arcane experiments. Following Graco's instructions we tried cutting the apple, boiling it, placing objects on top of it before turning our backs on it to see if its existence persisted when unobserved. Graco duplicated each experiment herself, using a tactile readout to confirm the readings on the scale, alongside other methods of measurement which only she understood. The results of the experiments were conflicted.

"So," said Graco, grabbing a mug and drawing steaming water from a pipe jutting from the condensation-clad wall of the room, "the blood apple exists. Or it doesn't. Both at the same time. This certainly is a datapoint for wild magic existing."

"But what *is* it?" I asked. "Why does it look like an apple?"

"Good question," said Graco. "One of you try and eat it."

"Not it," said Ven.

I sighed, and took a bite from the apple. My teeth clacked together – the fruit felt solid, the flesh firm in my hand but my teeth had passed through it as if it wasn't there. I tried again with slightly more caution, but the result was the same. "I can't. My teeth pass straight through it."

Graco nodded. "Okay, so it's possible the apple is only an apple for the wraith. What did the wraith do with the apples, Laceco?"

"I don't know, Rikolta changed back into a human before I could find out."

Graco nodded. "So, I see two possibilities. Either, these apples mean something very specific to the wraith, who knows what. Alternately, our experiments may have uncovered exactly what the apple is – both something and not something at the same time. It might be something like a magical stem cell."

Ven rocked back on her heels. "A what?"

Graco set her mug of steaming water down on the table with a definitive *clack*. "Water," she said, "is a starting point from which many things can be created. In this instance," she felt about under the table and retrieved a tin, from which she poured coffee grounds into the mug, "it has now become coffee. Now, imagine instead of water it was one step before the existence of water. Imagine it was the thing the water was before it was water, and instead of being able to become coffee or... coffee... it could become anything in the world." She sieved floating coffee grounds from the surface of her brew, and flicked them into a bin, before taking a satisfied sip.

"Do all your scientific explanations involve coffee, Graco?" I asked.

"I like coffee, get fucked."

Ven cackled before turning to me. "It sounds like we need to follow the wraith and see what he does with the apples."

I nodded, before realising exactly what Ven had said. "'We?'"

Ven ran her hand down my cheek before slipping her fingers around to the back of my neck. The chill in her fingertips made me shiver. She drew me into a kiss. "We," she said, once we'd separated.

"Well, I'm glad I didn't have to see that," said Graco, dryly. "Now, we're done, yes? Get out of my studio. I have art to work on."

Chapter Eleven

That night, Ven and I went on a wraith hunt. Rikolta was sleeping at Indi and Jans' place that night, so lurking nearby seemed sensible. The chill of autumn still crisped the air, so we wrapped up warm and found a hydroponics caravan with a good view inside which we could lurk.

"Why did you drop Rikolta?" asked Ven, an hour after the cavalcade had stilled.

I'd promised not to lie... "I don't know. Often... there are things I do and I don't know why I do them. I make decisions and I don't remember making them. Sometimes it might be because the fatigue is making my head a mess of white and grey noise. Other times it feels different, but when I'm in that state I'm not in a good space to watch myself. I don't remember if there's something wrong that I need to pay attention to."

"You feel like a zombie?"

"Sometimes, yeah. Other times... a marathon runner who finished their forty-two kilometres yesterday, and the day before that, and the day before that... and they need to do it again today."

Ven scratched her forehead. "Fucking hell..."

I pointed. "There he is..."

The wraith was on the bottom step of Indi and Jans' caravan. I'd been watching – I hadn't seen their caravan door open or close, I hadn't seen Rikolta, I hadn't seen anyone approach. Nevertheless, there the wraith was.

Ven drew in a single sharp breath, shivered and then stepped forward, her jaw set firm.

I joined her in her march towards her partner, "you okay, Ven?"

"This reaper isn't going to harvest me, is it?" she said, her gaze locked on her beloved's false face.

"Manifestations don't cause lasting damage," I said, hoping I sounded more confident to Ven than I did to myself, "nine times out of ten."

The wraith... Rikolta showed no sign of recognition on our approach. He kept his slow, stalking stride down the thoroughfare between sleeping caravans.

We walked with him as he plucked an apple from one tree then the next. Five apples later and he hadn't acknowledged our presence at all.

"Have you noticed the way he's walking?" said Ven, her voice like silk in the stillness.

"Yeah, like a hunter stalking prey."

"What? No. It's his gait – Rikolta's. He's... He walks as if he's weightless, moving like one of those ancient monks who used to step between tree branches as if they were terra firma."

I frowned. Ven was wrong, surely. This was my area of... But then, I hadn't studied movement in... certainly a while. Had I picked it back up after the hospital? I'd been so tired all the damned time. I shook my head, feeling the cobwebs loosen a little. I watched Rikolta's gait – what little I could see of his movement beneath the grey cloak. His bone-clawed feet tore at the ground beneath him, and I'd assumed that had meant his form was heavy. Weighed down. But… Ven was right.

His steps were slow and precise, but… I lay down on the ground, wincing as the damp grass immediately soaked my clothes. I shook my head and shifted onto my side. I should get up. Why was I down here? A shadow passed in front of the moon – the towering wraith moving past. Yes, I'd been trying to watch Rikolta's feet. I closed my eyes, feeling the fatigue fade ever so slightly – a retreating wave from a flood tide. I opened my eyes and focussed on Rikolta's feet before hauling myself upright. "You're right."

"Mm?" said Ven. She was walking next to Rikolta, matching him step for step.

"He's walking in this really calm manner… floating from step to step, but with a consistent pace. It's *purposeful*, for all the lilting lightness. What I can't figure out is why his steps are marking the ground so much if his steps aren't carrying any weight."

Ven let Rikolta move ahead and examined the claw-prints he left in his wake. "Huh. He could be leaving a trail for us to follow?"

I scratched my forehead, my nails scraping dry skin. "Maybe, but he doesn't exactly blend in. I think you're right in that there's something specific about his claw-prints. Something purposeful."

"Huh," Ven said, but didn't elaborate.

Rikolta's path took him in a rough circuit of the Ember Cavalcade. Once he plucked his twelfth apple, he hefted the basket in his hands and strode in the direction of Jans and Indi's caravan.

"What happens now?" Ven asked, having to half run to keep up with Rikolta.

"I don't know. Last time I stopped him entering. I don't think he's here to hurt them. Shall we just let his manifestation play out? See what happens?"

"You're sure he won't hurt them?"

"No!" I said, frustration cracking my voice, "I'm not sure about anything Ven! Particularly when it comes to manifestations."

"Best guess?"

"My only guess – the apples are an apology. He's upset Indi and Jans in some way. He sees himself as a monster, but he can't express that without the manifestation. His subconscious turns him into the wraith, but with that pain literalised he has the strength to gather his... apology apples."

Ven drew in air between her teeth, before taking a step back. My heart faltered as the wraith climbed the steps to the caravan's door. I rocked on my heels, second guessing everything I knew about wild magic. What if I was wrong about Rikolta not harming the occupants? I still had time, I could get in front of him and stop him as I had the night before. But what if that denied us the information we needed to unlock Rikolta's manifestation?

Four bone fingers, longer than my arm, gripped the doorhandle and forced it down. The wraith swung the door open and stepped forward. The moment he stepped over the threshold, the cloak and basket vanished. I winced at the sudden shift in my vision, having to rub my eyes rather than focus on the impossible change. One moment Rikolta was the wraith, then in the space of a single footstep, he was back to himself – half the size, no cloak, no basket. No apples.

The caravan was dim inside, but I could see enough from the gas lamps and moonlight that Rikolta's hands were empty. He closed the door with barely a click, leaving Ven and I shivering and deeply confused.

"Do we..." I said, before realising I'd started talking with no clear idea of what to do next.

Ven clapped her palms to her cheeks twice, nodded and then strode up to the caravan's door. She knocked softly, waited a few moments, and then knocked again. The door opened. Ven spoke quietly. The door closed. Ven stalked away, her gaze unfocussed. She was heading in roughly the direction of our cluster of caravans.

I fell into step next to her. "What happened?"

"Mm?"

"Who did you talk to?"

"Oh, Rikolta. He looked as if he'd just woke up. I asked him if he had any apples. He gave me a bit of a look and said no. I bade my beloved goodnight and here we are."

"Huh. Did you see the apples? The basket?"

"Nope. Saw most of the caravan. No apples."

Getting to sleep that night was an exercise in frustration. My brain couldn't let Rikolta's manifestation go, but it also couldn't make any actual progress. I kept finding myself thinking the start of a thought, before my brain would slip and I'd have moved to another thought without any intervention on my part. My chest felt empty, my arms and legs limp and lifeless.

I was used to feeling so tired I could barely move. For months at a time I'd need to lie in bed for an hour after waking, too tired to actually *do* anything but not tired enough to sleep. I'd lie there, gathering energy until finally able to rise. Given my body clearly wanted to rest, I resented my brain not letting me actually rest.

Rikolta turned to a wraith, so...

The apples disappeared so that must preclude the stem cell theory...

Did I really want to...

Establishing motivation...

Ven slept soundly next to me, her breathing the only soothing thing in my world. After maybe an hour of the same four thoughts starting and then slipping away from me on a loop, I gave up on sleep. I opened my eyes.

A sliver of moonlight slipped through a gap in my curtains, landing gently on the wall by my feet. It bathed the room in a faint, silver glow, which picked out Ven's features. I watched her breathe, letting my brain focus on her, rather than the puzzle I was grinding my brain against. Her face was a palace of silken curves – her delicate chin, her mischievous cheekbones and her eternally arched eyebrows.

Back in Oro, some of the older generations might not have believed this hurricane who shared my bed was a woman at all, because of a quirk of her birth. They'd think the same thing of Rikolta, although because of the Oro Virus they'd think Ven was a predator and Rikolta was merely confused. I breathed, my chest filling, feeling light. I closed my eyes for a long moment and realised I'd been breathing easier after I'd turned to Ven. I kept the afterimage of her face with me as I felt myself drift...

***

The next morning, I doorstepped Rikolta with a basket. "Here you go,"

Rikolta squinted at the basket. "What is it?"

"Basket," I said, jiggling it.

"Okay," said Rikolta, tentatively taking it. "Do I open it?"

I shrugged. "Sure, why not."

Rikolta lifted the lid with one finger, in the manner of someone unsure if he's about to be surprised by a picnic or an angry adder. "Oh," he said. "apples." He then frowned, "Wait, I know these..."

"That's right," I said. "Twelve apples. There you go."

"Thanks?"

"Eat one."

Rikolta lowered the basket's lid. "Look, Laceco, can you just tell me what's going on?"

I waved a hand at him. "Yes, in a minute, now eat an apple. Please."

My romantic rival sighed, fished out an apple and bit down. "Ow!"

"Your teeth pass straight through? Sorry about that, I know that hurts," I said.

"What... how... my teeth..."

"You can try the others if you want but I suspect they'll be all the same. Do you have some sort of urge to *do* something with those apples?"

"Stick them up your arse?"

"Make me dinner first."

Rikolta glared at me for a moment too long before grinning. He held out the basket. "Do you want some tea or something whilst you tell me what's going on?"

I didn't want anything from him. Well, the Oro Virus didn't want anything from him. It was getting hard to separate those two out. In such circumstances, a good way of working out what to do is to think about what the Oro Virus might want me to do and then do the opposite. I smiled back at him and took the basket. "Tea sounds amazing, thanks!"

I gave Rikolta a summary of events thus far whilst he infused peppermint leaves with boiling water. He concentrated on his work but once I was done, he nodded. "I've been dreaming... I was... I was collecting those apples, there was this grand old city and... I remember it being really important..."

"Can you remember why it was important?"

Rikolta shook his head.

"Right."

Rikolta looked at me for the first time since I'd entered his caravan. "That's not a problem?"

I had to think about that, and ended up letting out a rattling sigh. "It fits with an idea I have."

Rikolta sipped his tea. "Do we have to do this now? I've got a lot going on."

I pinched the bridge of my nose. "No, we don't have to do this right here, right now, but these manifestations are always happening for a reason. If you ignore them and hope they go away by themselves, the same need that caused the manifestation in the first place tends to get a little... frustrated that it's not being listened to and tends to ramp things up a little. You might find yourself collecting souls instead of apples, for example."

Rikolta shifted. "Okay, so you said you had an idea?"

I closed my eyes – this was going to be rough. "You and I have to spend the day together."

"Okay."

Damn, I'd hoped he'd refuse. "Okay, does anything need doing about the cavalcade?"

"Something always needs doing. I think we finished cleaning up the town yesterday – we could volunteer to help with the kitchens?"

And that was how I wound up sitting in a caravan peeling potatoes with my romantic rival. My romantic rival Rikolta. "RRR," I said, testing the sound out.

Rikolta looked up from his peeling knife, "Sorry?"

"Nothing."

I was having trouble. My experience with manifestations had shown that good results could be achieved by ignoring subtlety in conversation. Cut to the heart of the matter, never mind the small talk. With Rikolta, things weren't that simple. RRR flicked a piece of potato skin from his peeler before setting it down and scratching his leg. He frowned, then rolled up his trouser leg and scratched – ah, the point where his leg met his prosthetic.

"You alright?" I asked, trying to sound casual.

"Feels like I've been wearing this thing too much."

"You might have been collecting apples with it on, unless the wild magic doesn't work that way, in which case..."

RRR sighed, "Yes, thank you, Laceco. I've got some liniment I can use to soothe it. Should have brought it out with me."

Curiosity was bubbling within me – a pot of boiling water eager for scraps. I wouldn't feed it. What would RRR answer? The same answer most of us would probably give. 'Yeah, it's rough some of the time, or a lot of the time, but you've got to just get on with it.' I felt stupid for even thinking about asking. I sighed, sounding like a pale echo of RRR. "So," I said, clapping and getting potato starch on my palms, "Ven said you were a little intimidated by me when I first showed up."

RRR raised an eyebrow, "She did, did she?"

"I would be overjoyed to hear she's wrong." I said, hating how my accent made me sound sarcastic even when I was being genuine.

Rikolta excavated some dirt from beneath a fingernail. "It's more that I'd thought we were having a private conversation."

"Ah."

Silence lay in-between us like a decomposing fish. Rikolta went back to peeling potatoes. I followed his example, my cheeks burning, my vision spiking. It was stiflingly hot in the caravan, I was amazed Rikolta wasn't sweating through his shirt.

"Did you ask because it'll help with the manifestation?" Rikolta asked once his next potato was stripped to the flesh. "Or were you doing one of those power games I hear your country-people go in for?"

I wiped my brow with a sleeve, surprised to find it dry. Deep within me, something seethed. I ignored it. "Yeah, the manifestation was why..." the seething, prowling feeling broke free, "although now you mention it," I jabbed my potato peeler towards RRR, "here's the thing, Rikolta. Are you jealous of my relationship with Ven?"

Rikolta shrugged with a single shoulder, his bulky frame making him look like an over-stuffed bird of prey. "Nope."

Liar. No matter, I could cut out his hauteur another way. "So you must be thinking your relationship with her is better than mine."

Rikolta frowned at me, set his potato peeler down and closed his eyes. "Laceco," he said, "what's your favourite book?"

The seething creature within me had been running victory laps. It stumbled. "What? I don't have a favourite book, I'm not twelve. I've got a bunch of books I love but I haven't *ranked* them."

Rikolta opened his eyes and wiped his hands on the cloth that hung from the potato pot. "So, you're saying that one great book isn't necessarily better or worse than another because they're doing different things?"

Crap. "Er... Well..."

"We covered this back in school. I wonder if you did... In philosophy class we looked at Oro and how, because you're used to putting people above you or below you based on how much currency you have, you fall into this habit of doing that for other things. Is that right? So, and I hope you'll forgive me for my armchair psychology, you might be assuming that because we're both in a relationship with Ven, one of those relationships has to be better than the other. Is that right?"

No. No, it wasn't. Not exactly. The seething creature had been pinned to the deck by Rikolta. A javelin through its throat. It thrashed, rasping '*She likes one of us more. She likes one of us more.*' I couldn't look at him. "Something like that."

The stink of the dead silence between us filled the air again. The moment stretched. I concentrated on slicing the skin from my potato. I could only see Rikolta's hands moving in my peripheral vision – his fingers strong but dextrous. They flashed – dropping a potato into the pot, but then didn't pick up a new one.

"Laceco... do you know what my vocation is?"

I stared at a particularly tricky bit of my current potato. "You're a resettlement officer? You introduce people to the Ember Cavalcade, get them settled."

"Mhm. How busy do you imagine that keeps me?"

My grip tightened on my potato peeler. "Er... it would depend on how often you get new people in the cavalcade..."

He sounded as if he'd moved far away from me. "One or two a month."

"So... you must have other duties..."

"Sure, I help out the hydroponics farms, assist in the kitchens – they always need extra hands."

"Okay..." I dropped my skinless potato into the pot and made the mistake of glancing up. Rikolta sat, looking at me. His eyes dark and deep.

He held my gaze. "So I think Ven was simplifying a little. I don't find you intimidating, Laceco. Revealing, maybe."

He was offering up a thread for me to pull on. Urging me to unravel him. I didn't want to be here. I wanted to jolt to my feet and storm out, away from him, away from this bizarre cavalcade...

I was listening to the virus again. I shut it down. What had Rikolta said? "What did I reveal, Rikolta?"

"I volunteered to settle new arrivals because mum said we needed someone. That was three years ago. I'm twenty-two. I've been watching Indi and Jans settle into their vocations, losing themselves in projects they love, coming home and chatting about it like coked-up parakeets. And there's me. I know I want something but I..." he shifted, the air around him *cracked.* "I try to focus on what I could do..." His head ripped back. "And I can't even..." Bones *jutted* from his chest. Black cloth rose around him, smothering him. He rose, towering over me, a bone wraith, utterly unfeeling. Utterly certain. He turned from me and strode from the caravan.

My hands were shaking. I set the peeler down and followed the three meter skeletal wraith. Outside, Embers were going about their day. No screams – that was good news. And Rikolta hadn't gone far – he was stalking the main thoroughfare between the caravan spinneys, as before.

I caught up with him in only a few seconds – there were plenty of Embers about but they'd parted for Rikolta. That thought made me pause and turn on the spot. The Embers weren't staring at Rikolta – I wasn't sure they could see him. They were parting to get out of his way. That made sense – I'd seen something similar before during a manifestation back home... but...

People were parting ahead of Rikolta even without seeing him. There were shadows on each face. Furrowed brows. I didn't understand what was happening until I passed Sol, the femme who'd walked me through tidying the lonely town. She'd stood aside to let Rikolta pass, but when she saw me, she approached.

"Can I help?" she asked, a hand resting lightly on my forearm.

"I don't know," I said, "can you see Rikolta?"

I pointed. Sol looked, but her eyes defocussed and she swayed before turning back to me. "Sorry..." she said. "We were talking about something... is everything okay?"

I smiled my best reassuring smile, "No, but I'm working on it."

Sol smiled – her eyes twinkling. "All right. Just ask if you need anything, whatever your name is."

Rikolta was getting away from me – I dashed after him, calling over my shoulder: "Actually, could you get Ven?"

Sol pointed, "She's just ahead of you."

I nearly bashed into the femme who made my heart dance.

She was red in the face and breathing heavily. She sighed in relief when she saw me. "Gasil said something had happened but they weren't quite clear on what..."

"Rikolta's manifestation took over when we were talking. People seem to be able to sense him. They know something's wrong, even if they don't know what."

"That tracks. It's part of the reason we're all here. I told you, we get it. Even if we don't quite get what's going on, we can often tell something's up."

Thoughts were swirling in my head – a maelstrom I was struggling against but deep within me I could feel a core of warmth. Someone had fetched Ven. They couldn't see Rikolta, let alone the wraith. And they'd known what to do. I needed to think more about that. Preferably when Rikolta wasn't stalking the cavalcade.

"Right," I said, taking Ven's hand and striding off after Rikolta, "so, any ideas for how to bring Rik back?"

"None at all. You're the expert."

"I've encountered manifestations before, you're the expert on Rikolta."

"Fair. Indi and Jans might be useful but... hey, they're coming..."

Rikolta's other partners jogged up to us.

"What's up?" said Indi.

"Where's the fire?" asked Jans.

"Long story," I said. "Look, I was chatting to Rikolta and he had a bit of a moment. He was talking about his vocation and he seemed to be struggling."

Indi and Jans exchanged looks. Ven rolled her eyes, "What is it, you two?"

"It might be nothing," said Jans, "but he's been stuck in a bit of a rut the last year or so. He's not really sure what he *wants,* you know?"

"Ah," I said, feeling lines in my head swirl and curl to form a perfect circle. "I've got it."

I stopped, letting Rikolta move ahead of us. I explained my theory to Rikolta's paramours as briefly as possible.

"What can we do?" asked Ven.

I nodded to the trio. "Follow my lead."

Rikolta had his basket when we caught back up with him. I peered inside, trying to see how many apples he'd picked since we'd started following. I saw maybe five. "Rikolta," I said, unsure of how to start talking to a three meter bone wraith. "I hope you can hear me in there. I'm sure part of you can. Look... I was in hospital for nearly two years with this Post-Viral Fatigue thing."

Rikolta reached up and plucked apple number six from the nearest tree.

I resisted the urge to jump in front of him. Instead I walked at his side, his paramours keeping close. "And the thing about being in hospital for that long is... I was there with a bunch of people who were around my age – some still in school. Others were older of course. Some got better, others stayed. The ones who were discharged wrote to us, some came to visit. Their recovery was glorious, Rikolta, of course it was, but it was also a fucking knife in my side. They were recovering, back to living their lives. I could barely manage an hour out of bed each day."

Rikolta picked an apple from a towering silver tree.

Ven strode forward, a pilotfish for the gliding hulk of Rikolta's wraith. Embers still made space for Rikolta, but they seemed less worried to see Ven leading our bizarre procession. She called over her shoulder: "I spent so long being The Autistic Friend. Everyone I knew was different – coping better, understanding more."

Rikolta picked apple number eight.

Indi nudged Rikolta as we walked. "For five years I refused to buy in. I'd never move to Ember, I was my own person. I revelled in living a life far more difficult than it needed to be. And I did that because I knew I was *different* from the people who lived in Ember. They were *disabled*, I was *me*. My disability didn't *define* me." She stuck her tongue out and made a retching noise. "Of course, then I moved here with Jans and... well, you know."

Apple number nine went in the basket.

"I've never been particularly smart," Jans said. "And I don't know if that's the learning disability or just me. Indi's smarter, you're more compassionate, Rik. Sometimes I can't stand having mirrors in our caravan."

"Jans..." said Indi.

Apple number ten went in the basket.

I closed my eyes, focussed on the point of this particular moment. I opened my eyes. "Rikolta, let me tell you what I think is happening. You're scared. Two of your partners have vocations they love, and the third is a damned virtuoso. Yes, Ven was a little shy, but then she brought home a sage, a visionary who could unwind knots of wild magic."

"Sage?" hissed Ven. I waved a hand at her and mouthed 'I'm doing a thing!'

"I think you took a long, hard look at your life and you weren't particularly impressed. Your subconscious panicked. It needed to feel that your life had purpose – *any* purpose. So each night you took on the form of a bone wraith and collected twelve crimson apples. What the apples were *for* wasn't important. The key was the specificity. You were taking clear action, acting on a precise objective. Every night you enacted the life you wished you had. You wished you knew what you were doing."

"I don't know what I'm doing, Rikki..." Indi said, tears beading at the corners of her eyes.

"Sorry, did anyone think anyone knew what they were doing?" Ven said, sounding genuinely surprised.

Rikolta reached out and plucked apple number eleven.

"Comparing your life to another isn't a great idea at the best of times," I said. "A doctor told me that. I wanted to throw the yoghurt I was eating at her, but her point was - whilst the red ties *can* compare their lives to others, we definitely can't. We all live in Disabled Time. Time shattered to fragments. We can't live in the same way the red ties can. Our expectations of how long certain things take might be based off Red metrics – very precise metrics that brook no deviation.

"We mustn't bend ourselves to live up to a standard forged by the reds. Time very literally means something different to us. Due dates, the time it takes to perform certain tasks, working hours, hours of sleep the body needs – they all mean something different to everyone here.

"We're time travellers. We're old when we're young and young when we're old. Our time is relapses and stages of our conditions, and our time is non-linear. We live in grief, the time we lost to our disabilities. The time we spend thinking about the things we can't do any more, what we might never get to do, who we could have been if we'd come to Ember earlier. Lost friends.

"We live in broken time. We all have different body rhythms which affect how we all think and feel. We live in sick time, in a world where we are never sick and we are never well, we're always somewhere in between. We live in vampire time – late nights, unconscious days and weird life schedules that don't match up with the rest of the world. Feeling as if the lines between life and death are blurred for us. But we also live in creating time – a lot of us reflect and create based on how *we* experience the world, not as the reds experience it."

I paused to take a breath. My legs were dragging at me, but I couldn't, *couldn't* stop. Indi and Jans had each reached up and helped to support Rikolta's basket. Ven was walking ahead, exchanging brief words with Embers who glanced our way. Everyone she spoke to nodded, and their expressions were those of the time traveller. One seemed familiar – Graco.

I looked up at Rikolta. His skull glared out from his hood. I couldn't tell if he was looking back. "Rikolta... let me tell you about my friend. He welcomed me to the Ember Cavalcade. He's got a wonderful set of partners, a vocation which genuinely means a lot – he helped me get settled when I was lost and scared about finding myself in a new place. He's never judged me for the restrictions I live with. I've had some times when my friend and I didn't get on brilliantly, but he never acted spitefully, he never treated me badly in any way. I wish I could say the same about my own actions. I admire him for that. When I think about my friend Rikolta, when I look at his life... he's doing really well, I think. Better than me – I don't have a vocation. Haven't for three years."

Jans was openly crying, "Rik... I don't think you understand how wonderful it is to have you in my life. You care – you care *so* much. You steady me when all I want to do is stop existing. I'm not sure I'd have even found my vocation without you cheering me on every step of the way."

Indi didn't seem to be able to tear her gaze from her shoes. "Rikki... who was it who stopped me from burning down that inn, after the barkeep made those hurtful comments about Jans last Spring? That might be why feeling stuck must hurt so much – you're in the moment, but you can focus on the world past the next five minutes. I admire the heck out of that."

Ven turned, walking backwards without apparent effort. "Rikolta ... do you really think we'd be dating if you weren't amazing? Rikolta, look at me. I only date the best. You're the best, Rikolta. Are you calling me a liar? Are you? Are you calling me a liar, Rikolta?"

Rikolta approached the twelfth tree. I let him walk ahead. "You already know what you need to do, Rikolta. Even if you don't know *how* to find a vocation that will fulfil you, you know what the next thing to do is. I trust you."

Rikolta reached for the twelfth apple... but his shoulders slumped. He shrank, his cloak melting into his shadow. His basket of apples blew away like smoke. The tree in front of us collapsed into splinters that pattered to the ground. The season's first rainfall.

"We're here, Riki," said Jans, taking his hand.

"I thought..." said Rikolta, the wraith's skull relaxing into his true face. "I needed to do *something*."

"If you want to be a stalking reaper who picks blood apples, we support you," said Indi.

"Every step of the way," said Jans.

"It's an amazing vocation," said Ven. "I know someone who wants to be a witch who lives in the woods and eats children."

"Is this 'someone' you, Ven?" said Rikolta, staring dead ahead.

"Shut up, I'm not that predictable."

It would have been a poetic moment to apologise to Rikolta about dropping him and about being pretty damned petulant about our dating situation... but it would have also meant making the moment about me, rather than Rikolta.

"Er..." said Rikolta, looking from Ven, to Indi, to Jans, "can we talk about... this whole... thing?"

"Let's go to the statues," said Indi, taking Rikolta's arm. "It'll be quiet this time of day."

The four Embers walked away, although Ven did bump her fist against mine as she brushed past. Eventually, Graco approached from where she'd been observing. "What in the seventeen realms of spirits just happened?"

Interlude: The Diagnosis Dragon

The Ember Cavalcade prepared to leave the Town of Lonely Windows the day after Rikolta resolved his manifestation. Ven stayed with me as the cavalcade set off, the plumes of scorching dust rising in our wake.

Rikolta reported feeling more hopeful in the wake of his experience. He moved out of Indi and Jans' place, and let Ven occupy his old spot. His relationship with the three typhoons persisted, but he explained he needed a place that was his, whilst he worked out what he really, truly wanted.

I didn't answer any of Graco's questions the day of Rikolta's resolution, much to her aggravation, but I tracked her down after getting permission from Rik. I found her in a canteen caravan where she was chairing some advocacy meeting or other. Once she'd called a break, I filled her in on the facts of the case.

As autumn wore on, the Ember Cavalcade stopped at many more locations. The Labyrinth Valley, where I got lost trying to find the labyrinth. The Lost Notes – a whitewashed wall in the middle of no-where covered in handwritten notes, written by or for those who were missing. The Embers' task at the wall was to scour the notes for new additions and carry any news further down the Ember Trail.

Ven and I grew closer. We talked dreams, histories and made up games to torture each other with. I didn't see much of Rikolta, which I don't think made Ven massively happy. She said she'd enjoyed having us in the same place when I'd first moved in. Apparently it meant she could reliably get the loving she needed in the one spot and didn't need to worry about one of us being out.

The Ember Cavalcade introduced rationing as we moved into winter. My old cavalcade would have been close to mutiny if some no-good logistician had asked them to eat less for the good of the community. For me, it meant eating less than I'd like, but Ven said it'd only be for the winter. The cavalcade had plenty of supplies, but after a few close calls in previous years, the citizens voted to enact rationing before it was required, to give us the best chance of making it through winter intact.

Graco tracked me down on the roof of my caravan as I lay watching the mountains in the distance gradually grow in size. "You up here, Laceco?"

"I'm here, what's up Graco?"

The roof swayed gently as Graco climbed the ladder up to join us. It turned out she was wearing a yellow and red striped long-sleeve football shirt, shorts, long thick socks, and tennis shoes. "Hi," she said.

"I'm here too, Graco," said Ven.

"Hi, Ven."

She stood, the first two fingers of her left hand tapping out a staccato rhythm against her thumb.

"You going out dancing?" I asked.

She turned to me and bared her teeth momentarily. "On my way to football. Haven't been able to practice for a while and our next stop doesn't have any cages. Managed to persuade a friend to do a kickabout in her studio." Ven and I exchanged blank expressions. Graco sighed, "Yes, I meant football. Yes, I can play football if there's a bell in the football. Yes, that means that when the caravan is on the move the only place quiet enough for me to reliably hear the bell as well as anyone else moving about is a studio where musicians record gramophone records."

The light dawning in Ven's eyes must have mirrored mine.

"Gotcha," I said. And, because I was starting to get used to living in Ember, I followed up with: "Sorry for asking."

Graco nodded. "Right." She folded her arms. She didn't move. After that, she still didn't move.

"Need any help with anything, bab?" Ven asked.

"Mm?"

"It's lovely to see you," I said, before wincing. "I'm sorry, I..."

Graco clapped her palm to her forehead. "It's fine, people can mention seeing without me having a panic attack. These days. So, yes, I wanted to visit you after the Rikolta thing because I thought you might want to hear why I'm investigating this Wild Magic thing in the first place. Give you a more complete picture, that sort of thing."

I nudged Ven before she could turn her eyeroll into a groan. "Yes please, Graco."

Ven rolled her eyes again at me, to ensure I'd noticed her... I realised I didn't actually know what she was rolling her eyes at and made a mental note to ask her about it later. She then lay back on the roof, closed her eyes and interlaced her fingers behind her head.

Graco shifted on her feet before nodding and sweeping her left foot ahead of her in a crescent. Finding only clear, flat roof she sat down. "Okay," she said. "Right. Okay."

"Okay?" Ven asked. I nudged her.

Graco nodded, her fingers were tap, tap, tapping out a rhythm on the tar-sealed wood roof, causing a dull pattering sound like a very localised monsoon. "Okay. So. There was this girl when I was studying at Obsid. Same class as me – Investigation and Interrogation."

I shook my head as that information failed to fit into my mental image of Graco. "You studied how to interrogate people?"

Graco cut the air between us with two slicing fingers. "Concepts. Ideas. Take what we think we know and make sure we're right. Take ideas and kick the tyres. What used to work but isn't working now? That sort of thing. Interrogation is meant to challenge status quo bias."

Ven cracked an eye open. "What's status quo bias?"

"The idea that the way we're doing things now must be correct," said Graco.

"Gotcha," said Ven. She closed her eye again.

Graco clenched her fists before resting her hands lightly on her knees. "So, my friend Nives and I did a project in our second year about the fundamentals of magic. Interrogating current theories of where it came from and how it worked. I'd never heard of Wild Magic before. She told me about her brush with it." She thumped the roof next to her twice with the flat of her palm. "I should say that I don't believe this story. Never have. It's just... what with the blood apple, I disbelieve it slightly less than I used to. So I thought I'd tell you."

Graco lapsed into silence. I let the moment sit before wondering if she was waiting for a prompt. If Ven really wasn't up for hearing a story about Wild Magic... I poked her in the ribs. "Ven, I'd love to hear Graco's story but if you wanted to do something else..."

Ven smiled and shifted into a more comfortable position, "No, go ahead you two. I'll offer insightful commentary from the side-lines."

"Please don't do that," said Graco. "Okay. Nives. Wild Magic. She grew up in this village near the border with Oro. Did a bunch of trading, occasionally had currency lying around the place because Oro people are obsessed with it. No offence, Laceco."

"Absolutely none taken, I don't get it either."

"Good. So, this town was haunted, or maybe there was this enormous creature that no-one ever saw. People only knew about this haunting creature because they'd wake up to find claw marks gouged into the walls of buildings that hadn't been there the day before. Trees were ripped up and crushed, leaving little but splinters. Water troughs left dry and covered in scorch marks. Livestock unharmed but clearly upset by whatever had happened."

I nodded to myself. "Anyone see the creature?"

"Nope. They did all the normal things. Hiding indoors all night, sheltering in cellars, praying to the spirits in the hope that the creature would go away. Some mascs from Oro with firearms did stay up all night a couple of times. They claimed to have seen a sinister shape that fled at the sight of them."

I let my head roll back. "How very plausible."

Graco nodded. "That's what I said! In that tone!"

Ven winced "Oh this is just getting worse..."

Graco waved a hand at her. "Silence, whatever your name is..."

Ven's brow twisted, "My name's Ven! We've met before!"

"Ah, yes, I remember now," said Graco. "Anyway. No-one reliable saw this creature. The town got used to having their buildings damaged but not disastrously so. Life continued. That's where Nives' story starts in earnest. She'd been struggling for years with her life. She wasn't focussing properly, finishing projects was a massive struggle and she'd been losing friends left, right and centre. People kept calling her selfish."

Ven shifted uncomfortably, grimaced, and then sat up, facing Graco. "And was she?"

Graco's lips moved silently for a moment. "Was she what?"

"Selfish."

"Oh! I don't think so. She wasn't when I was at uni with her, anyway, but all will become clear, Ven, don't you worry. So, Nives was struggling. People could see she was struggling as well, but in pretty odd ways. Every once in a while someone she didn't know would come up to her, tell her everything was going to be all right and then wander off. She just found that confusing. The only time she really felt herself was when going for long walks after her day's responsibilities were complete. One particular day, when walking one of her regular routes, she spotted a cave. She'd never seen it before, and it would have been hard to miss. It was as if it had appeared from no-where"

I smiled, "A mystery cave! The plot thickens."

Graco pointed in my direction, "Exactly, whatever your name is! Exactly!"

I raised a finger, confused, remembered Graco couldn't necessarily see it, then my brain caught up and I realised it was possible Graco was doing a *bit*. I resolved not to interrupt, on the off chance she wasn't doing a bit. Ven giggled at my confusion.

Graco opened her mouth to speak, hesitated, closed her mouth, and shook her head. She took a breath. "Then, and I do want to stress I don't believe this literally happened, Nives said she went into the cave. There, standing in front of her, awake and watching her, was a dragon."

Ven started, "What?"

My head felt fuzzy and everything around me was suddenly disjointed, as if reality had slipped a gear. "I thought... but aren't... seriously?"

Graco shrugged. "Exactly. That's partly why I think Nives was speaking metaphorically. Prior to encountering your blood apple, I was certain. Now... anyway, she was standing there, frozen, in front of this hulking mass of emerald scales, piercing golden eyes and row upon row of jagged teeth. The dragon watched her intently. It prowled in a half-circle around Nives, but it always kept its gaze locked on her. Its furnace breath blistered her face. The ground trembled with every step it took.

"After examining my friend for an agonisingly long time, it returned to face her. It lowered its head so they were at roughly eye level. It stared at her, its gaze burrowing into her. Then, in a sudden flash of movement, it opened its jaws – they flexed back far wider than should have been possible, it could have bisected a caravan with one bite. Nives said she didn't have time to think, she only remembered seeing three rows of teeth before the dragon snapped her up in its jaws and swallowed her whole."

An ember, kicked up from the trail, brushed against my cheek, a momentary scorch before it was whisked away by the turbulence of the cavalcade's passage. Graco looked in my direction, her expression stone. When she didn't continue, I said: "I'm listening."

"Of course you are. So, Nives doesn't remember exactly what happened next. She remembers crushing panic. A sick white void. Emptiness. When she woke, her body felt heavy, as if she'd been sedated. She shifted, tried to stand but banged the top of her head on something hard. She winced, but it was more disorientating then painful. She checked her head for lumps... and a jade-scaled arm passed across her vision. She felt supple scales with her fingertips, an elongated crest. She gasped, and brought up her hands. Claws. A dragon's claws."

"Dun dun dunnn," said Ven.

Graco's scowl lasted only a moment. "It was scarier when she told it. Anyway, she crawled out of the cave – oh, did I say she was in the cave where she'd found the dragon? Anyway, she crawled out of the cave and she was in a valley – no-where she'd ever been. Lost. Alone."

I drew in a breath through my teeth. "Fuck..."

"Yeah. There was a village at the end of the valley. Nives approached, but everyone screamed and ran when they saw her. She fled, herself, before returning an hour or so later and just sat a stone's throw from the rice paddies stepped outside the village. She waited. The villagers spotted her, screamed and ran. She didn't move. Eventually, some peasants approached her with burning torches and pitch forks."

"Not what I'd have hoped from our people," said Ven.

I nodded, "People aren't at their best when they're scared."

Graco sighed, "Nives retreated again. She looked for the dragon she'd seen but, of course, it was no-where to be found. She made some clumsy attempts at flight, but found herself a new-born starling fallen from the nest. Someone in the village must have noticed, because someone approached. Nives couldn't tell anything about them – her dragon's eyes saw things in jagged lines and bizarre curves. The human could have been old or young, masc or femme... but they talked to her in a language Nives couldn't understand. She tried to reply, but only scalding steam emerged from her mouth.

"Nives wanted to help the people in the village. Her claws could plough the earth, but her lashing tail felled trees and cracked walls. She could boil cauldrons of water in mere moments, but if she lost concentration she boiled them dry. The villagers didn't seem particularly angry with her efforts, but Nives heart blazed with fury at herself. She was a monster, incapable of anything.

"The human who visited her returned, and they brought friends. They saw the pain she was heaping on herself, and though they couldn't understand each other, they stayed with her. Their persistence spoke louder than words. Nives fell into anguished sedation. The visitors returned. She roared, feeling undeserving of their companionship. They left, but returned the next day. Slowly, Nives grew used to them. Over months, her hatred faltered and died. She felt the ground under her scaly belly, the air in her crest. She listened to the singing of the villagers.

"One day, one particular visitor picked their way to Nives' cave. This one was strange, because Nives could see her clearly. She'd no idea how long she'd been trapped as the dragon, only seeing jagged lines and bizarre curves, but she saw this person's matted russet hair, their drained expression, their stooping gait. The visitor saw Nives, and without ever knowing why, Nives picked them up in her jaws and swallowed them whole. When next she woke, she was human. Back in the cave where her dragon had swallowed her."

I opened my mouth to speak but Graco pressed on. "That's not the end. You haven't heard the interesting bit. So, once Nives was human again, she felt *free*. Like she'd come out the far side of something. She moved to a smaller village, saw a doctor, got herself checked out and lived her life for two years before going to Obsid University."

Graco was sitting stiffly, facing our destination. She seemed to be letting the dancing dust of our travel play across her face. I frowned and wanted to ask if she was okay, before wondering where that thought came from. "Was... is..." I said, before trailing off.

Graco jerked her shoulders. "Well, anyway, Nives said that every once in a while she'd spot someone – or someone would spot her.

They'd recognise *something* about each other, and if they took the chance to talk, they all recounted the same experience of becoming the dragon. The details always varied, but the way Nives reported it... her face always lit up whenever she recognised someone. Every once in a while, she'd get a sense of Deja Vu, before realising that the person she'd recognised was someone who'd approached her before her encounter with the dragon – they'd told her everything was going to be okay. They'd recognised something in her that she hadn't even known was there.

"And the scientific method is quite precise in these matters – I couldn't easily identify people with this (probably fictional) experience in advance. This meant I couldn't test if Nives did, actually, recognise something about them. Well, I might have been able to if you gave me six months and I didn't have any other projects on, but I was an undergrad at the time and didn't give Nives' story any particular credence. I thought it was just a metaphor she was using for getting diagnosed."

"Hell of a long metaphor," said Ven.

Graco stretched. "I agree completely. Anyway, the reason this story really stuck with me was... Nives and I shared a lab for our final year at Obsid. One day a porter dropped some materials I needed at the lab. I heard Nives gasp... and then I heard a scuffle. I was going to shout for help but then I heard what they were saying. 'It's you!' 'You made it, I'm so proud' 'Thank you for everything'. Mushy shit, you know the sort."

"I do not," said Ven. "I never get treated in the manner I deserve."

"I blame the Oro virus," I said, without really thinking.

"The what?" asked Ven.

"The porter," said Graco, clearly wanting to be done with her story, "was the dragon before Nives. Both of them were crying. The porter

– Haban I think her name was – couldn't stop saying she was sorry. She'd tried to explain what was happening before she ate Nives, but her body couldn't speak... and Nives couldn't stop saying thank you. Haban had given her a miracle, she said.

"So, you can imagine I was a little sceptical of this but Nives wasn't the sort of person to fake a meeting such as that, in order to convince a friend that her story was true. It never seemed to *bother* her that I never believed her. Whenever I was sceptical, she just smiled. Multiple times she hugged me, which annoyed me a great deal. But I asked around about Haban after that meeting, and the word was she'd only joined the Obsid University Cavalcade a day or so before. Hell of a short period of time for Nives to bump into her and set that scene up."

I nodded. "just possible enough that you can write the experience off?"

Graco bristled. "I'm being sceptical of something extremely... Hah. Incredible."

I shrugged. "I suppose that's fair."

Graco stood and brushed herself down, swaying with the motion of the caravan, like a sailor. "For the longest time... It's stuck with me because the feeling she described... I didn't get it until Obsid linked up with Ember last year. That sense of seeing someone and being seen in return... Yeah. I get it."

"Hang on," I said. "The town Nives lived in – an invisible creature was damaging it, but Nives wasn't invisible when she turned into the dragon..."

"Right," said Graco. "So, if Nives' story *was* something to do with diagnosis, that part of the story... or metaphor, might be there because your symptoms are present whether you've noticed them or not, whether you've put the pieces together or not. Nives wasn't diagnosed, but her symptoms were still there, plain for anyone to see. It's just nobody saw. Except the dragon, and those who had been the dragon."

"We all need a pissed off dragon in our corner," said Ven.

Chapter Twelve

As autumn turned to spring and spring turned to summer, I found myself settling into the rhythms of the cavalcade. I rested, I went out with Ven and, with initial lingering reluctance, Rikolta. After one frustrating dinner under swirling stars where Rikolta and I had talked past each other about vocations, he offered to introduce me to a friend – a vocation officer.

Her office was organised to the point where I'd disrupt the flow if I stood in the wrong place. I sat in the cramped chair in front of her desk – itself placed with geometric precision with relation to the office walls, and shifted under her charming smile.

"So," she said, slipping a sheet of paper free from a manilla folder with the grace of an assassin slipping a knife from a sheathe. "What thoughts do you have with regard to vocation?"

"I'm sorry," I said, watching the sheet of paper as if it was about to slice towards me, "I don't understand the question."

Her gaze flicked up at me before slicing back down towards her folder. "Which part of the question would you like clarified?"

I really needed to start wearing a tie, but I hadn't settled on a colour. White was too simple, yellow didn't add enough and I didn't feel affected enough to use purple. "Er... sorry, I... I'm not sure if I've had any thoughts for a while, vocation wise." Was that wrong? Surely everyone had considered their vocation.

The officer nodded, jerking her head so swiftly she might have just betrayed a history in the special forces. "Yes. Good. So, we can have an informal chat about what you might enjoy, what you might be good at. I'm keen to do that myself, I rarely get to practice generalised relaxed chat for reasons that elude me. If you refuse the chat, we could always conduct an autopsy of your past, cracking open the ribs and really digging around in your chest cavity to see what interesting organs we can find. I can also just give you a list of things which currently need doing but that's really just putting a plaster on a deep slice to your carotid artery." She peered at me a little closer. "On second thought.... I'd probably choose your jugular. If I had the time, and I usually do." She scratched a note into the paper she held at her mercy under her left palm.

"I'm sorry, is there someone else I can talk to?"

She placed her pen down and folded her hands on top of each other, "Why does everyone always ask that? Yes. I can find someone else for you. Shall I?"

Well, now I felt bad. "No, sorry. Let's... do the chest cavity thing?"

She only looked hurt for a moment. She interrogated me for maybe fifty minutes, which was when my history with motion emerged. Before the Telegram Flu, I'd been studying acrobats – the way they moved and the choices they made as part of their roles. The vocation officer listened to me explain and smiled kindly before asking me to return in a week after thinking some more about motion, along with the art at its core.

I left feeling more baffled than anything else, and followed the bridges back across the Ember Cavalcade to where Ven was fishing for sparks off the side of our caravan. I told her about the consult as the cavalcade finished its climb through the Talsotan Mountains, and parked up at the Yuneding Farmsteads.

Salt and pepper mountainsides flanked the ash field on which we parked, beyond which stood a proud parade of halls, workshops and community spaces, each built from stone and sealed against the elements with ash paste. Wood was a precious resource up here, it seemed. Beyond the halls, maybe forty homes climbed the steppes up to Mount Talso. Thatched rooves nestled on top of grey stone – volcanic rock from Talso itself. Flowing from the houses down to meet our ash field in a sea of lush green vegetation were the farmsteads' fields, each bursting with life enough to feed family upon family year round.

I had mixed feelings about reaching Yuneding. On the one hand, Ember would be able to restock our food supplies, which hopefully meant rationing would be over. On the other, Ven and Rikolta had spent the last few days talking about how much they wanted to visit Yuneding's bath houses – fed from Talso's volcanic hot springs.

Because bathing was such an attraction at Yuneding, Ember wouldn't be running showers at the communal facilities during our stay. I could have a shower if I really wanted to – find a source of water, get fuel to heat it, work the pumps to build the pressure and *then* shower... or I could deal with the fact that I was going to have to engage in Akoma's tradition of communal bathing.

Mostly, what happened after Ember and Obsid were done parking in the ash field was chaos. Thankfully, Ven was of a mind to stay in our sanctuary whilst the initial flurry of swirling people spread out through Yuneding. I read my book, she practiced scales and, together, we waited for the storm to pass.

After a full hour, during which the sounds of jubilant chatter outside only seemed to increase, I reached the end of my chapter and let my brain skitter away from me for a few moments, digesting the revelation about the goose, the gosling and what that meant for the Spirit-Mother Sigran's murder. Something tugged at my attention, and I realised I hadn't heard any scales for... I had no idea how long. Looking up, I found Ven staring at me.

I closed my book, keeping my place with my thumb, "Hello, virtuoso, what's up?"

Her wide-eyed stare persisted. "I'm bored."

I spread my arms, "Cuddling is proven relief from boredom."

Her stare persisted, but her gaze had wandered a little – she seemed to be thinking about something. It took a little while for her to come back, after which she shook her head. "Not feeling... I don't..."

I smiled, "It's okay, Ven. You don't feel like cuddling, that's fine."

"Sorry, I..."

"I know that you don't always like physical contact and that's fine..."

"Yes, but..."

"I'm here for you, no matter what you need."

"Are you 'here for me' to the point where you'll let me finish a fucking sentence?"

Sharp, dazzling shock. "Ah. Sorry." I fell silent, trying to return space to Ven.

She breathed in, held the breath, and then exhaled. "That's better. I was going to apologise for not... well, you know, and then you said the very nice thing." She was speeding up, her gaze flicking from point to point. "But you interrupted me in the process and then we were in a cycle of you thinking you knew what I wanted to say, thus preventing me from actually saying the thing I really wanted to say." She puffed up her cheeks and blew a steam of grey and red spiking air off into a corner of the caravan. "And now I've said all the things. You may speak again, you magnificent chatterbox."

I nodded, gravely. "I'm sorry for not listening to you."

She waved a hand, "Yes, yes, we're all very sorry. Let's talk about something else. You know much about Yuneding?"

"Only that it's a spot on the Ember Trail, and the Ash Pilgrimage – it has one of the thirty-three shrines up in the Talsoan mountains."

Ven nodded, "Right. It's also one of the main farmsteads for the region. Farmers work here year round, building up supplies that cavalcades then ship back down the mountain where they can be loaded onto trains and cargo caravans and things."

"They just farm up here all year, every year?"

Ven winced, "That word 'just' is a bit judgy."

I waved my hands, "No, no – sorry, it's just.. my old cavalcade was self-sufficient, we lived off the land as well as our own hydroponics. Farming all the way up here just seems a bit of a thankless task."

Ven snapped her fingers and pointed at me, her finger pinning my thought in place. "Exactly! Exactly! And that is what we're here to do?"

"Er... *What* is what we're here to do?"

Ven grinned. "Thank them!"

Across Yuneding, Embers and Obsids were spreading. Finding out which farmers needed help and which ones were coping just fine. Artists, performers, and entertainers of all sorts visited the communal halls and began earnest discussions with the locals about what could be done to celebrate Yuneding's efforts. Many who'd been travelling with our cavalcade would be staying here after we'd left in order to help with the summer work, whilst we'd be picking up others who'd been assisting through winter and spring – they'd either join up with Ember or Obsid or we'd drop them somewhere else. Slowly, outside my and Ven's little sanctuary, Yuneding took on a festival atmosphere.

Ven and I hid inside for the night, though jubilant singing from one of the hills occasionally woke us in the small hours.

***

Something fell from a table, waking me. I felt about for it. Next to me, Ven turned over, groaning. Two more things hit the floor, making sharp *raps*. Wait, no. Door. Someone was knocking the door. "What?" I moaned.

"You both in there?" Rikolta called, sounding infuriatingly perky.

"Fuck off," grumbled Ven.

"I can't hear you!" chirped Rikolta.

Ven struggled up onto her elbows and raised her eyebrows at me.

I shrugged. "Yeah, we're both here. What's up?"

"You decent?"

"Not even a little," said Ven. "but we've got clothes on. Well, some clothes."

Rikolta breezed in, bringing with him the freezing mountain air I hadn't particularly missed.

Ven immediately pulled the covers back over her. "What do you want, light of my life?"

"Breakfast!"

I rubbed my eyes with the heels of my palms. "You want us to make you breakfast?"

Rikolta laughed, a clear twinkling stream of a sound. "No. No, no. They have a great place for it here. It's new, and it's got mountains."

"We're on mountains," I objected. "Well, *a* mountain."

Rikolta winked at me. "Come and see."

Altibites turned out to be the ground floor of one of Yunending's halls. Two sets of doors kept most of the breeze out, which meant the diners sat at the tables set out in a circle weren't actively shivering. In the centre of the ring of tables was a glass case – maybe two meters tall, and *in* the glass case...

"Wow," said Ven.

"Told you," said Rikolta.

I slipped between two tables, unable to hold back. The case contained mountains. Tiny ones. At their base were simple pebbles, although there was a hint of a tiny stream running between two rocks. From there, the smallest of the mountains rose to about the level of my shins, its slopes lined with needled evergreens. Its neighbour rose to the level of my waist, *its* neighbour reached the height of my chest and whilst the tallest peak was obscured by tiny clouds which drifted through the upper atmosphere of the case, matching the weather outside, I was pretty sure its peak could see the uneven way my hair grew in after I let Rikolta give me a haircut.

"What..." I said. "How..."

"They've got a sign about it next to the door," said Ven, stifling a yawn. "Go look once we've eaten. Come on, Riki's found us a table."

"But the mountains..."

"They'll still be here in twenty minutes after we've found out how to get food in this joint, come on."

She took my hand and led me to a table. I bumped into tables and tripped over discarded bags because I couldn't take my eyes off the miniature mountains for long enough to check where I was going.

"Okay," said Rikolta, as I tore my gaze from the mountains for long enough to find a chair. "They have eggs, celery, potatoes, paprika, tomatoes, leeks, onions, garlic, soy, tofu, salt, pepper, coriander, rice, and some other bits and pieces. What do you guys want?"

One of the mountains quivered, sending a shale scree skittering down into the valley between it and its neighbour.

"Do we have to make it ourselves?" asked Ven.

"Oh, no. You can if you want but they have some cooks working who can whip up basically anything from that list."

"Weird system."

I waved a hand, "I'll have whatever you're having."

"Whatever I'm having?" asked Rikolta. "Or whatever Ven's having? Because one of those choices is definitely braver than the other."

"I'm not known for my bravery," I said, trying to peer around someone who'd stood in between me and the mountains.

"Ha," said Ven. I glanced at her, confused. Her eyes widened. "Oh, you were being serious? He'll have what you're having, Riki. And give me whatever that is plus some chilli. Bonus points if they have those potato dumpling what do-you-call-its."

"Gnochi?" asked Rikolta.

"Bless you," said Ven.

Rikolta cackled. "I'll see what they can do."

His chair scraped, his coat swished.

Tap-tap-tap. Tap-tap-tap. I tore my gaze from the mountains. Ven was tapping the table. "You know... I'd be perfectly happy just having breakfast with Riki if you want to spend the entire time just staring at the mountains. You don't *have* to sit with us."

"Mm?" My brain hadn't got up to speed yet. I wanted to turn around but it felt as if I were missing something. I squinted up at the ceiling before turning back to Ven. "Sorry, I think I... no. I should be talking to people. Out. Socials, you know? That sort of thing. And I want to make more of an effort with Rikolta. Get past the Oro virus, you know?" Ven folded her arms and stared at me. I shifted in my seat. "What?"

"You've mentioned the Oro virus before," she said, picking at her fingernails without shifting her gaze from where it was pinning me to my chair. "I thought you were speaking figuratively. Well, no. I know you were speaking figuratively, but I didn't think you actually believed it."

"I don't – it's not a real virus. Well, not a.. it's not a disease. It's a mindvirus."

"But it's not real. Right?"

I screwed my eyes shut and scratched at the back of my head. "Er. No? Yes. Sort of. It's a whole..." I tried to gesture with my hands in a way that encompassed my homeland's attitude to hierarchy and gender and sexuality and everything else. I wound up knocking over my water glass.

"Mm," said Ven, "because the way you talked about it just now made it sound like original s..."

The entire room fell silent. I opened my eyes. I was alone. Silence. A breeze kissed my cheek. Empty tables, chairs placed neatly around them. No hints of the people who'd been happily dining seconds earlier. Out the window, the bustle of the cavalcade continued but in Altibites the world was still and silent as a funeral shroud. Apart from... "Was that someone closing a door?" I said. I hadn't meant to speak out loud but the sudden emptiness had drawn the sound out of me, leaving me feeling hollow and...

Rikolta was suddenly present. He half dropped three plates onto the table in front of me. The contents jumped, spilling rice and greens over the table.

Rikolta swayed. "What just happened?"

Chair legs scraped against floorboard. Ven, now also present, clutched at her head. "I don't know, one moment... and then the next..."

I stared at my companions – one moment they'd been absent and then... it had been as if I'd suddenly remembered they'd been present. They might have been here the whole time but I hadn't been able to see them.

Then, as if I'd walked through a door and suddenly found everyone else who'd been eating at Altibites mere moments ago, *everyone* else was suddenly back. Or rather it felt as if they'd never been gone.

"Manifestation," I said, the sound dry, cracking in the thin mountain air. "Everyone vanished for a few seconds. You two came back first."

Rikolta gripped the edge of the table. "Seriously? Does it always feel like that?"

I stood without meaning to, but then found myself standing next to him, shifting my weight, my hands hanging useless by my sides. "No, it's usually not that sudden."

Ven groaned. Her head dropped to the table and she mumbled some fragment of despair into the tablecloth.

"You alright, bab?" I asked, reaching out a hand but I remembered in time and stopped before I touched her.

"Mmmm," she said, before rolling her head. I caught a hint of her defocussed gaze through the marvellous haystack she called hair. "Why can't we just have breakfast without something like this happening every time."

Rikolta smiled, thinly. "To be fair, we haven't had anything like this for a while now."

"Sorry, you both," I said, a water stain on the tablecloth holding my attention. "If I wasn't here the curse wouldn't be spreading."

Rikolta squinted at Ven. "What's he talking about?"

"He's trying to apologise for wild magic having some unknown connection to him," grumbled Ven, "and he thinks it's because something, something, curse, something, something."

Rikolta raised an eyebrow at me. "Curse?"

"The curse of the Ember Trail – I crossed it when I was little."

Rikolta frowned. "I have literally never heard of the curse of the Ember Trail."

"You must have! It's..." I tried to snatch the memory from the air but the fatigue threatened to fog my access. "It's a whole..." the fog was rising. "It's a whole thing."

Rikolta and Ven exchanged glances. Rikolta shrugged. Ven hauled herself upright. "Whatever, Trevor," she said, "let's eat."

Our food turned out to be crispy, spicey and heart-warming. Rikolta explained a local farmer's son had cooked it for us, one of several cooks who were trying to keep a lid on the rush of Embers and Obsids during our first few days.

"I thought we were supposed to be improving things for the people here," I said, sitting back and letting the chili's aftermath delightfully scorch my mouth. "Having them run about making food for us doesn't track with that. I don't really get how any of it works unless people are getting paid."

Ven rolled her eyes whilst Rikolta answered: "We've got cooks from our side helping too. It's a complicated dance of social dynamics. Everyone doing their part leaves us all doing well, you know?"

I shifted in my chair. "Seems as if that'd be harder for Embers as we're not able to do as much as others."

Rikolta shrugged. "We do what we can. Every once in a while we get someone who's very obviously not doing their bit."

I snapped my fingers. "And you evict them from Ember?"

Ven and Rikolta looked at me as if I'd just kicked a puppy. Rikolta shook his head. Ven sighed and tapped the table between us. "No-one gets evicted. If someone is taking the piss, they can take the piss. Those people tend not to stick around long, though. Just because we're not going to evict them or deny them care doesn't mean we have to like them. They don't get invited to parties much, if you follow me."

"Speaking of," said Rikolta, "our chef was telling me about a party tonight – not massive but should be fun. There'll be booze and games and interesting people... Indi and Jans are working on a project for the next few days. You two interested in coming with me?"

Ven's gaze tracked across the ceiling. "When you say, 'not massive'?"

"I mean there'll probably be more than about ten people," said Rikolta, his tone resigned.

Ven looked at me. Rikolta looked at me. "Er," I said.

"Go on, Lac," said Ven, "I'll be fine."

I hadn't been particularly worried about Ven, I'd been hoping to avoid being around other people as much as I could... but I couldn't immediately think of a way to dodge Rikolta's shimmering, entreating gaze. "Sure, sounds fun," I said, slipping on my most convincing grin.

The ashen gravel crunched under my footsteps as I strolled back to my caravan. Ven had announced her intention to go and practice with her fellow singers and Rikolta had said he was going to check on something with a friend of his in hydroponics. All that left me at a loose end until the evening, except for thinking about my past and the seeds contained therein.

I'd been trying to think about aspects of life at the circus I'd enjoyed, my memories slipping and sliding away from me whenever I reached for them as if I was trying to seize hold of a particular part of a fog bank. This meant that I didn't notice the silence until it suddenly vanished. I'd been passing a communal hall, and the sudden rush of noise felt familiar. Thinking back I couldn't be sure if I hadn't noticed the chatter and clatter of people living their best lives or if it had suddenly returned after a wild-magic-shaped absence. I shook my head and hurried home.

Since Rikolta's manifestation, I'd been doing my best to hold myself together. My caravan was littered with evidence of this – books stacked in a crate by my bed, a padded sack on the floor where I could do my physiotherapy, and scavenged sets of spare bedding folded under my bed. If I was going to spend a sizeable chunk of every day in bed I wasn't going to fall into the old trap of slowly fusing with unwashed bedclothes.

A party. I'd been to parties back in my old cavalcade, before the Telegram Flu. We'd also had parties in the hospital but they'd been more of the sort where a desperate group of people gathered together to chat to each other whilst eating cake. I frowned and thought back to the parties I'd been to before – they'd mostly been myself and other teens boozing until we made a series of unwise choices and then fell asleep. Was that a party?

I held my head in my hands. Apparently I'd managed to lose my grip on what a party was. I was getting too in my head about this. I had hours to go before Rikolta had said he'd come get me. I stripped down to my smalls and slipped into bed, shivering at the chill of my tangled sheets. I closed my eyes and tried to empty my mind.

Consciousness returned in waves, as if I were a beach and it was lapping waters, gradually rolling further and further up me until I had no choice but to accept that I was awake. The ceiling above my bed lured my slowly blooming attention – its planks roughly cut and then planed flat, knotted timber from what must have been dozens of trees, off-cuts bound together. My old caravan had been an Oro original – everything machined with precision and efficiency. Everything smooth, everything fitted perfectly. A monument to relative luxury, as long as you didn't think too hard about how fucking wasteful the process was.

And just like that I'd let my mind wander and keep wandering until I'd lost track of what I was... what was I... what had I been doing? I'd been lying in bed and... The soles of my feet tingled, my heels round nubs of bone, rippling and flaring. My legs splayed out, knees aching, thigh muscles taut and aching but still managing to feel heavy and drained. A straining band was strapped across my chest, keeping my breathing shallow and halting. The back of my head drove into the pillow, so heavy I could only shift it left and right by centimetres at a time – lifting it a total impossibility.

I'd been improving since Rikolta's manifestation. I'd been *improving*. How could I be stuck like this again? I closed my eyes and breathed. So unfair. So unfair. So *unfair*. I breathed. I let the feeling of air rushing in through my nose, down my throat and into my lungs lull my thrashing thoughts. I was here. I had time.

It must have taken over an hour for me to gather enough energy to haul myself up so I was sitting on the bed with my back against the uneven wooden wall. From there, I didn't have too much trouble standing. The layers of sweat on the clothes I'd worn that morning, along with the previous two days smelled sour but with that dreadful, luring familiarity. I had clean clothes, I could put those on... but I hadn't showered for the last couple of days so I'd need to visit the bath house. That meant I'd have to find the bath house and... or I could just put the old clothes on.

If Ven was here, she'd snark at me until I gave in and did the thing I knew I needed to do anyway. If Rikolta was here, he'd be frustratingly supportive. He'd show me where the bath house was and ease my passage. I could wait for Rikolta – he was coming to get me before the party – but that would also mean delaying our attendance by at least an hour.

I closed my eyes and lolled my head back, "Fffffffffuuuuuuuck."

With the bad grace of someone who knows they're taking the mature, healthy course of action but doesn't have to be happy about it, I set out in search of the bath house.

As is often the way, my impossible mission turned out to be far less awful than my mind had convinced me it'd be. I managed to avoid any particularly awkward encounters in the bath house, got myself properly, gloriously clean and returned home with enough time to read for an hour before Rikolta came and grabbed me.

We followed the winding path between the caravans towards Skylark Hall – the smallest and most distant of the halls at the base of the farm-steps. The setting sun threw our shadows ahead of us, leading the way.

There were still plenty of Embers and Obsids around, together with plenty of people I didn't recognise. None of the new people wore ties. After months of about two-thirds of the people in the cavalcade wearing a coded splash of colour somewhere conspicuous, this felt odd. Still, the locals seemed to not mind our presence – plenty of them were sitting around thriving campfires with our people, chatting away or playing card games.

Rikolta asked how my chat with the vocation officer had gone. I mentioned the homework she'd given me, and asked if she was actually an assassin or something along those lines. Rikolta laughed at this, and explained there was ongoing speculation about that question.

We passed a sizeable gap in the groups of caravans – an open space in the ash field where boulders had been pulled into a rough circle. Around twenty people of mixed ages and genders were clustered there, each listening to an older femme with flowing grey hair, and the twinkling eyes of someone who has truly seen some shit. Next to the femme was Graco, although she looked noticeably more scruffy than I'd seen her previously – her hair fell every which way and her shirt was torn in multiple places.

I waved, then smacked my palm into my forehead. The masc sitting next to Graco whispered something to her. She clapped her hand on his shoulder, picked up a long white cane, stood and picked her way around the outside of the circle to join me and Rikolta, sweeping the ground with her cane to catch obstacles in her path.

"Hey, hey," she said, her voice blazing with unexpected energy. "I'm yearning, I'm learning, and my ears are burning. Still having trouble with the idea that I can't see a whole lot, Laceco?"

"How did you know it was me?" I said, innocently.

"I asked myself who would wave at a blind woman and the idea popped into my head. Who have you got with you?"

Rikolta grinned, possibly on instinct. "Hiya, Graco. It's Rikolta."

"Oh, hey! So what's up? I'm in the middle of something."

"Oh!" I said, suddenly flustered, "I only wanted to say hi... althoug h..." Was that absence of sound behind me natural, or had it happened suddenly? "Can you think of a reason why groups of people would suddenly disappear? Or for sudden unexpected patches of silence?"

Graco shrugged. "Yeah, probably, but you'd need to be more specific. Magic can overcome conservation of energy to a certain extent but to make a bunch of people suddenly disappear would require a *lot* of energy in one place and that runs contrary to what little we think we know about wild magic. There might be a witch or something wandering about. Haven't heard of anyone like that."

"Me neither," said Rikolta.

"Cool," I said, trying to project the smile on my face into my words, "more study needed. Thanks Graco. I'll let you get back to... what are you doing?"

Graco swept an arm in the direction of her friends. "That," she said, "is the group I'm working with to get more workers helping out at the farms and with food distribution generally. Next stop after this is a town outside Shai, and then it's Shai itself. The people there know the work done in Yuneding is really important, but only in this kindof abstract way. We're hoping to recruit about twice the number of seasonal workers than last year when we come back this way, and that'll require some of us staying in Shai to get the wheels turning. Want to help out? We always need more people."

"I actually do," said Rikolta, beaming, "but Laceco and I have somewhere to be right now. Can I catch up with you tomorrow?"

Graco nodded, "Sure, ask your friends where to find me." With a half wave, she turned and tapped the ground around her with her cane. She found the nearest large boulder and set off back around the circle of activists to her old spot.

"I didn't know you were interested in activism," I said to Rikolta as we set off towards the party once more.

Rikolta shrugged, "Me too. I'll find out soon."

Yuneding's main collective spaces were gargantuan – the largest easily the size of my circus's Big Top. They'd been cut from stone, millimetre precise. They must have either asked a stonecutter witch, or hauled a water blade machine up through the mountains.

Rikolta led me past the largest of the halls, each bustling. "Now," he said, "I've met both you and Ven before."

"Fucking... prove it," I said, before blushing and resolving not to try and be funny again until my head settled down a bit.

Rikolta glanced over his shoulder – he might have been looking for someone or he might have been trying to get an inconspicuous look at my expression to gauge if I was serious. Either way, he made the smart play and ignored my attempt at jollity. "The party I've snagged us an invite to is more exclusive, more classy than any of these affairs." He waved, airily at the brightly lit hall we passed, inside which people appeared to be waltzing.

I found I'd pressed my palms together at chest height, my fingers splayed away. I forced my palms together, my wrists aching, dully. "Isn't being exclusive a bit of a... what's the word... isn't that a bit like a sin here?"

Rikolta grinned, "That's not the right word, no. And you're right, I was trying to put it in terms you'd understand."

"Ah." Maybe it wasn't too late to... no. Rikolta was trying to be considerate. "Rikolta, I've lived in Akoma for damn near my entire life. I might still be in recovery from a few little gifts Oro left inside me but I get the whole... collectivism thing. You don't need to translate for me. If I'm lost, I'll ask. You might have noticed I've been doing a fair amount of that since I arrived in Ember."

"No stranger to questions?"

Unbidden, the memory of the moving silence rose in me. I thought about staring off into the distance and saying 'only answers' but I'd have then had to explain what I'd meant, which would rather spoil the point. I did, however, take a little too long thinking about saying that, which left an uncomfortable silence hanging between Rikolta and me. I kept making things worse. Wait, did I? Who'd thought that? Me or the Oro Virus? I'd done it again. I should have slept longer. "No," I said, after far too long. "No stranger to questions."

We passed a hall, inside which a glass smashed. A dozen voices cheered, followed by the sounds of tables and chairs scraping. If I had to guess, I'd say that at least five people had just started industriously clearing up the broken glass. Rikolta's footsteps fell in between mine, my step slipping ahead of his, or lagging behind just enough to feel as if I were missing the evening's rhythm. I closed my eyes, opened them, and nodded. "You were saying something about the party we're going to?"

"Yes, and I should say if you don't want to go, you don't have to. I'd like to go with you but..." He drew in a breath between his teeth. "Not if I'm going to worry about you having a shitty time every time I catch a look at your expression."

I chuckled, the sound bridging the silence between our footsteps. "I promise if I'm having a terrible time I'll leave, but I really should get out of the caravan."

"Right. So, this party is small. Mostly people our age or a little younger."

"No octogenarians playing Sparrow in dark corners?"

"If there are, they'll be our sort of people. It's just up here."

The ash path we followed ended abruptly at the door of a hall – two stories tall with poky windows. It's walls lent against each other for support – no precisely cut angles on display. The place was either very old, predating the other halls, or had been an afterthought.

Rikolta strode up, pushed the door open and held it for me. I nodded as I passed him into a cosy hall. Faded carpet lined the floor, three distinct patterns that had been stitched together. Waves crashed against stitching before becoming grey hexagons on a cerulean background. The floor ahead of me was clear. Voices echoed from corners. Laughter, private rather than raucous. I drew in a breath, released it, and looked up from the carpet, taking in the room itself.

Glow globes shimmered in the ceiling, bathing the room in warm light which more than compensated for the cramped windows. A triad of sofas was occupied by a group, only half of whom wore ties. Two long tables stretched the length of one wall, bearing bottles both marked and unmarked, together with a cluster of clean glasses. Three bowls made a centrepiece, of sorts, containing rice crackers, stick biscuits and pineapple bread. A battered set of curtains had been tied back from a stairwell leading up.

A grand total of eight people were in the room, including Rikolta and me. Before the Telegram Flu I'd have probably complained loudly about how dead the 'party' was. Now, I... "Huh."

"What's up?" said Rikolta.

"Thanks for bringing me," I said. I'd wanted to tell him I felt as if I'd come home.

"Waaaay," cheered two of the chaps with ties on the sofa.

"Hiya!" said Rikolta, beaming. "Come on, Laceco, let's inspect the supplies."

We grabbed drinks and snacks before climbing the stairs and exploring the first floor, where we found six tables, only three of which were occupied by people playing card games. I thought I recognised a few of the ones wearing ties but it was hard to be sure.

A femme who had been shuffling three different coloured decks of cards waved at Rikolta, stood from the wheelchair she'd been lounging in and hugged him before sitting back down. "You made it!"

"We made it," grinned Rikolta.

"Yeah, you did. Who's your friend?"

"Laceco, he's dating my girlfriend."

"Oh!" she turned to me, "You're dating Indi?"

Rikolta smacked his head, "No, sorry, I have another girlfriend as well as Indi."

She nodded, thoughtfully. "Cool, cool. You play games, mysterious stranger?"

"Absolutely!" I said, before my brain could latch onto the question and I found myself doubting if I'd ever actually played a game of the sort she meant.

She fanned out a deck of cards, cut the deck into two – half in each hand, twirled the cards, dropped three and scooped them up.

Rikolta sat at her table. "You've got better since last year."

She slapped his shoulder.

I sat next to Rikolta and drained my drink, the burn of home-distilled spirits a comforting distraction. I set my glass down on the table with a *thump*, that shouldn't have sounded nearly as loud as it did. The hall had fallen silent. Rikolta, his card-shark friend, and all the other occupants of the room had vanished. Silence reigned... except I was sure I could hear someone moving about downstairs. Someone who might just be the epicentre of a manifestation.

Chapter Thirteen

I crept to the head of the stairs, trying to breathe as quietly as possible. If this manifestation was based around silence I didn't want to make things worse by shattering it. I descended, one stair at a time until I was able to see a little of what was happening on the ground floor.

There was a single person downstairs. She wore white, although her trouser cuffs were turning grey from the ash streets outside. She wore necklaces – crystal shards, glass beads and varnished wooden pegs. I recognised her, but I couldn't remember where from exactly. She wore a green tie, which she'd knotted around the shirt sleeve of her right forearm.

She strolled around the room, clearly taking her time. She brushed past the empty sofas, letting an idle finger trail along the backrest of the nearest one. She hummed low, slow notes which seemed to fill the space left by the people who'd recently been present. She turned, letting her fingers drop from the back of the sofa and crossed to the drinks table. She picked up a bottle, unscrewed the top, poured a very generous measure into an empty glass, nodded, and strolled away from the table, leaving the glass behind but taking a long draught from the bottle.

Through the fog of memory... Sol. I'd cleaned the Town of Lonely Windows with her. She'd kept me safe during my encounter with a spirit. I was annoyed at myself for taking so long to remember her. My annoyance only increased, when I realised what I was doing.

I was observing Sol, a femme, who was unaware of being observed. That seemed very much like the sort of thing the Oro Virus would approve of me doing. Sol... yes, she wore a green tie. I couldn't remember the details of her hearing loss, so I couldn't rely on the old fall-back of clearing my throat.

She took a second swig from the bottle before sauntering back towards the sofa. I gave up on being subtle and resumed my descent into the room. She must have heard something because her head whipped round.

I gave a small wave. "Hi, Sol."

Sol dropped the bottle and *bolted*. She was out of the door in seconds, slamming it shut behind her. As soon as the door closed, the chattering group on the sofas returned, their conversation resuming with no hint they knew of the disruption.

I dashed upstairs, "Rikolta!"

He was already looking for me. "Laceco? Did it just happen again?"

"Yes, I think I know who's the source. I'm going to look for them – you stay and have a good time."

Rikolta nodded, "Come get me if you need any help."

"Thanks!" I said, and dashed down the stairs and out into Yuneding's twilight.

The path away from the homely hall was short, and I devoured it. When had I last allowed myself to run? I slowed as a path crossed mine, leading to other halls as well as up Mt Talso itself. I couldn't see

Sol, there were too many people moving between the halls. Too much noise to cover her flight. Voices raised in song, laughter, cheering and. .. I turned. Three paths led away, and down two of them Yuneding still sounded festive. Jubilant. To my left, towards the Ember Cavalcade, silence reigned.

The hush only lasted a moment, but it was enough. I ran, pausing occasionally to listen for the sound of silence. Plumes of ash jumped up in my wake. My legs pumped, my chest heaved. I was *running*. I hadn't sprinted anywhere for years. The ground flashed past under my feet. Now I knew what to listen for, the sudden silence was unmistakable. Left, past that hall. Straight on at the intersection and into a thicket of caravans.

There, past a gargantuan hydroponics caravan, a solitary caravan stood, pushed back a little from its neighbours. The solo dwelling had been pushed a little back. I climbed the steps up to the door, my legs feeling weak after my sprint, and raised my hand to knock.

I remembered Sol had hearing issues moments before rapping on the wood. There was a bellpull hanging next to the door. I gave it a tug, causing a bell within to clank arthritically.

The door opened a fraction. Sol stared at me from the crack. "Go away."

She shut the door. I sighed. I pulled the bell-pull again. She jerked the door open again – this time fully. A bell swinging from an apparatus connected to the bell-pull was the only movement inside. Sol glared at me. "What do you want?"

"To help with what's happening to you."

"Great. You can help by leaving me alone." She shut the door again.

One more try. One more. I tugged the bell pull.

She opened the door the moment the bell jangled. "This is harassment."

"I'm sorry," I said, holding up my hands, "it's just that I have experience of these sorts of manifestations and it's not going to get better if you ignore it. If you won't accept my help can you talk to someone else?"

Sol's eyes flashed, "No, I can't. I was supposed to help out as a chef this morning, would have been nice to make some new friends there, see the miniature mountains. Never got the chance. Went to a different sort of party tonight to try and change the scene. You saw what happened. It's not a problem. It's fine. Please go away." She closed the door. It was going to be one of *those* manifestations.

My bed was calling, calling, but I tried to maintain momentum. I groaned, and stomped my way back to the party. The delighted look in Rikolta's face when I returned, honestly, made the evening worth it.

***

The next day, I met up with Ven who demanded I tell her all about the party. We'd been seconded to stack bags of rice in one of Yuneding's massive storehouses, and our chat was progressing nicely, punctuated by the sounds of thumping hessian sacks hitting each other. I was just getting to the good bit of the story when the warehouse suddenly fell silent, and I was alone.

I turned, searching for Sol. "You out there, Sol?" Only silence replied, which felt appropriate. After a few moments, Ven returned followed by the rest of the noise.

"It happened again," said Ven, gripping a battered wooden crate for support.

"Sorry," I said, "she doesn't want help. She might work it out on her own, some people do resolve manifestations by being fiercely independent."

"I bloody didn't."

"Independence isn't a virtue I particularly respect."

The following week, the silence fell in the area I was specifically in three times. Once at the bath house, one in a communal eating hall and once at an open-air performance of Anarchy Reigns, a sober reflection on Akoma's history and the challenges faced therein.

The last one stung. I couldn't even see Sol, so I couldn't judge if yelling at her to fuck off would be audible to her. On reflection, I'm glad my desire to not be ablest overcame my pissy mood. The play resumed after only thirty seconds, which was lovely, but...

"Can I vent to you for a bit?" I said to Ven as we walked home.

"Is that a genuine question?" Ven asked, in between bites of her spiral fried potato snack.

"Yes, why?"

"Oh, good," Ven said, chomping a twist of fried potato free and chewing, contemplatively. "Sometimes when people ask if they can do something they don't really care what the answer is and I hate that shit with such a fiery passion. So I'm free to say no if I want to?"

"Are you intentionally taking the wind out of my ranting sails?"

Ven shrugged. "I can be doing many things at once, I'm extremely talented."

"That you are." We passed a middle aged couple who were standing, watching the stars. One of them seemed to be crying, but maybe not because of misery. I couldn't help but smile. "I won't be annoyed if you say no I can't vent at you, Ven." I said, and was only slightly surprised to find I was being honest.

"Cool. Go ahead then, but I reserve the right to ring the 'you're going on a bit, Laceco alarm.'" She pulled a little bell, the sort some people put on cats, out of a pocket and flourished it at me.

"Is that new?"

"Got it from a crafter this morning. Didn't know what to do with it. Do now, though."

I had to stop walking and close my eyes for a moment to remember what I'd wanted to rant about. Eventually it came back. "Okay, so Sol doesn't want my help. And, obviously you can't force someone to accept help. It's just deeply frustrating when... you can see someone is suffering and they don't need to suffer but in order to not suffer they need to get over whatever block it is they have in their head which is stopping them from engaging with the problem to the point where they can accept that they need to make some sort of change."

Ven's lips moved slowly for a full twenty seconds before she nodded. "Gotcha. Yeah, I think that's a whole thing. Rikolta was saying... I think it was a year or so before he met me... he got into a *thing* of really not wanting to put his liniment on his leg."

"The liniment he uses to make it so his prosthetic doesn't rub?"

"That's the feller. He still wanted to wear his prosthetic, though. So he went through a period of about three months where he was constantly in pain but really didn't deal well with anyone suggesting he use his damned liniment for the purpose it was specifically designed for. We're all going through stuff, you know. People heal at their own paces."

"Yeah. It's just frustrating. The person in the current manifestation is behaving irrationally."

"Hey, neurotypical people are behaving like spirit-possessed squid people from my perspective. I fully have no idea what any of you are up to half the time." Ven wiggled her arms like a squid in a way which she, presumably, thought emphasised her point. "Although, to be honest, I'm not convinced you're not on the spectrum."

"Yeah," I said, feeling my world grow noticeably foggier, "I'll look into that."

Something brushed against my cheek. Immediately, I smiled without knowing why. The moment filtered through to my brain. Ven had kissed me on the cheek. My smile felt warming. Relaxing. I reached out, and Ven's hand was there for me to hold.

Two days later, as I was getting ready to help out at the warehouses again, someone knocked on my door. Ven wasn't in the habit of knocking. It might be Rikolta... I heaved myself to my feet, checked I didn't look like someone who had been dragged through a hedge backwards and opened my door.

Sol stood on the far side. She glared at me. "You know what's happening to me?"

I nodded.

"Can you fix it?"

"No. But I can help you resolve it."

She toyed with the pudgy black beads of her third necklace. "Fine. What do we need to do?"

I pulled my shoes on. "You said you were helping out as a chef at Altibites, right? You helping there today?"

Sol shook her head, "Haven't been back since I made everyone fucking disappear. I don't wanna talk about it." Her grip slipped on the nightshade bead she'd been toying with. Her fingers cracked out before fumbling at her neckline until she found the nightshade once more.

Ven was working at the warehouse and she'd found the moment where Sol's manifestation left deeply uncomfortable. What else needed doing? Everything. That made things easier. "Come on," I said, "let's see what needs doing. We can talk whilst we work."

After a few false starts we found that Yuneding's small medical clinic needed people scouring the hillsides for specific herbs. I hadn't needed to forage since joining Ember. So, feeling nostalgic, I volunteered us. I returned to where I'd left Sol in her personal bubble of seclusion. She bore the news of our task with weary dignity.

Together, we climbed the steppes, past the farms and up to the wilder slopes of Mt Talso. Sol stared listlessly about at the shale-strewn slope, its scree punctuated by tufts of mustard yellow plants.

I brushed past her, following the path that had been roughly cut into Talso's slope. "What can you tell me about your manifestation?"

Sol flicked beads from one of her particularly loose necklaces around the back of her neck and down the opposite side from where it had started, breaking the peace with a steady *tic, tic, tic* of glass beads colliding. "I go to a place, the people disappear. Effect seems to stop as soon as I leave."

"Immediately?"

Tic, tic. "Seems so." *Tic, tic*. "What's causing it?"

I spotted a spindle of green leaves peeking from between two boulders. I knelt and began teasing the herb out of its home. "Wild magic. We went litter picking in the Town of Lonely Windows, do you remember?"

"Oh, yeah? Sure."

"A spirit took a liking to me. Wild magic is the same. It takes a liking to people and expresses some subconscious desire they have."

A space opened up like a suddenly missing tooth. It took me until I'd packed away my herb to realise that Sol had stopped playing with her necklace.

"You think I want this to be happening?" Sol said.

I stepped on my instinctive reaction – a weary sigh. The nervous, exhausted energy moved to my thumb, which ground itself against my index finger, a dull scraping sensation that felt as if I'd strip the skin from my fingers if I kept it up. "You, Sol, don't want this to be happening, but something is wrong in your life, and you're in pain, and your subconscious is expressing itself the only way it knows how. It might be expressing some desire – you're tired of people and want them to leave you alone, say. Or maybe it's literalising some fear you have – you're scared people will abandon you, for instance. I'm not saying either of those are what's going on, I'm saying that's the sort of thing we're looking at."

Sol stared up at the greying sky, clouds twisting together over her. "This sort of thing happen a lot?"

"I saw three manifestations last autumn. This is the first of the year."

Sol absentmindedly started twirling a leather necklace around her fingers. "Will it stop if I leave Ember?"

"Maybe. Do you want to leave Ember, Sol?"

Sol shrugged in a clatter of beads. "I'm starting to think making a community out of disabled people isn't the best idea. Just because we have one thing in common that doesn't mean we have anything else in common. And it means we're not living in society at large, demanding Akoma changes to meet our needs. We're squirrelled away, nice and quiet, where we don't make any reds feel uncomfortable by needing them to make adjustments in the way they live."

I teased dirt away from the roots of another herb, muck lodging under my fingernails. "Last time we spoke you seemed to appreciate the... sense of shared understanding found in Ember."

Sol snatched up a stick and poked at the earth next to her spot on the path as if it would spontaneously sprout herbs any moment now. "Our disabilities are understood, yes."

Ah. "Are you not feeling understood, Sol?"

"Fuck off, I'm not fourteen."

I held up my hands, the herb I'd just grabbed spattering loose soil over my shoes, "Sorry, sorry."

Sol grumbled something I didn't catch.

"How about this, when did your manifestation start?"

"Er..." She toyed with a necklace of tiny, transparent glass teardrops, "Around the time Ember arrived in Yuneding."

"Okay, great." I stowed another herb, straightened up and dusted myself down. "Did anything happen around that time?"

Sol folded her arms. "Define 'anything'?"

I counted to five in my head before replying. "Anything stressful, anything out of the ordinary, anything that made you worry about the direction your life has taken. Anything you think is significant."

Sol rose onto the balls of her feet, though her expression didn't change. She was standing straight, and her slight rise made me think of a marionette being drawn skyward. She rocked back, shook her head, and stomped back down the path, towards the village. "This is bullshit. If I wanted to talk about this stuff I'd go to therapy."

I fought the impulse to chase after her. After another count of five, I called: "I'm here anytime you want. I know we can resolve your manifestation, but if you want to sort it yourself more power to you." I counted to five again. "But you should probably also go to therapy! All of us need it!"

I spent the rest of the day gathering herbs in blissful silence. My concentration kept slipping, my mind circling back to Sol storming away again and again and again. The thought of her retreating back made my chest tighten. My finger joints clicked as my hands clenched. Dirt from the path had plumed up, staining her ridiculous white trouser turnups. She'd held herself with this profound arrogance, the strut of a fucking idiot who...

The palm of my right hand felt damp. A fractured, lifeless body crushed by my grip. I concentrated, letting my fingers uncurl, revealing the herb I'd crushed. I hadn't even been watching what I was doing. Had I been staring down the slope? I couldn't remember. I held myself together. Not too much effort needed. This time. Sighing, I sat where I'd been standing, letting the fatigue that had been creeping up and up around me flow freely.

Two days followed. Two days of recovery. Two days pulling myself back together. Taking things slowly. I let Ven set my pace for rising in the morning and retiring at night, but she was focussing on her musician friends, so I couldn't body-double with her during the day. I read, I bathed and I recovered. Sol's personal bubble of silence circled my caravan.

I'd hoped for Sol to come and see me and ask for my help once again. On the third day I needed to spend the morning outside my caravan, no matter how much recovery I needed. The uneven walls were turning from cosy to tedious, crushing my mood. I took my book with me to breakfast in one of the communal halls, and only noticed once I'd opened the door that it seemed dreadfully quiet inside.

Sol sat at the central table, surrounded on all sides by empty, pristine table settings. She didn't look up, she merely pointed to a wall where a serving counter was laden with rice balls, battered vegetables and soup.

My footsteps echoed en route to the serving counter, an executioner's tread, so loud they made me wince. I took a plate from a stack, the sliding shriek of ceramic on ceramic brought tears to my eyes. I focussed, trying to quieten my cack-handed racket. Grabbing the quietest food available, I sat at the closest table, not wanting to antagonise Sol.

I ate, the organic squishing and crunching of my mastication made me feel unclean. I should have left Sol alone. I was making things worse for her. I was...

Scraping – chair legs against wood. Footsteps behind me, Sol strode into view, circling the table and sitting opposite me. She placed her plate down precisely. She speared a rice ball with a fork and popped it into her mouth. She chewed, and swallowed, never taking her gaze from the prongs of the fork.

She flicked the business end of the fork so that it pointed at me. "There was a party," she said.

"What sort of party?"

She lowered the fork, still looking at it, rather than me. "You just said something. I heard the low frequencies. Couldn't hear what you said, though, mate." She reached into her jacket and pulled out a white cloth bag. She drew out a horseshoe-shaped metal plate, augmented with protruding sections and prongs. Must be the part of her hearing-aid that usually lived in her mouth. It looked more like an instrument of torture or dentistry than a hearing aid.

I thought about replying to Sol, but thankfully my brain kicked in before I went too far down that mental cul-de-sac. I gestured for her to continue and started attacking my breakfast.

"There was a party on our first night here. My friends and I went. Tino, Whatsit, Randing and Steve. Known all of them more than a decade. We grew up in the cavalcade together. Gifted kids, all of us, it's how we knew we belonged in Ember. Of course I also had the deafness thing. They tried to set me up with deaf friends, as if I'd magically like someone because they had the same disability as me. Woo. Good job, guys." Sol sat back in her chair, slumping like a dismembered puppet.

I chewed, quietly. The rice ball I'd chosen had been stuffed with celery or some other crunchy vegetable and the crunching, combined with the burning spices they'd used to flavour the thing were making it hard to concentrate. I tried to maintain an expression of open interest whilst I cursed myself for not finding a glass of water from somewhere. I couldn't very well go and get one now. I lost concentration and my foot clattered off my leg, landing on the floor below my chair. I fished about with the stump of my leg, trying to jam it back into my foot.

Sol looked at me for possibly the first time since I'd entered the hall. "You alright?"

I nodded, although the fatigue had come rushing back. If Sol stormed out I wasn't sure I'd be able to chase her.

Sol shrugged. "Alright. Anyway, we went to this party and we were catching up with some old friends from Yuneding – people we'd grown up knowing. We cracked some of the same old jokes. You know, what's the difference between a dead baby and a—"

I coughed, my mouth and brain both burned. I held up a finger, staggered over to a table where a jug of water sat next to some glasses, drained a glass and returned to the table with a refill. Outside, someone laughed and a ripple of conversation eased away the deathly silence of Sol's sanctuary.

I collapsed back into my chair and pressed my palms together to Sol.

"Anyway. Ours was the sort of group where we don't take prisoners, you know? There's always been banter. Harmless banter. Banter, banter, banter." She shifted in her chair. "Anyway, after we'd got through a few hours of decently intense drinking, Tino said this... she made this joke. I think it was a joke. The details are pretty hazy... but I remember thinking... I remember thinking really clearly... 'Oh shit... you don't actually like me that much, do you?'"

The laughter from outside abruptly fell silent. I frowned. "Fuck..."

"So, yeah. The manifestation started just... wait... what's up?"

I closed my eyes and concentrated. The void spoke in a silent roar. My heartbeat thundered, my breathing rushed but the world outside was dead. My chair legs scraped against the floor as I stood. My footsteps were hammer strikes against the floorboards as I strode to the nearest window. The world outside was still, and empty. No people. No birds. No movement.

The hall door jammed as I tried to open it – I yanked at the handle, which flexed as the wood stolidly refused to budge. I tried to focus, to calm down. I eased the handle down and swung the door open in one smooth motion before stepping out. The street was completely empty.

Sol joined me, staring. "What's happened?"

I tugged an earlobe. She flicked a necklace which had fallen in front of her jacket pocket and withdrew the metal plate she'd shown me earlier, which she slipped into her mouth. She froze, tilting her head. "Do you hear anyone?"

"No."

"Crap. The effect's spread. Is the entire town affected?"

"I don't know! Sol, telling the story has made part of you panic and increase the size or severity of the manifestation. You're going to resolve this, I know you can do it. We just need to work out how. First step: try not to panic. Feel the ground under your feet. Do you feel it?"

Sol stared at her shoes – mostly still white although the sides were covered with ash. "Mm," she said, her gaze wavering. "Yeah, I feel... I feel the ground. Okay. Okay. Okay." She drew herself up. "It's okay, I'm okay. Right. Look, I think I know how to resolve this. I'm not feeling... look, back in the hall I had my bag by my chair. It's got something in there that might be the key to this whole mess. Can you get it for me?"

"Of course!" I strode inside, fighting the urge to run. If Sol saw me running, she might panic. Besides, whilst I could probably run for short distances without making my fatigue flare up it wasn't wise to push myself too hard, too quickly. I was already feeling fuzzy. My conversation with Sol and the sudden silence had burned through more fortitude than I'd have liked.

Sol's chair lay splayed across the floor like a crime scene victim. Her bag wasn't by where she'd sat at the table. It must have been kicked under the table at some point, maybe when she'd scrambled to join me. I dropped to my hands and knees – no. No bag under the table. I turned, tracking the ground through the forest of chair legs. No bag.

I bashed my head against the floor twice, groaning at my own idiocy. I scrambled back to my feet and dashed outside. Sol was no-where to be seen.

Chapter Fourteen

I beat my fists on the floor. "Fuck! Fuck, fuck, fuck, fuck, fuck!"

I took a moment to breathe. Then, I realised I didn't have a moment. If Sol's manifestation was accelerating and if she'd just deliberately sent me away, she might not have long left. I'd managed to resolve every manifestation I'd encountered without anyone getting hurt, but when they started getting really bad, there was an ever-present risk that they might get past the point where they could be resolved. Sol's isolation bubble might manage to envelop me as well, continue growing until it covered the entire area, then all of Akoma, then the world. She'd walk the land alone, trapped by a hell she didn't understand.

Turning on the spot, I was stonewalled by silence on all sides. Was the ash particularly disturbed in one particular area? Not as far as I could tell. Someone with a granite grip had grabbed my heart and was clenching tighter and tighter every beat. I couldn't delay, and my brain was too fuzzy to try and figure out where Sol might have gone. Where had she gone last time? Her caravan. I turned, and swayed a little before setting off at a run towards the cavalcade.

The first ten seconds weren't too bad, but it wasn't long before my legs felt rubbery and weak, my breath ran ragged from my lungs and I was pretty sure my heart was going to collapse in on itself. Sol's caravan was quiet when I reached it, unsurprisingly. I hauled myself up the steps to her door, my vision swimming in and out of focus. I wanted to just lie down in the ash, close my eyes, and not move for the rest of the day. Instead I rang the bell twice, swayed a little, supported myself on the door frame, got bored, and pushed Sol's door open.

Her caravan was empty. I collapsed down onto the stairs and leant back against the doorframe. That might have been a mistake – I'd struggle to get back up. Still, I needed to think. Where would Sol go? She'd intentionally got rid of me, so she didn't want to be found. She probably wanted to just give in to the manifestation. What would I do if I were in a vulnerable state? Go talk to Ven. Yes, but Sol didn't have Ven or Rikolta or even Graco, Indi or Jans. She was in this state precisely because she felt cut off from her friends.

Had she said anything that would give me a clue? What did I know about her? Partially deaf, used blood magic hearing aids, helped out with cavalcade work but transparently didn't enjoy it. Anything else? I didn't even know who her friends were, and I couldn't talk to them even if I *did* know because Sol's manifestation had stowed them away somewhere. There must be something else. What had we talked about? Nothing, really, she'd mostly spent her time grumbling.

When had the manifestation started? After a party. Yes, but *when*? At Altibites, the mountain restaurant? That was when I'd first encountered her manifestation. Why had she been there? She'd... she'd been going to help out with the cooking. She'd talked about wanting to see the mountains. Did she ever actually do that?

I jerked to my feet and threw myself into a run. If I thought I was about to be enveloped by a wild magic manifestation, and I knew there was a truly beautiful piece of magical art that I'd been supposed to see but circumstances had kept me from... that might just be a place I'd visit before giving in.

It felt as if someone had spliced five kilometres of surplus pathways between Sol's caravan and Altibites. My vision swam, vague shapes pulsed past – caravans, halls and gaslamps. I was grateful the paths were empty because it meant I could concentrate on running and not worry I'd bump into anyone on the way due to my progress being less than steady. I let my sense of the world fuzz and fade. I kept my legs moving. Driving myself forward.

I nearly ran past Altibites, but its façade was recognisable enough that some part of me noticed it, feeding the information through to my brain only a little late. I stopped, my skid throwing up a drift of ash. I staggered towards the door and hauled it open.

Inside, the joint was quiet and still. A weight fell in my stomach – had I guessed wrong? I leant against the doorframe and tried to focus. Was that someone? Yes, it was Sol. Yes. I heaved in a breath and then let it go. I'd made it.

Sol was standing, staring at the mountains. She didn't even look up at me. "Don't worry, I'm just doing this one thing, then I'm off."

Right. Fears confirmed. I had to convince her to stay, stick with the manifestation. Not give in. I had to say something insightful, something that connected with her on a truly human level. That was a problem, because in the time since I'd learned the cause of her manifestation, I hadn't had a chance to fight through the fatigue, fight to get my thoughts in order. I'd done very little but panic.

Sol frowned at me. "Are you okay?"

I was leaning against the doorframe. How long had I been doing that? *Focus, Laceco.* Sol was there, and she needed help. I raised a finger. I opened my mouth. Nothing happened.

Usually, when I opened my mouth, the real trick was getting me to stop talking. Ven had made that observation repeatedly, and with a certain amount of weary resignation. I could talk for hours if people really let me get going. If I opened my mouth, I started talking. That was how it worked. Birds fly. Capitalism crushes people. Laceco talks.

My head felt as if someone had stuffed it fill to bursting with cotton wool. I closed my mouth, and then opened it again, but nothing came out. Fuck. I couldn't hold myself together anymore.

I fell apart. My ankles detached from my feet, and cracked down onto the floor, my bones jarring agonisingly against the wood. The fall separated my lower legs from my knees, and when my thighs hit the floor, any remaining integrity left to my body shattered. My torso hit the ground, my arms thumping into segments, useless hunks of meat. My head was last to fall. It landed on top of my torso, which softened the landing, but then I rolled down and away, the room spinning vomitously. I squeezed my eyes shut, gave in, and waited for it to be over. My forehead cracked against something solid, and, for a time, that was that.

***

A smooth cotton funeral shroud enveloped me. I lay, my muscles limp and loose. I felt whole, but shattered. I opened my eyes, and blinked until the space around me resolved into a room, recognisable despite its unfamiliarity. A hospital room. I couldn't see much of it because half a pillow and the corner of my bedsheets were obscuring my view, and beyond those, a drawn curtain cut my bed off from the rest of the... ward? Room? Where was I?

"Are you awake?" Sol's voice. Behind me.

Could I roll over? No. Damn. I tried to speak but only managed to open my mouth a fraction.

"He's awake!" called Sol. I knew these words contained a mystery, but for the life of me I couldn't remember why.

The privacy curtain was swept back, then replaced in a flurry of movement. A tall nurse with mischievous eyes bustled to my bedside, and squatted down to meet my eye-level. "How you doing, Laceco?"

I cleared my throat, My mouth felt as if someone had coated it with sandpaper. "Yeah. Better."

"Sol didn't know what the cause of your incident was. I can ask her to leave if you wanted to tell me in confidence?"

I breathed, the air leaving me inexorably turning into a sigh. I thought I'd left hospitals behind. Eventually, I had enough space in my head. "Post-viral fatigue. No treatment required. Pushed myself too hard, too fast. Just need rest."

The nurse nodded, "Great. We'd like to do a few checks but they can wait. Rest up. I'll come back with some lunch. There's water and some painkillers on the table just behind you. Need anything else? A book?"

"A book would be amazing."

We then haggled over what sort of book, during which time enough of my energy returned for me to fight my corner and insist on a half-decent murder mystery. The nurse, clearly having dealt with difficult patients before, returned a few minutes later with "Blood in the Belfry", before leaving once again.

I was able to roll onto my back and then shuffle up into a semi-sitting position. There was a shadow on the other side of the privacy curtain. "That you, Sol?"

"Mm."

"Pull back the curtain, bab, it's fine."

She twitched the curtain open, before sitting back down and gripping her necklace with the smallest beads tightly.

"You resolved your manifestation," I croaked.

Sol shook her head and jerked a thumb over her shoulder. "Look out the window."

Outside, Yuneding was silent, still and solitary. "Crap."

"The nurse came back when I gathered you up and brought you here. A doctor too. No-one else. And they don't seem to know they're the only ones who have returned."

"Thank you."

Sol sighed. "I couldn't very well leave you there in pieces. Are you human, Laceco?"

The corners of my mouth twitched up. "As far as I know."

"You're living with a manifestation as well?"

"Seems that way."

Sol sighed. "Damn. I'm... really sorry. Looks like I made your manifestation a lot worse."

I lifted a hand, with the intention of waving the apology aside but could only flump it back down onto the bed. Her guilt was useful. She wouldn't give way to despair for as long as her guilt outweighed her misery.

Damn. That was a really fucked up thing to think. I closed my eyes. I hadn't managed to come up with any amazing award-winning speeches that would help Sol see the truth of her manifestation. I didn't have enough information. She'd wanted to solve this herself, and it seemed likely she'd have to. I could try getting her started, but probably not much else.

I did my best to concentrate. Half an idea was forming, and it was focussed on one question: "Who are you, Sol?"

Her hand stilled, fingers holding a solitary silver bead. "You know who I am."

"I don't... I'm sorry, I'm struggling. Can you answer the question for me?"

"Sol. My name's Sol."

I coughed, and tried again. "Not your name. Who are you? Really?"

Her fingers twisted a bead free of her necklace. It dropped to the ground with a *clack, clack, clack*. "I'm a person who cooks and drinks and climbs and goes... used to..."

"What about the necklaces?"

Sol's hand froze again, her gaze darting from point to point. "What do you mean?"

I squeezed my eyes shut. I was getting this *wrong*. "Sorry, Sol. I promise... I'm not being intentionally difficult..."

She leant forward. "You need to rest, Laceco. You shouldn't be doing... this."

"It's important. I think you've forgot something."

She jerked back and patted her pockets. "What?"

"It goes back to my first question."

Sol sighed and sat back. "Can you... is this making sense to you, Laceco? Should we just do this later?"

"I think we're close. I'm really sorry. It's... can I just talk out loud for a bit? I'm trying to put pieces together."

Her lip curled, "Keen to fix me, are you?"

"Sol," I said, maintaining eye contact as best I could, "this is really important. I can't fix you. I can't resolve the manifestation. That has to be you. You're in control here. All I'm doing is... I have experience with these things. I can sometimes... I see things a little differently, and sometimes people need an outside perspective to catch the things they've missed. You can resolve the manifestation, and you will. You don't need me, but you might get there quicker if I help."

She sighed, the weight of years making her shoulders slump. "Go ahead."

I shifted, seeking a more comfortable position. Pins and needles burst up my leg, making me wince. "Okay, so... At first I thought you were lonely. You went to a place, your subconscious removed all the people. It was trying to literalise loneliness for you, right?"

Sol gave me a terribly blank look. "I'm not lonely, Laceco."

"I know. If you were, I don't think your manifestation would have ramped up the way it did. We've been talking a bit these last few days. If you were lonely then our chats might have made you feel a little better."

Sol shrugged.

"So... There are a few ways manifestations try to communicate with us. Sometimes they want to show us some hidden truth. Sometimes they want to get us to do something. I think yours might be the later, but I need... can you answer my question?"

"What question, Laceco?" Her voice was flat and quiet. Drained.

"Who are you?"

Sol shrugged, but didn't reply.

"I think that's what you've forgot. You went to that party with your friends and you left thinking they don't actually like you that much. It made me wonder how long that's been the case. Who is the Sol who was first friends with them, and who's the Sol sitting in front of me? When you told me about the things you did with your life – cooking, climbing – you didn't seem to have real passion for any of them? Is that fair?"

Sol shrugged.

"And the necklaces. Is there a reason you wear so many?"

Sol shrugged.

"I might be completely wrong, but I wonder if you made some decision years back and you find yourself wearing... how many necklaces, six?"

"Five."

"Five, sorry. And you can't quite remember how you got there. Is that fair?"

Sol shrugged. The corners of her eyes shimmered.

"So, I think your manifestation might be angry. You were hurt in the wake of that party, and you started wondering if anyone actually knows who you are. And that line of thought led you to the question I've been badgering you with. Hence the manifestation. I think your subconscious was sending people away not because you were lonely, but because you can't stand being around people who don't know who you are. No, wait..."

I squeezed my eyes tight. Something there was wrong. "If that was true you could have sent me away too. Is that right? Your manifestation isn't sending people away..."

"It very much is," said Sol, barely above a whisper.

"It's making space," I said, the thought that had been out of reach all this time was nearly close enough to touch, "It's saying 'yes, you're lonely. Yes, you feel misunderstood. Yes, you're struggling. Yes, your friends are shit heads. So... reset. Restart. Who are you? Let me give you this space so you can work on that question.'"

Sol shifted in her chair.

My thoughts burned. I wanted to follow up what I'd said, find the perfect thing to say and then say it and make everything better and stop her hurting so much. I couldn't think any more. The hacked-together thought I'd barely expressed had been bad enough. I couldn't say anything else. Either I was right or Sol was about to leave.

Sol shifted again. Slowly, silently, she nodded. She closed her eyes, drew in a breath, and released. She drew in a breath, her shoulders rising. She released the breath, her shoulders falling. She drew in a breath, her shoulders rising and her hands rising to her sternum. She released the breath, her shoulders falling and her hands lowering to rest on the arms of her chair.

"Who am I?" Sol asked.

Outside, footsteps passed the window and a bird trilled the first notes of a song. Sol breathed, and, like a rising tide, noise returned.

Interlude: Mari the Puppet

The day our cavalcade was due to leave Yuending, Ven, Rikolta and I returned to Altibites, the mountain restaurant. We'd been instructed by Sol to ensure we were packed and all our responsibilities had been seen to. When we arrived, we found the place empty other than Sol.

"Come in," she said, "come in, don't stand there creating a draft."

She shepherded us to a table. *The* table. There was only one left in Altibites, the others must have been squirrelled away to a store room. Another cavalcade wasn't due to come through Yuneding for months so the locals had reclaimed the space.

"What's going on, Sol?" I asked.

"Hush," she said. "I've got to get back. I think something's about to boil over."

She bustled back to the kitchen. I sat back in my chair, thought better of it, turned my chair a little so I had a better view of the mountains and settled back in my chair once again.

Ven rested her head on my shoulder "What do you think she's up to?"

"Not sure," I said. I'd recovered a little from my last collapse, but I would still need to take it easy for the next few weeks.

Rikolta stretched, "I think she feels a little guilty. You shouldn't have told her about our problems disappearing and reappearing, Lac-ci."

I wanted to shrug, but Ven still occupied my shoulder. "She asked."

Sol returned, carrying three steaming plates. "Here," she said grandly, "is a feast to remember Yuneding by."

"Please tell me you made some for yourself," said Ven.

"Whut?" said Sol.

I face-palmed.

Five minutes later, Sol had joined us with a fourth plate. Ten minutes later, Rikolta had finished his meal whilst we were still working away. "I think my mum might have encountered a manifestation, you know?" His tone was precisely casual.

I made a querying noise through my mouthful of baked strips of tortilla.

"Yeah. She told me this story one time... Way back, before she was Ember Priestess, she was studying religion and the lack of religion in Oro."

I groaned. Ven slapped my shoulder.

Sol gave us a look. "What was that?"

Ven rolled her eyes. "Laceco has opinions on his country of birth."

I swallowed. "I'm carrying a mind-virus they put in me."

Sol blanched, "Really?"

"Yes," I said.

"No," said Ven.

"Anyway," said Rikolta, tapping the table. "She met this femme, couldn't have been much older than eighteen. She was sweeping the road in the middle of no-where – a telegraph road between two half-forgotten towns. This femme.. she was slight. Short. Looked as if a stiff breeze would pick her up and carry her with it. Her hair was long and scraggly but tied back into a ponytail. Mum would probably have stopped to talk to her anyway because it's not every day you meet someone sweeping dust from an obscure piece of road leading from nowhere to nowhere squared. The thing that really grabbed mum's attention were the glowing filaments attached to the femme's wrists, ankles, and head. They led away, twinkling, trailing in the dust. Mum couldn't tell if she lost them amongst the road's dust or if they stretched all the way to the horizon."

"Damn. I should have gone traveling after school," said Sol. "Somewhere other than the Ember Trail."

Ven shrugged, "You still can."

"Plenty of amazing places in Akoma and beyond," said Rikolta, "but there wasn't anything particularly special about this one stretch of Oro. So, obviously, mum asked this femme what her deal was. She probably said it in a slightly more... elegant and fucking... eloquent manner or something. Anyway, the femme was Mari and she said she was a puppet."

I smiled. "A wooden puppet or a metaphorical puppet?"

Rikolta flourished an index finger, "Neither! Okay, so this was the sitch: Mari grew up in this big, *big* fucking house. The sort of space you only have if you build it yourself in the middle of no-where or if you are taking up *way* more space than you need."

"This house was in Oro?" I asked.

Rikolta winked at me, "Someone wins the paying attention prize. Anyway, she lived there with her mum. People brought her food, books, toys, clothes, the works. She went on walks, played in a play-ground with some kids her own age, very little to complain about generally. There was something... off about the whole place but as a kid she had no idea what. Any guesses so far?"

I sat back in my chair and stared at the ceiling. "Not enough people for it to be a cult. You don't have that stuff unless you're exceptionally rich. You didn't mention holidays. The Oro oligarchs are pretty famous for extravagant jaunts around the world. So not a cult, not a standard oligarch, doesn't sound like a religious leader or an industry titan..."

"I need to strike Oro from my list of places to visit," Sol stage-whispered to Ven.

"No guesses?" Rikolta asked, a grin drawing us all back to him. "Well, then, I will continue."

"You can just continue, you don't need to say you'll continue," said Ven.

"Right," said Rikolta, "So, Mari started to realise what was up when she hit her teens. She was never allowed out without an escort. Neither was her mum. At first she thought they were bodyguards or something, but then she paid more attention to how they interacted with her mum. They treated Mari with frigid acceptance but her mum received steel contempt. One day she got curious and tried to leave without permission. She found the doors were locked, windows too. She asked her mum for the key, but her mum tried to talk about something else. After some back and forth, Mari slipped out of the house when one of the guards wasn't paying attention. She climbed a nearby tree and watched to see what would happen. Twenty minutes later, she was starting to get bored, but then guards flooded the area around the house. Some calling for her, others dead quiet but all were carrying pistols – the fancy compressed-air powered things."

"Huh," I said. "A political prisoner?"

"A what?" said Sol.

"Someone locked up against their will because the people at the top of Oro's weird hierarchical society didn't like their political opinions," I said. "One of the reasons we get so many people fleeing here and to Oro's other neighbours. That, along with the starvation, the homelessness, the lack of any satisfying vocations, the prison system, police, three-tiered approach to medicine... Sorry, I got sucked in there."

"Mari was a political prisoner yes," said Rikolta, "Well, her mum was, which meant she also was. Security was tightened after her experiment as well – she wasn't able to see other kids as much. When she asked one of them for help, she was stopped from seeing them at all."

Sol turned to me, "Your homeland seems fucking awful."

I nodded, my eyes wide enough to hopefully convey my utter lack of surprise at her strikingly original observation.

Ven growled at the back of her throat before leaning forward, "Are you going to let my beloved tell his story that I'm sure will start being fascinating any minute now?" Her gaze snapped to me, "We don't interrupt you as much when you tell stories, beloved."

I remembered my last attempt at recounting a historical manifestation differently, but I was pleased at being called 'beloved' so I reasoned I was best off letting it go.

"Thank you, Ven," said Rikolta, grandly. "So, Mari was a prisoner in her own home. Her mum was no use, her spirit had broken long before. Things took a turn, however, when two journalists were invited to the house. Mari was given a fresh frilly frock – try saying that six times fast – and briefed on exactly what she could and couldn't say to the journalists. When Mari was being interviewed, she felt herself move without any desire to move. She spoke words that weren't hers, and when the journalists left she looked down and saw that glowing threads were linked to her hands, feet, body, and (she had to check a mirror for this one) head. The strings led up into the ceiling where they disappeared.

"She freaked a little about this, as I'm sure we all would. She ran to her mum, who didn't know what she was talking about. So, Mari lived, scared, alone and having her every movement dictated by some malevolent figure."

I grimaced, "She couldn't find the puppeteer?"

Rikolta shook his head. "The strings always led to a place where she wasn't. She went through a period of experimentation. She could pick up scissors but her puppeteer wouldn't let her try to cut her strings. She had to give up certain personal activities because she hated the idea that someone else was controlling her movements during her private time. She didn't feel great about showering, and only bathed when she couldn't stand her own smell any longer. She wanted to spend all day in bed but the puppeteer didn't like that. So, three months after seeing the strings for the first time, three months after becoming aware that everything she could see, say, and do was controlled by someone else, she resolved to fight back.

"She tested the limits of the puppeteer's control, only to conclude that their control was total. That would have sent her into another despair spiral were it not for the second realisation of that day. She realised that, by controlling her every move, the puppeteer was, willingly or otherwise, telling her exactly what he was like. She realised that he wasn't forcing her to bathe. He wasn't forcing her to disrobe for his vicarious pleasure. He wasn't forcing her to leave the house and perform propaganda exercises. He wanted her quiet. Dormant."

"Servile," said Ven.

"Obedient," said Sol.

Rikolta snapped his fingers, "Exactly. So she learned all she could about this coward. She realised that she could take small actions of her own if she redirected her puppeteer's demands. The puppeteer wished to move her such that she sank to her knees and polished the parquet floor, but she would only do so if she could first dance a two-step in the kitchen. He wished for her to prepare snacks for the guards and she obeyed, but made some extremely creative choices about what went into the snacks. And that was when she learned that her puppeteer knew nothing, *nothing* about cuisine, herbs, mushrooms. What ingredients could, for example, when combined, cause a severe gastric event."

"She got out?" I asked, grinning. "Well, of course she did, your mum met her on the road."

"Right," said Rikolta, "She got out. She learned enough about the puppeteer to finesse the way he moved the strings. He wanted her to walk to the west, she moved in a way which made him think he'd succeeded, all the while she was running to the east. She walked out of the house one day, out of the front door, and she made the puppeteer think it was all his idea. She plucked at her strings as she walked. They were frayed. Easily snapped. And yet, she walked. She kept walking until she found that one particular stretch of the telegraph road, and she made herself a home there."

"Why not snap the strings?" Sol asked. "Be free of the manifestation?"

I groaned. "Because if she'd freed herself, the puppeteer would have tried again. Or maybe he'd have made someone else his puppet. Men in Oro always seek to recapture power they've lost. It's the virus."

Ven grumbled under her breath.

"That was what Mari told my mum, yes," said Rikolta, "for as long as Mari was content living her life, controlling the puppeteer's every movement, she knew he'd never hurt anyone ever again."

Chapter Fifteen

Ven clambered up to the roof of my caravan and adjusted the goggles that kept the embers out of her eyes. "Okay," she said, "here's the thing. The femmes and I have been chatting and we're going to try and do a run at one of Shai's theatres after we get there. Maybe do a bit of a conservatory sort of thing during the days."

"Heeey," I said, the embers settling on my skin matching the dancing, burning thrill in my chest. "That's amazing! Can I come see your show?"

"Mm." Said Ven, her gaze fixed forward on the trail. "the thing is, I was practicing with the squad a fair bit at Yuneding. And do you remember what you did?"

"Solved a manifestation?"

"Exhausted yourself to the point that you fell apart in front of someone who was essentially a stranger. Tell me you don't make a habit out of that sort of thing."

"Of course I don't!"

"You say 'of course', Lacci, but I don't fucking know, do I? It's why we're having this conversation, so I'd appreciate you not treating my requests as childish."

"Spirits, Ven, I'm sorry, I didn't mean it like that."

Fire blazed behind the lenses of her goggles. "Oh? How did you mean it?"

"I meant... I'm sorry. I promise I'll take better care of myself."

"Good. So can I go on this thing and be reasonably confident you won't run yourself ragged if another manifestation shows up?"

"Yes. Please pursue your stint at a theatre, Ven."

"Right. Okay. And when I get back, we're going to have to spend some serious time working on yours."

"My what?"

Smoked lenses swayed in the dancing embers, "Your manifestation, Laceco."

"Oh, that."

"Yes. That."

Answers rose from within me. None of them would have been wise to voice. "Right."

"Right," said Ven. "Okay. Well I'm going to say goodbye to Rikolta. Before I do, do you have... I don't know... Twenty minutes to spend with me inside?"

"Yes. Yes I do."

***

Shai, when we arrived, turned out to be occupied by more people than I'd thought existed. If Shai had been a body, then it's arteries would be clogged by bustling citizenry. It's heart, the cacophonous cultural district, was heaving with humanity. We arrived at dusk, which turned out to be one of the two busiest times of the day, when the scorch was starting to fade. It would have been nice to wait for the heat to fade completely, but the food we'd transported from Yuneding needed to be unloaded as soon as possible. Our cold storage apparatuses had been sorely stretched, none were operating at peak efficiency and every hour the food stayed out of Shai's more robust facilities was a day cut off each Foodstuff's window of safety.

All hands helped, no exceptions. We'd all lived through periods of famine, many of which had been caused directly by Oro, to risk treating food distribution lightly. Those who couldn't lift and carry managed inventory, those who couldn't manage inventory carried messages and those who couldn't carry messages worked on the steam powered heat exchangers, coaxing them into working just a little harder for these last precious hours.

I hauled bags of rice, crates of chilled vegetables and churns of breakfast soy, oat, and almond milks. I managed an hour before I started flagging. The temptation was to continue, but I pictured Ven's expression at my decision. I went to find a team working on a cooler engine who needed someone to hold things.

The night was taking on a serious chill by the time my engine crew finished up. The food had been mostly distributed by that point, leaving the activity surrounding our parked cavalcade less frantic.

Our driver had parked my caravan a decent way away from the engine I'd been working on. I had to ask for directions a couple of times, but found my way eventually.

Fatigue gnawed at my bones, but I was pretty sure I'd done a decent job of managing my energy. I'd know if I'd fucked it up in a couple of days. Still, I wasn't at my most awake. This meant I only noticed Graco when I was only a stone's throw from her.

She was leaning with her back against a chain-link fence, her eyes shut and her cane propped next to her. She looked as tired as I felt, which made me pause. And in that pause, I heard the bell.

The bell tinkled like a spirit completing its unfinished business. There followed an almighty thump, then another bell rang – this one much louder and fuller than the first, although as that bell faded, I heard the tinkling bell once again. Graco was standing still, but tilted her head slightly as I approached.

Still not sure how exactly I was supposed to announce my presence, I opened my mouth to make an attempt. As I did, Graco straightened, turned, and strode away from me, the bells ringing in her wake. She trod in a gloopy white splat on the ground as she walked, her footsteps smeared the pavement. Her staccato stride set my teeth on edge but I had to hope she'd just had a long day. I found my caravan, crawled into bed and was asleep before I could wonder anymore about Graco.

***

I woke up the next morning feeling as if I'd been hit by a smallish earth-moving automata. This prompted five minutes of internal flagellation. What a charitable soul might call justified anger but I called a tantrum. It was so *unfair*. I'd managed my energy yesterday! I'd done everything right. That meant I basically wasn't disabled, right? If I did everything right, then I'd never experience symptoms ever again.

Rather than fight against these lumpy, slimy thoughts I gave myself to them, letting them inhabit me. For five minutes, I was a small, petty grievance of flesh and spite. I raged at the world, Akoma, Shai, the fucking Ember cavalcade, Ven...

Cursing Ven was what brought me back. The crimson tint through which I'd seen the world faded. My brain refused to accept my rage. If everything was shit, that meant Ven was shit, and that was obviously not true. I was booted from my tantrum through a head-on collision with simple logic. Not my worst exit from childish rage.

Ven echoed in my head, in my room. She'd said the words. Out loud. Had she not understood how it worked? If you never acknowledged the problem, that meant the problem didn't exist. Nevertheless, she'd said it, and you can't stuff the badger back into the sack once it's tasted freedom, as badger-wranglers in Oro used to say before the animal welfare act of 564. She knew. Sol knew. Rikolta very possibly knew. I was experiencing a manifestation. The manifestation... My distress was causing Ven distress. I should take steps to deal with it.

Obviously it would be much healthier to deal with the manifestation because I wanted to recover. Self-motivation. Otherwise I risked putting Ven on a pedestal and... I shook my head. I was second guessing my own reasons for pursuing recovery. Or was I procrastinating? I groaned and got out of bed.

Graco. Graco knew about wild magic. She was more likely to have a useful take on my manifestation than Rikolta or Sol, though they might also have insight... I'd start with Graco.

Of course, starting with Graco meant working out where she was. The Obsid University Cavalcade had parked up in a different district of Shai, maybe because there wasn't room in the smoke stacks district, maybe because Obsid and Ember were parting ways. Who could say which? Probably multiple people, but not me. I thought I'd heard someone say yesterday that Obsid was parked around the Embassy District? Something like that. I found a signpost and followed its directions.

My route took me down the same road I'd seen Graco on last night. I could hear the same thumps and bells ringing out as I'd heard last night. I stopped at the chain-link fence, glad for the excuse to take a breather.

On the other side of the fence was a squat building, and stretching out from that was a long paved area, lined by rope netting to the left and right, as well as above. At one end the paved area had been subdivided five times, creating netted cages, but open on one side. The paved strip curled up away from the cages to five clusters of bells opposite each cage. Four of the cages were empty, whilst Graco stood in the fifth.

She was wearing the long-sleeve football shirt I'd seen her in way back, with the addition of a blindfold – black with silver threaded flowers tracing its borders, which seemed a little superfluous, but what did I know. A football rolled down the sloped path to where Graco stood, a bell tinkling as it rolled. When the ball reached Graco, she spun, kicking the ball as she turned. The ball flew towards the cluster of bells, striking the one in the centre. Graco turned towards the sound of the tinkling bell as the ball rolled back down the slope towards her.

Well. I didn't need to find the Obsid University Cavalcade. I'd take that freebie. I was initially at a loss as to how to get to where Graco was, but I found my way in through the squat building, where a bored looking masc let me in after I told him I was there to see Graco.

"Come here often, does she?" I asked.

The masc shrugged. "Been here a lot since her cavalcade got in."

He went back to reading his book. Knowing when I'm not wanted, I followed the signs to the Football Cages.

Graco paused as I approached. "Is that someone wanting to use the cages?"

"It's Laceco," I said, "I wanted to say hi. Do you have time for a wild magic consult?"

She shrugged, "Eh." She kicked the ball, striking a bell at the edge of the cluster. "I'm kinda done with that stuff, but if you think it'll help I can listen. I'm a good listener."

"Really? You seemed pretty into the wild magic research when we last chatted about it."

The ball rolled back to Graco, who stopped it with her foot, rolled it to the right and then sent it flying. "Yeah, well... I want to try and focus on one thing, you know? I was splitting my time, splitting my attention. Trying to engage with too many things. Left me not sure what I was doing at any one time, you know? So I'm going to focus on the football. I'm extremely good at it." She kicked the ball again, striking the bell in the centre of the cluster, punctuating her point.

"Right," I said, "I've been meaning to ask, why the blindfold?"

"Standard equipment," said Graco. She drew back her foot to kick the ball again but a quintet of crows chose that moment to land on the ropes nearby with a great flapping of wings. She caught the ball on the side, making it spin into the net next to her. She rounded on me, "You said you wanted a consult."

I grimaced, "Right. So I've been going through a manifestation for a while."

Graco felt about for the ball and scooped it up. "How long?"

"About two years."

"Five."

I rocked back on my heels before shaking my head and refocussing on Graco, "No, Two. Two years."

"Yeah, you said. And what happens?"

"I fall to pieces if I push myself too hard."

She sucked in air through her teeth. "Sounds nasty. Ven know about it?"

"Yeah. Saw it happen pretty early on."

"That's good. It'd suck to go through one of those things by yourself."

I counted on my fingers, pleased to have the opportunity to do so without anyone seeing me. "I think only about one in five get to be in my position."

"Fuck's sake," Graco set the football down in front of her and cracked it into the centre bell. "Well, I'm not exactly sure what you want from me other than my sympathy."

"Really? When I've come to you before about this sort of thing you've done all sorts of experiments and stuff. Usually involving coffee. Shall I get you a coffee?"

"Did it ever occur to you that only coming to see me when you want something is not the best way to make me think kindly of you?" Graco asked, balancing her foot lightly on top of the freshly returned football.

"Ah."

"So," said Graco, "unless there's anything else, it's hard to do this whilst having a conversation." She kicked the ball, missing the centre by centimetres.

"Sorry, Graco. I'll... think about what you just said. Sorry." I left, my face burning.

I walked, not having a destination or even a direction in mind. If I didn't concentrate, the soles of my shoes dragged against the pavement, my body trying to root itself to the spot. I held myself together as best I could, and was so grateful when I spotted a bench someone had placed near an out-of-the-way rock park that I wanted to cry.

Collapsing onto the bench, I let go. Not completely – my hands fell from my arms, resting on the boards of the bench next to my bum. My ankles slipped from my legs, leaving the stumps of my legs dangling, limp. Uncontrolled. My head lolled back but I held onto that. If I'd let go it might have fallen down the back of the bench and been a pain to retrieve. A pain in the neck, possibly.

Snatches of my conversation with Graco played in my head, but at a distance. I was clearly beating myself up about something or other, but the fatigue was making it difficult to parse exactly what. I sat, letting everything happen. There might have been parts of the everything which could be steered, potentially lessening my need for rest, but working out what those elements were would have required concentration. Concentration would have increased my need for rest. They called that the paradox of disability. Did they? I called it the paradox of disability. I had only now named it the paradox of disability. There might already have been one of those. Damn. The twelfth paradox of disability, that's what I could call it. There might be one or two already extant but there probably weren't eleven. I was pretty sure I'd been thinking about something important before every one of my five available brain cells had been occupied by thoughts of the Paradox of Disability numerical system.

Had I eaten breakfast? I might have got excited and set out to find Graco without eating anything. That would explain how things had got quite this bad in such a short space of time. I didn't have any specific breakfast memories from this morning, which probably meant I'd forgot. I pulled myself together so I could crack my knuckles, got up and tracked down a local who could point me in the direction of a communal food... zone. Place? Hall.

A square surrounded by battered-looking houses on three sides was packed with benches and tables, whilst being sheltered from the south-Akoman sun by awnings and canvas sheets strung between balconies. About half the benches were full, and I vaguely recognised most of those present. Which, after my deeply confusing morning thus far, felt as if I were a pearl diver finally coming up for air. A serving table stood by the open side of the square. I queued up, was given a double helping of a stew that looked thick, lumpy and carcinogenic, but smelled as if it would render all food I'd eaten before it mere ash and sulphur.

Casting around for somewhere to sit, I spotted Rikolta with Indi and Jans. I stumbled over and hesitated only briefly before collapsing onto a bench next to my paramour's paramour.

"Good morning, Laceco," said Indi, the ghost of a breeze making her locs dance.

"Hi," said Jans, their tone echoing the timbre of a funeral bell.

Rikolta patted me on the shoulder, "Eat. Don't worry about conversation."

What the fuck had I done to deserve being friends with people who could see what was happening with me, and didn't take the opportunity to inform me that I was being lazy or a burden? Some past life act of supreme charity. Or I was expressing internalised self-hatred again. I smiled at the three seraphim and ate my stew, which turned out to dance across my tastebuds, the hearty base brought to life by tickles from herbs and lent depth by crisp aubergines and courgettes.

My three friends chatted, and I listened to them, the fog in my head slowly clearing as my stomach and heart filled. After maybe twenty minutes, Jans announced that they were going to tour Shai's shrines. They invited Indi, who said she had duties to attend to. I might have imagined the sub-tone to her voice that heavily implied she'd rather stick her hand into the business end of a farming automata than spend any more of her life visiting shrines.

Rikolta said goodbye to them both. He kissed them, one after the other, both in exactly the same way. He kissed them tenderly, the triad taking their time. When I'd seen him kiss Ven, the pair had looked as if they were on fire, wishing they could melt into each other. I slipped a spoonful of stew into my mouth and chewed contentedly as they finished their goodbyes.

Indi left, walking one way whilst Jans walked the other. Rikolta sat back down next to me. I finished my mouthful before checking his plate – polished clean. "Hello," I said, "keeping me company?"

"I have a wager running."

"Ah," I said, "that explains nothing."

He winked at me. "Can't have knowledge skewing the results. How you doing?"

I wiggled a hand, "Been better. You know about my... problem?"

"Your problem? Or..." Rikolta lowered his voice an octave, "your *problem*?"

"Wait... what problems do you think I have?"

Rikolta blinked with agonising slowness, "Excellent question."

"I'm working on resolving my manifestation," I said, dividing my stew into two equal sections on my plate, then four.

"Oh hey, good work," said Rikolta. "Need any help?"

'Only coming to see me when you want something is not the best way to make me think kindly of you.'

"Mm," I said, splitting my four piles of stew into eight, and selecting one to consume with my mighty jaws. "Only if you haven't got anything you'd rather be doing."

He was looking at me. I couldn't get a clear look at his expression out of the corner of my eye. Fuck it. I was curious. I swallowed and turned. His gaze danced from point to point to point but didn't seem to be moving away from me. A smile had tweaked the corners of his mouth, and only grew when our gazes met. His eyes were deep wells of peace. Tranquillity. What had happened to the fidgety chap who had been overcome by an insecurity wraith?

He didn't speak, he just smiled.

"That'd be very kind," I said, my gaze dropping to the table.

"Hm," said Rikolta, running a finger across the tabletop, "want to talk about it?"

I froze. "Talk about what?"

"That bad, huh?"

"Errrr..."

He waved a hand. "Never mind. So, what's the next step in working out your manifestation?"

I only then realised I'd been clenching my teeth. I let out a breath, relaxing my shoulders, letting my teeth separate. "Well for the last few I've tried talking to Graco but she's busy right now. Information is useful. Theories, that sort of thing. Obviously, I know my own history so that's easier but the scientific approach did help..."

Rikolta nodded, slapped his knees, winced briefly, and then stood. "Alright. Well, Graco isn't the only scientist in the Obsid University Cavalcade. They also have a library that might well have a section on magic. Maybe even wild magic. You can fill me in on any history you feel is relevant on the way if you want a second opinion?"

I followed him out of the square, then past caravans, houses and an enormous civic building, its plain stone walls decorated by thousands of painted handprints. It was only when I broke my attention from wondering about what the handprints could have symbolised that I realised something was odd. "Rikolta?"

"Mm?"

"This wager you have. It's not between you and Ven, is it?"

"Who can say?"

"She's worried I'll burn myself out if I get lost in another manifestation?"

Rikolta shrugged. "I couldn't possibly comment."

"Have I been... worrying her?"

"Her, me, and Sol."

"Huh."

Rikolta paused at a point where two roads met. Bicycles, caravans, and handcarts flowed across our path. He stared for a moment before turning to me. "She was concerned about the virus stuff."

"The Telegram Flu? That's long gone."

"No. The other one."

"Ah. Yes, that one. I'm doing my best to keep it under control."

"Mm." Rikolta turned back to the traffic, studying it intently. "You ever consider that you might be making your condition worse by constantly worrying about a fictional virus?"

"It's not *exactly* fictional. I grew up in a culture that considers certain groups to be less worthwhile than others. It's hard to break free of that."

"Mhm. And I'm not saying you should stop worrying about that it's just... you know anything about Hierarkkinen? It's a faith they have over in Sydän. They have this concept of original sin. They believe everyone is born with this... corruption, I suppose. The way you talk about the Oro Virus made me think about that. Ven mentioned the same thing."

"You think my commitment to being a better person is akin to original sin?"

"I think it's sad that you don't trust yourself to live well, given you might be making your health worse by fixating on how fucked up the systems you grew up in were. Come on, I spot a gap in the traffic."

I tried to think about what Rikolta had said after we'd dodged through Shai's traffic, and I'd filled Rikolta in on my background. I wasn't even sure when I'd started referring to the Oro Virus as such. The idea had been with me for a while. Besides, when we located the Obsid University Cavalcade parked up in the courtyard of the Akoma Technical College, I decided I should be focusing on the mechanics of my manifestation. That meant finding the library.

The cavalcade was quiet, which meant there were few opportunities to ask for directions, that was until Rikolta spotted Graco. He called her name before I'd even spotted her. She was back wearing her grey trouser suit, black shirt, and blue tie, rather than her football gear. She'd added accessories, however. Two gold collar studs. Very slick.

Graco cocked her head, then sauntered over, tapping her cane across the cobblestones. "Rikolta?"

"Yeah. Got Laceco here too."

"Always a pleasure. Can I help you?"

"No," I said.

"Yes," said Rikolta at the same time.

Graco smiled. "Curious."

My cheeks warmed, "Sorry, it's just after what you said about... you know."

Graco tapped her cane against the cobbles, narrowly missing a splat of bird droppings. "I do not."

Rikolta took a step towards Graco. "Laceco is looking into resolving his manifestation."

Graco started and rounded on me. She grinned and her fingertips drummed on her cane. "Another manifestation? How exciting. Tell me all about it, what six is the Wild Magic getting up to this time?"

"I thought..." I said, frowning, "never mind. You remember I told you I fall apart if I'm too tired?"

Graco nodded, slowly. "I don't remember that, no. Curious. There's something squirrely going on. Come on, I want to check on something." She strode off, rolling her cane back and forth across her path.

"Where are we going?" I asked, trying to keep up.

"The library!" Graco said, delight warming her voice.

"Sure," said Rikolta, "but can you slow down a little?"

"There's no time to be slow!" Graco said, "Not when science is at stake! I also need coffee."

Someone tapped me on the shoulder. I found a small girl in dungarees staring up at me, holding out a piece of paper. She stared at me. I took the piece of paper. She nodded and wandered off. "Who gave this to you?" I called after her. She shrugged.

The piece of paper was blank. I turned it over. Block capitals lined the other side from edge to edge: 'LEAVE IT ALONE. DROP THE INVESTIGATION. DROP IT. DROP. IT.'

I scratched my chin. "Huh."

Rikolta and Graco were still striding away. Rikolta glanced back at me, and held out a hand, palm towards me. I nodded. He nodded, and turned back to Graco.

I searched about for a bench, but I didn't find one. Eventually, I gave up and sat on the cobbles in the shade of a caravan. Something was going on with Graco, and I'd promised not to get drawn into another manifestation. I couldn't think particularly clearly, and my bum quickly grew numb from sitting on the cobbles. I needed to find somewhere... were Obsid's university caravans here by themselves or were the students and faculty here as well? The courtyard had been pretty full... I hauled myself to my feet and took in the caravans. The taller, grander caravans were at the far end of the courtyard. What had I been sitting next to? Looked like a pretty ordinary two-story dwelling. What had Graco's caravan looked like?

My feet dragged as I checked the nearby clusters of caravans. After maybe ten minutes I found Graco's caravan and knocked on the door.

Kay, Graco's wife opened the door. "Hello," she said. "Are you okay? Need any help?"

I nodded. She waved me in and I collapsed into a chair. The room was about the size of mine, but it looked as if it had been set up as a living space rather than an all-in-one. Plants lined every available surface, except in the small kitchenette, where a pot of coffee was steaming. There must be a bedroom upstairs – not uncommon for families.

"Do you need anything?" Kay asked. "I think we've met, but I don't remember your name, I'm sorry."

"Just to sit for a little while," I said. "Sorry, it's been a lot."

Footsteps clattered against floorboards – a curtain sectioning off one wall was swept aside. Graco strode through – a set of stairs only briefly visible behind her before the curtain swished back.

"What's been a lot?" asked Graco. "Is that Laceco?"

I stared. Graco wore a buttoned down shirt, tucked into flowing black trousers. Her hair had been tied back into a little stub of a ponytail. She'd been wearing a suit earlier... and her football kit before that.

"Graco," I croaked. "Did you play football today?"

Graco laughed, "No, I've been trying to focus on what's important. I was doing too many things at once, you know? Neglecting my relationship with *someone*. She wrapped Kay up in her arms and kissed her slowly. Her eyes closed, her fingers teased down Kay's shoulders.

"Ah," I said. "Good, good, good." I closed my eyes. Graco was definitely in the grip of a manifestation.

Chapter Sixteen

I wasn't able to stay with Graco and Kay long. Two manifestations to deal with at once, a new city and a complete lack of Vens added up to a hurricane in my head – thoughts I couldn't keep a grip on. Feelings that rose, jumped at me, and then fled. Fatigue seeped from my bones. Kay had left to find someone who could ferry me back home, which I'd be grateful for as long as I lived.

Graco was feeding birds at her windowsill as I left – three flurries of feathers, darting in for sunflower seeds and then flitting back. She wore a faint smile, her hands moving in easy, flowing arcs. I didn't think I'd ever seen her so relaxed. I left a message with her in case Rikolta had the same idea that had graced me. I didn't want the chap to worry about where I was, but I couldn't exactly track him down. It was… everything was too…

I fell apart as soon as I fell into bed, and sleep followed soon after. I woke up sometime after sundown and pulled myself together for just long enough to stand, drink some water, grab some rice cakes from a cupboard, devour them and collapse back into bed. I slept, and dreamt of being so tired I physically couldn't move. Given the day I'd just had, this felt a little cruel on the part of my subconscious.

Next morning, Jans came to see me, resulting in the only conversation I'd had with Jans when no-one else was in the room. They said Rikolta had things to take care of on that particular Thursday, but he'd looked into wild magic in the library and had some thoughts. Jans, looking a little uncomfortable, asked if I needed anything. I pulled myself together from the waist up, just enough so I could sit up in bed without alarming them. I said I was fine, and thanked them. I just needed rest.

I gave the strange 'DROP THE INVESTIGATION' note to Jans, asking if they could pass it on to Rikolta when they next saw him. Jans nodded, but seemed hesitant to leave.

"Really, Jans, I'm fine," I said. "This happens. I just need to sleep. Take care of myself better, you know how it is."

Jans shook their head, "Not that. Not exactly that. Not *only* that, anyway. Er... Have you and Ven talked about polycules any?"

"Er..." the wall of fog in my head was impenetrable. "Some, yes."

Jans's shoulders drifted down, "Oh, good. Okay, well good luck with all that. There are a few Embers who are having a rough time right now – can I stick your name on the list? It'll mean you'll get food deliveries and such."

I badly wanted to say no, but I only had so many rice cakes. I couldn't say the word, but I nodded. Jans smiled, which was possibly the first time I'd seen that, and left. I slept again, only to be woken by my bladder. That was, essentially, the rest of my day. At some point someone dropped some food round and filled up my water jugs, but I couldn't retain any information about who they were. I slept, too tired even for boredom. Darkness rose and fell inside, then outside, then possibly inside and outside a few more times, it was hard to tell.

***

"Laceco."

"Mm?"

"It's Rikolta."

"Oh. Good."

"How are you doing?"

"Not great."

"Yeah. Want me to come back?"

"No, what's up?"

"Would you like to open your eyes?"

"Mm. Fine."

Sun streamed through a gap in my curtains. Soulful eyes glittered with shimmering silver around the pupil… Rikolta's eyes. I started. "Hi, you're here!"

"I am. Need any help?"

I shook my head, "Someone's been taking care of me. Not even sure what their name is…"

"Don't worry, we've all been there."

I frowned. "I doubt you have, Rik."

He sighed, "I've needed three surgeries on the leg. After two of them, I couldn't walk at all for a month or so. If I fall behind on my self-care, I run the risk of being unable to move because moving is too painful. The pain plus not being able to move leads to a chain reaction of negative effects – emotional, physical, mental, and spiritual."

"Right," I shifted, the dried sweat in the bedclothes making my skin feel scratchy and uncomfortable. "So, what's up?"

"I thought you'd want to hear what I learned at the Obsid library?"

"Oh," I said, "yeah, go on. Let me just..." I looked around for a fresh shirt.

Rikolta stepped back and turned around. "There wasn't much about Wild Magic in general, the library mainly has reference books and Graco mentioned that, as a phenomena it was essentially impossible to study."

"Yeah," I found some clothes that didn't smell as if I'd spent the last few days marinating in them and tugged them on. "It's inconsistent and actively tries to hide itself from anyone not involved. Scientific nightmare."

"Right. But you know what I *did* find a book on?"

"What?"

"The Curse of the Ember Trail."

I shoved my arms into shirt sleeves and turned to face Rikolta, buttoning my shirt up. "No shit? You can turn around now."

Rikolta turned, whistled, and nodded. "So yeah, Curse of the Ember Trail? Surprisingly easy to study it turns out. Get a bunch of people to cross it, follow up with them in a week, a month, a year, a decade and so on. See what ill effects they experienced."

"Yes? And?"

"Well, one subject fell off a tower the day after crossing the trail."

"Right?"

"Everyone else reported no ill effects. Same people who ran the study looked into the history of the curse – turns out it's a rumour that first sprung up in Oro around a century ago. Who can say why?"

I rocked back on my heels. "You're fucking kidding."

"I am not fucking kidding. But this is good news! It means what's happening isn't the result of a curse, it's a manifestation! That means it can be resolved!"

"But the curse... it made so much sense!"

"Mhm. But the manifestations weren't just following you – Graco and my mum's stories… these manifestations are happening all over the place."

"I've encountered one or two more than typical."

"Right! So why is that?"

"Damn." I sat on the edge of my bed. "That's an excellent question. I'm going to have to mull it over."

"What? Why not talk it out now?"

"Graco is also going through a manifestation. And mine has been going for a while now, it's not urgent. Hers… I have no idea how long hers has been running. It might already be accelerating."

Rikolta's grin slumped. "Ah. Bugger."

"Exactly." I found my shoes and tugged them on. "So we need to make sure she's okay."

"You need to rest, Lacci."

"Yes. And I have been, but I won't recover if I'm stressing about Graco vanishing into thin air or splitting herself into hundreds of pieces and never being seen again. Come on, let's argue about it en route."

"En route where?"

"Well, I've seen her doing three distinct things so far. If my hunch is correct, we'll find her in under ten minutes if we just ask after her."

A little over twelve minutes later, we'd been pointed to a Graco's location. She was supposed to be marching towards one of Shai's administrative centres as part of a protest, the context of which flitted past me without leaving a mark.

We found the march on Straat van Gebroke Drome – a wide boulevard of which half had been cordoned off for the march. Around fifty people were striding, waving placards, and chanting about administrative statis. Graco was just about visible among a cluster of activists at the head of the march. She was moving at a significant clip. I'd never be able to catch her. A swift shape darted above her, evidently keeping its eyes on the head of the procession too. Someone must have snacks they were being careless with. But... something niggled at the back of my head. It fled when I reached for it.

Rikolta clapped me on the shoulder. "Don't worry, I'll catch up to her, work out what I can and come back."

I grinned, sheepishly before collapsing onto a nearby bench. I apologised to the person I'd very nearly sat on, closed my eyes and focused on breathing.

"Hello, Laceco," said Graco.

I jumped. She was sitting next to me – the person I'd nearly sat on. "How did you know it was me."

Graco gave me a withering look. "I have *some* sight." There was little colour to her eyes, hair, or lips. Her skin hung from her bones like a sheet thrown over a clothes airer.

"Are you okay, Graco?"

"Better than you, Laceco. I only have so much sight left and I resent having to see this whole..." she traced a circle in the air around my face "...disaster."

My eyes narrowed. "What are you up to, Graco?"

"Oh, you know. Sitting."

I nodded. The other Graco's I'd met had been *focussed*. Time for a gamble. "I got your note."

Graco nodded. "And yet, your investigation persists."

"Technically I was investigating something else when you sent me that note. I'm focussed on your manifestation now, though."

"Don't." She was drawing in shallow breaths, her chest barely moving.

"Do you know what's happening, Graco?"

"Parts of me are being ripped away piece by piece. Joy and sorrow. Gold and silver."

"Do you know why?"

Graco sighed. "Well, that's the secret isn't it?"

"What secret?"

Graco rolled her head back, the bones in her neck cracking and snapping. "Laceco, you need to leave this alone."

"I can't do that, Graco. Your situation looks urgent."

"Your situation looks real fucking serious as well, you twat. Even feeling the way I do now, I can still leave you in the dust." She hauled herself to her feet, and unfolded her white cane. "Think about that, Laceco. Slow. Down."

She walked away, tapping her cane resignedly. I tried to stand, tried to follow her, but I couldn't. I had to watch her agonisingly slow retreat. I couldn't move from the bench, even when Graco turned a corner without a backward glance. I still couldn't move five minutes later. Ten. Twenty. Plenty of time to think, for sure, but in this state thinking was not my strongest skill. I was missing things. Unobservant, illogical, unemotional.

Closing my eyes, I fought for focus. Multiple Gracos, only one of which seemed to know what was happening. The other Gracos – football, university, activist, and homemaker. Three of the four I'd talked to had been focused on one particular aspect of her life, letting everything else fall away. Were they aspects of Graco or was she... not shape-shifting, exactly, but switching focus?

She'd be practicing football at the nets, then she'd shift away from that and become University Graco? Something was wrong with that idea. So much was wrong about this whole situation. I'd promised Ven I wouldn't do exactly this, and I was clearly burning out. I might already be actually burned out, consuming the last of my energy before the flames reduced me to embers and I'd drift, finally free, becoming part of the Ember Trail.

I'd promised Ven, but Graco was in serious trouble. Only people who had manifested could help – Ven, Rikolta and Sol. I didn't know where V and S were. I could ask Rikolta to fetch them when he returned, but that would leave me stuck here with Graco doing goodness knows what.

Ven had trusted me when I'd said I could hold myself together, and I was in the process of breaking that trust. What if I resolved the manifestation and she concluded that she couldn't leave me alone in case I found another manifestation and self-destructed again? I'd effectively be blocking her from her vocation. I'd be denying her self-actualisation, and I'd be denying the world the gift of Ven's voice.

Alternately, she might consider my betrayal of her trust sufficiently serious that she wouldn't want to continue our relationship. That wouldn't be ideal. So, I had to ask the question: Was Graco's manifestation sufficiently serious that I could afford to not help her resolve it as quickly as possible? The Graco I'd met on the bench – Graco Prime, I could call her – had looked lifeless. On a precipice.

"Fffffuuuuuuck."

It would have been nice to fall asleep on the bench, rest a little and then decide what to do with a little more energy. Sadly, despite feeling so tired I was surely half-a-breath away from slipping into a coma, I wasn't sleepy. I contented myself with trying to think until Rikolta returned, which he did – a glimmering beacon amongst the chaos of Straat van Gebroke Drome.

"She didn't remember our chat up at the university," he said, sitting next to me, "She said she'd given up on research work in order to focus on her activism."

I nodded. "That makes four." I then filled him in on my chat with Graco Prime.

"When you say she's in trouble," Rikolta said, "how much trouble, exactly?"

That question fell across my shoulders, driving them down. "That's the thing, it's hard to tell. She might have days left before her manifestation starts getting really serious, or she might have hours. Maybe even minutes. These fucking things are all... what's the word. Unique. Individual? Something like that."

Rikolta nodded. "Okay. Full disclosure: Ven was worried that something like this would happen. Have you noticed the pattern to these manifestations?"

My head slipped to the side – I felt as if I'd fallen down a crack between two cobblestones. "No? What pattern?"

Rikolta grimaced. "It might be nothing. Have you noticed that you just start to recover... you're on an upswing, improving just a little and then another manifestation... manifests?"

"I thought you said I wasn't cursed from crossing the Ember Trail?"

Rikolta shot me a look. "I did, yes. I still think that. What do you think of the pattern?"

I closed my eyes and tried to think. It was like searching a fog-soaked field for one particular patch of dirt. I only managed a few seconds before giving up. "Not sure yet, need to let the idea sit with me. Why don't you think this is evidence of the Curse of the Ember Trail?"

"Because if this pattern *is* a thing, it feels deliberate. Feels as if it's part of your manifestation."

I probed at my top teeth with my tongue. "Huh."

"So, yeah, Ven was worried this might happen. I told her I'd take care of you if it did. You know how she is, if you were deteriorating then she'd have dropped her..."

I waved a hand, "I get you. Thank you, Rikolta."

"My pleasure. I'm essentially getting a crash course in manifestation resolution in case I find self-actualisation in it."

I'd got lost in that sentence about halfway through. I'd ask him to repeat himself later. "All right, so we're not bothering Ven with this. What about Sol? Can you go ask her for help?"

"Yeah. I'm not sure where she is, exactly, but I can find her. Tell you what, I'll find us a transport. Sound good?"

I hadn't understood *any* of that. I splayed my fingers. "Sure."

He returned five minutes later in a coach – the sort aristos used to trundle about in when Oro was in one of its boom periods. I clambered in, and collapsed onto a seat inside.

Rikolta studied the view out of the window. "Graco mentioned a secret?"

"Yeah, but she wouldn't be drawn on what the secret was. There are oddities to this manifestation. Various Gracos have said things that didn't quite fit into the conversation but the bastard of it all is I can't remember exactly what they were. I think she's in pain and she's leaving us clues. She picked a bad time to... wait. Why is this happening now?"

"Sorry?"

"Ven's manifestation was kickstarted by you asking her to move in. Your manifestation happened because... well, you know. Sol's manifestation started because she felt a moment of clarity. So, what kick-started Graco's manifestation? That might help us work out what's up."

"Right. That's a good idea. Hang on, I think we're here. Don't go anywhere."

The carriage trundled to a halt. Rikolta stepped down and it might have been my imagination but he seemed to be treating his prosthetic carefully. He was gone only two minutes before he returned with Sol.

She clambered in, half-way through what sounded like a protracted grumbling session. Her complaints were severed when she saw me. "Bloody hell, Laceco."

"Yeah," said Rikolta, hovering in the carriage doorway. "Where next, gang?"

"Graco's caravan," I said, my voice rasping, "If something happened, Kay might know about it."

Rikolta nodded and asked the driver to take us to the Obsid University Cavalcade.

"Thank you for helping with this, Sol," I said, studying the carriage floor for clues.

"I wasn't gonna fucking say 'no' was I?"

I shrugged. "People do. I asked for help a few times at my old cavalcade. Was a roll of a die."

Sol leant forward. "Yes. But that was there."

I nodded. "And now we're here. Still, thank you."

Sol sat back and folded her arms. "You got it. Just warn me if you're going to fall apart again, it was a little alarming."

"That's fair."

Rikolta and I caught Sol up as we rolled through Shai, safe from the thundering sunshine inside our carriage. People swirled on the pavement outside, following some infinitely complex pattern I could only guess at. I found myself wondering who our driver was. A Shai local or a disability transport Ember? What was their name? Who had looked after me yesterday? They'd not asked for gratitude. Still, I wanted to find them and thank them. Not a fucking hope of that happening anytime soon, however.

The Obsid University Cavalcade was roughly as deserted as it had been on our last visit. Sol said there was some grand festival taking place in the college quads, which her ex-friends had been determined to gate-crash. Our driver stopped practically on Graco's doorstep. We clambered out, and I stumbled around to the driver's box – enclosed on three sides to protect from the equatorial sun. The driver wore linens and stared down at me impassively.

I reached up a hand. "Thank you. My name's Laceco"

She reached down and grasped my hand. "Calis. Happy to help."

Our middle fingers clicked together as we drew our hands back – a traditional Akoman gesture of friendship. She nodded at me, then started working on a three-point-turn.

"Which is Graco's caravan?" asked Sol, staring about.

"This one," said Rikolta. "You coming, Laceco?"

"Yup," I said, walking over, running my hand along a nearby caravan wall for support.

Rikolta knocked, Kay opened the door and raised her eyebrows before inviting us in. It was cramped with the five of us present – Graco was feeding the birds.

"She looks a lot like Graco..." Sol said.

"Mm," said Graco, "there's a reason for that."

"She sounds a lot like Graco too," said Sol.

Graco pivoted to face Sol The Observant "Is this your vocation, by any chance? Do we have a truth seeker in our midst?"

Sol shrugged.

"Sorry to intrude on your day once again, Kay... Graco..." I said, hoping to wrestle control of the conversation away from Sol. "It's just there's a manifestation happening," Graco opened her mouth. "And I know that you're not studying wild magic any more, Graco," I said. Graco closed her mouth and nodded. "But you might be able to help.

We're canvasing people we know... did anything unusual or surprising happen three days ago? Anything you weren't expecting? Just after we arrived in Shai?"

Graco frowned.

Kay looked at her wife. "Can you think of anything?"

Graco shook her head.

"Anything big or small," I said, "we've already got some pretty trivial answers, we're just working on the puzzle from every angle we can."

Kay nodded, and then snapped her fingers. "I remember! We met up with Molip."

Graco turned back to her birds and started refilling their seed tray. "Was that three days ago?"

"Yes, you must remember, She told us she was pregnant. Very exciting for her. Presumably."

Rikolta cackled, I smiled. Graco didn't seem to have heard Kay.

"Are you two planning on having children?" Sol asked. I fought back the urge to gasp and surreptitiously kick her in the shins.

Thankfully, Kay laughed. "No, no, no. No. No, no. Not our sort of thing."

Graco finished fiddling with the bird feeder and felt her way over to Kay. She reached out a hand. Kay took it and squeezed. Graco's smile was radiant. "Kay's never been sure she'd cope and I've only *just* managed to focus in on what's important in life, you know? And having a kid sounds a lot like splitting my attention off again. I've got to *focus* whilst we're both three. If I can focus then hopefully I can pursue the secret."

My head snapped up. "What secret?"

"Mm?" said Graco.

"You mentioned a secret before, what secret are you talking about?"

Kay laughed, although her voice sounded as if it were coming from a decent distance, "Oh, you know, the secret never to be told."

Rikolta, Sol and I exchanged looks. I shrugged.

Rikolta leant forward, "Graco... before you focussed on your relationship with Kay, what were you spending all your time doing?"

"Er..." said Graco. She rested her bottom lip between her teeth for a moment. "I can't really remember."

Kay frowned, but her face cleared almost immediately, "Oh, you were up to lots of things weren't you, bab? You had your activism, university research, creative projects, football, and you were working on plans to spruce up your brother's shrine when we got back to Shai."

"I'm sorry for your loss," I said, automatically.

"Where's the shrine?" Rikolta asked.

Graco took a moment to think about the question. "The Shrine to the Sparrow Spirits... I think. Somewhere near the top? Or maybe just over the northern crest?"

Crap. I wouldn't be able to climb that far. "Is there anything else Graco used to do whilst she was in Shai?" I asked Kay.

"Ah, now, that's an excellent, yet entirely misguided, question," Kay said, raising a finger. She then stopped and stared at her finger. "What was I saying?"

"About whether Graco used to do other things whilst in Shai..." I prompted.

Kay frowned. "I don't think so. Did you, my love?"

Graco was staring around the room as if she'd never seen it before. She turned, bumping into the bird cage. The trio of songbirds screamed in protest.

"Sorry," said Kay, "I think we have to get them settled down. Can we get together some other time? Dinner or something?"

"Sounds great," said Rikolta.

"Sorry to have intruded," I said.

"Not that sorry, though," said Sol. I glared at her. She ignored me.

Sol helped me back into Calis' carriage.

"Where to?" boomed Calis.

Rikolta turned to us. Sol turned to me.

"Er..." I said, "Can we drop you, Sol, at the Sparrow Shrine and you try and track down the Graco there? Rikolta and I will work on the bigger picture?"

Sol sighed and nodded. "I knew I should have stayed in bed this morning."

"Hear that, Callis?" Rikolta called.

"I got it, we're all going to Sol's bed" said our driver.

"Make me dinner first, Callis, for spirits' sake," said Sol.

Callis winked, and waited for Rikolta to shut the door before setting off.

***

We dropped Sol off at the Sparrow Shrine. As we drove away, Sol was still standing, staring up at the thousand steps that led to the summit of the shrine, hands on her hips.

"Thank you for your help with this, Sol." I said.

"I doubt she can hear you," said Rikolta.

I shrugged. "So, have you had any thoughts? Thanks for getting Calis on board, by the way, it's definitely helping."

Rikolta nodded. "You got it. So... there's a lot going on, right? I don't know Graco *that* well but everything feels quite scattershot. Is that normal for a manifestation?"

I had to close my eyes, "It depends. Yours was very specific – almost a ritual. Same elements every time. And Graco's is definitely more complex than that but that doesn't mean it's random. What did you get from Activist Graco?"

"She was crying. Marching and crying. The others at the head of the procession were initiating cheers, talking to passers-by, but Graco was crying."

I'd been thinking about opening my eyes. I kept them shut. "Not what I expected."

"Same. She seemed happy enough with Kay and when we were researching stuff."

I raised three fingers. "She was having a grand old time playing football. She was annoyed that I was interrupting it." I raised a fourth finger.

"So her crying is significant?"

"Maybe. I talked to her in the middle of a meeting with her activists friends a ways back and she didn't seem particularly upset, exactly... Let's leave that for a moment."

"What about Kay? She seemed confused."

I nodded. "Confused is right. Affected by the manifestation as well, probably."

"Sure, but when you asked about the secret..."

"'The secret never to be told,'" I said. "Yeah, I noticed that."

Rikolta settled himself after the carriage pitched around a corner. "'Never to be told' sounds damned specific to me. That's not something you just drop into conversation unless you're a scholar of archaic literature."

"So it's a clue?"

"It has to be. Where did you tell Calis to take us to?"

"Only one we haven't checked in on – the one in the art studios."

***

Artist Graco was in the same studio I'd visited her in when investigating Rikolta's magical apples. She was working on a clay structure, shaping, and reshaping it, her hands slick with slurry.

"Graco," I said, "nice to see you. Can I chat with you for a moment? Rikolta is with me."

"Absolutely," said Graco, her smile wide, "but try not to ask me anything too complicated, I'm in a bit of a flow right now."

"I see. You're focussing on your art, right now?"

Graco nodded, "Exactly. I was splitting my attention too much."

I frowned. "What does that mean? I don't understand."

Graco's smile widened. "I did ask you to not ask me complex questions..."

I met Rikolta's gaze. "Sorry," I said. "Are you enjoying working on this project?"

Graco twirled a finger across the clay, leaving a spiral pattern in its surface. "Absolutely! I can't believe I let myself get so distracted. Pure creation – nothing quite like it. The only thing that could make it better is a two, could you put one on for me?"

Rikolta's head snapped up. "A what?"

"A brew."

"You said two."

Graco's smile only widened. "No, I didn't."

Memories rose – the Town of Lonely Windows, the spirits, the prophecy. What had it been... "Are you counting? Graco?"

"No, I'm asking you to make me some coffee."

What had been the prophecy? Birds. Something about birds. I strode to the window – another caravan was parked up nearby, blocking most of the view.. but there were two birds perched on its roof, staring at me. Were those contextually significant motherfucking birds?

"Graco," said Rikolta, "what's the secret?"

Graco laughed, her hands digging into the clay. "I can't tell you that, Rikolta."

Why hadn't I written the prophecy down? What had the spirit said... We'd been linked, spirit to spirit, I should be able to remember if I just...

Colour flooded the world, trees rose - pear blossom and shuffling banana trees. People sat and stood about, chatting. Hundreds of them. Antigia stepped lightly in front of me, her skin cala-lilly rich, her eyes twinkling stars. "She'll be counting and you might not notice. Look for the birds. Look for the silver and gold. Remember the rhyme - she'll stop before seven. She won't be able to say seven out loud. You can."

I rocked on my feet, the world solid again, flashes of purple and magenta cascading at the edges of my vision. I'd been there and here at the same time. "Graco," I said, "can you say the number seven?"

Graco laughed again, her hands rending the clay in two, "Of course I can!"

"So will you say it? Say 'seven'."

Graco laughed again, but said nothing.

"What have you got, Laceco?" Rikolta asked.

I pinched the bridge of my nose, exhaled, and then dragged Rikolta out of the studio. I reminded him of the prophecy whilst the wheels in my mind span.

"She's counting," said Rikolta. "She said two in the studio."

"There were two birds watching her through a window."

Rikolta started, as if someone had lit a firework in his brain. "Birds. Yes. One was circling over her during the march. Three with her in the caravan. I'm pretty sure I saw six when I was heading into the library with her. How many birds were with Football Graco?"

"What? I have no idea."

Rikolta sighed. "Right. Okay, so she can't say seven. Six Gracos and a Prime Graco. Is Prime the seventh?"

I shrugged, helplessly. "There's a pattern there and it feels familiar..."

"The numbers? No, I know what you mean, and it's not the numbers themselves. It's something more..." He trailed off, clicking his fingers.

"Something more specific to Graco. She's never exactly struck me as a numbers person. She's into coffee, she's got her various vocations..."

"Yeah, the vocations are important, but I think if we focus on them too much we might be staring intently at the trees and missing the forest entirely."

"Rikolta, have I mentioned how much I appreciate having someone else talk this out with me?"

He frowned at me whilst simultaneously grinning. "Ssh, I've nearly got something... We were talking about her vocations, and her relationship with her wife, and her departed brother... but what else is specific to Graco?"

"Other than the coffee? She does this thing every once in a while where she gets poetic? Quoting old folk rhymes, I think. But that can't... except... poetry... 'the secret never to be told' has a poetic ring to it..."

Rikolta snapped his fingers. "Yes! Exactly! I knew I'd heard it somewhere!"

"Heard what?"

Rikolta grinned.

"One for Sorrow

Two for Joy

Three for girl

Four for boy

Five for Silver

Six for Gold

Seven for a secret never to be told."

"No," I said. "That can't be it, can it?"

Rikolta started counting on his fingers, "Sorrow was the activist, joy the artist. Three for girl – she was focussing on her wife. Five... was there anything silver about Football Graco?"

I screwed my eyes shut, willing myself to remember but all I got back was blankness and the needling pain that signalled the start of a headache.

"Hey," said Rikolta, and I felt his hand take mine. Warm. Welcome. "Relax. You've got this."

I couldn't help but smile. "Silver... I think there was some silver detailing on her football mask. But that might be co-incidence..." had there been anything silver with the other Gracos? University Graco, maybe. Something at her collar... No, it hadn't been silver. Gold. "University Graco had gold collar studs."

Rikolta squeezed my hand and I grinned at him. He looked golden in that moment too, the sunlight streaming through the window granting him a halo. I drew some strength from him before letting him go. He smiled and cracked his knuckles. "So, what's the secret? That's the key."

I nodded, but then stopped. "No... that's one step too far. We've turned over two pages at once. Why is Graco split into seven? She's focussing on all these parts of herself, not wanting to split her attention. What had Kay said about possible triggers for the manifestation?"

"Oh," said Rikolta. "Oh, no."

"What?"

"It's not just any old manifestation. It's *my* manifestation."

Chapter Seventeen

Sol flagged us down on our way to pick up Kay, and was a little confused when Rikolta and I immediately demanded to know how many birds had been near Graco's brother's shrine. Four was the answer. Tick.

We begged for Kay to come with us, reasoning that she'd be pretty vital for the next stage of the plan. The side of Graco devoted to her initially wanted to come with us but it became clear she couldn't leave the caravan, which seemed pretty miserable. Or it would have been if we weren't about to heroically provide her the keys to her manifestation.

"What's going on?" asked Kay as she climbed in to Calis' carriage.

"I'll tell you on the way," I said, pulling free of the fatigue which had been digging its claws into me. "When we came to see you last, we asked if there was anywhere Graco would go to whilst in Shai, and I think you realised that was the wrong question. Instead, we should have asked – is there anywhere Graco specifically *avoids* going to whilst in Shai?"

Kay nodded. "Yes, but I can't say without Graco's permission. It's a whole... there's..."

"Do you know the address?" I asked. "Graco's in trouble."

Kay glanced back at her caravan but her eyes seemed to clear momentarily. She rattled off an address, which Rikolta called up to Calis. Our coach rattled through Shai's streets, weaving through bicycles, stopping for pedestrians, every extended second of the journey agonising. We stopped outside a suburban house, brick walls whitewashed recently, windows shuttered. The front door stood open. Kay led us inside.

Glow globes set into the ceiling let out a feeble teal light – low on fuel, minutes from dying. A characterless hallway, three doors. The first, a tiny kitchen. The second, a cupboard containing two skeletal brooms. The third, a parlour with a single threadbare sofa. On the sofa, her skin lacking all colour, her flesh hanging from her bones, was Graco.

Her eyes flashed when she saw me. "I see you're taking my advice to heart..." but then she saw Kay. Her sarcasm faltered, and fell. She covered her eyes, and sobbed.

Kay rushed to Graco's side – she held her wife's hand and stammered unintelligible questions.

Rikolta, Sol and I stood with Kay, then knelt with Kay so we weren't looming over Graco like an execution squad.

"Graco," I said, "We know why this is happening."

"Good for you."

I sighed. Rikolta took Graco's other hand. "We know what's happening, because I went through something damned similar mere months ago. There are ways, and *ways* of talking about it but... imagine life is a tree. At first, you're climbing the trunk and it's nice and easy but then you have to make a decision – do you seize one particular opportunity - climb out onto this particular branch? Or do you ignore it, and climb higher? Every time you climb higher, you leave branches behind. Every decision you make cuts off possibilities. I think you've been climbing the tree of life for a long time now, and terror has been growing within you about the moment you'd force yourself to make that final decision. Which branch to pick? Sorrow, Joy, Girl, Boy, Silver, or Gold."

Graco's lips moved silently but her hand gripped Kay's tighter.

"You'd been telling us," I said, tears moistening my cheeks, "you'd been telling us all and I didn't spot it. And so you came here – I'm guessing your childhood home? Ghosts in the walls. The one place you'd never go, so we'd never look for you here.

"I'm so sorry, Graco, but you *knew*. You knew the life tree was a lie. At first I thought the secret never to be told was how terrified you were of making that one decision – of committing to one branch and rejecting the other five. But that's not true – look at Rikolta. Since his manifestation he's been trying... what have you been trying, Rikolta?"

"Activism, hydroponics, medicine, mechanics, sex work, and mindfulness meditation," said Rikolta without missing a beat.

"Sol's manifestation forced her to stop, to think. What did you think about, Sol?"

Sol smiled, "About what I'd been denying myself because I thought I'd be made fun of for it. Hobbies, habits. I can try them all now."

Footsteps approaching. A Graco in the parlour doorway. Graco in her football kit. She stepped through and stood, watching. Listening.

"You know this," I said, "and I *know* you know this, but some part of you panicked because the last of your partnered adult friends had a kid. What did that say about you and Kay? Were you stuck in statis? Children who couldn't make a simple decision?"

"No," whispered Graco.

"No!" I echoed, "Fuck that!"

"Fuck that," said Activist Graco from the doorway.

Rikolta stood, fire in his voice, "Life isn't a race, you're not pruning some spirits-cursed tree. If you want to devote yourself to six things then devote yourself to those six things!"

Sol brushed a finger against the beads of her solitary glass necklace. "I wish I had six things I was so passionate about that I'd split myself into parts so I could do all of them simultaneously."

Tears streamed down Kay's face "I'm so sorry. I'm so sorry that you were torn up about this and I didn't notice."

Gracos rushed forward, embracing their wife.

"I'm sorry I couldn't tell you," they said. There was a moment of stillness, before the Gracos contracted. They drew inwards. Reality inhaling for one long, eye-twisting moment. One Graco remained. She sat upright on the sofa, and threw her arms around her wife.

"I love you," said Graco.

"I love you, you twat," said Kay.

I sighed, feeling my shoulders relax. My vision swam. I couldn't ruin Graco's breakthrough. I staggered from the room, before leaning on the nearest wall, fighting the encroaching Darkness.

"Hey, Laceco," said Rikolta. "Breathe."

He caught me as I fell.

Epilogue: Laceco

"How do you think that went?" asked Rikolta, sat on the edge of my bed.

"Pretty good," I said. I was lying in higgledy-piggledy pieces on top of my bedsheet. "All things considered."

"I really wish there was a way I could help you with this," Rikolta's gaze tiptoed across me. He reached out and took my hand.

Peace flooded in through my fingers. "Just being here with me is plenty."

"Does it hurt?"

I tried to shake my head, but only succeeded in shifting a little.

"What are you trying to do, Laceco?"

"Shake my head."

Rikolta chuckled. "Here." He slipped a hand between my cheek and the bedsheet, then clasped my other cheek with his free hand. He lifted my head up to level with his face, then gently turned me left and right. "Head shaken."

My cheeks burned. Were his hands warm or...

"Laceco..."

"Yes?"

"Did I ever tell you I think you're amazing?"

"Amazing? You put a good half of Graco's manifestation together."

"Yes, but I already know I'm amazing."

He shifted me, balancing me with surety. His lips were so close. That thought was strange. I couldn't think why through the fog. I could still feel... "Rikolta?"

"Yes?"

"Will you kiss me if I ask nicely?"

He leant in and his lips brushed mine. Soft, playful. I closed my eyes and gave myself to the moment.

***

Rikolta helped me pull back together, and once I *was* together... Rikolta didn't have some of the same assets I was used to dealing with. He'd be considered mentally ill or deluded back in Oro. Here, he was Rikolta, and he was amazing. We held each other, talking about Graco. Talking about what we'd accomplished. It was perfect, until Ven opened the door. She stared, turned, and slammed the door as she left.

Rikolta leaped to his feet. "Stay there. I'll talk to her." He dashed out. I tried to rise, but felt my limbs wanting to separate again at the mere threat of movement. I sighed and settled back, letting myself drift.

I had no idea how long I was alone for, but when the door opened next, Ven was there. She strode into the room and sat on the edge of my bed, right where Rikolta had been mere hours ago.

"I'm sorry," I said. "I don't know... I don't really understand this stuff. It was a betrayal and I'm sorry..."

Ven scratched her temple, leaving a ragged red line on her skin. "Laceco, I don't mind that you and Rikolta got busy. I know you didn't plan to. I'm not angry about that. It was a surprise but... mostly what I saw was my paramour and my paramour clearly enjoying this quiet moment of... well anyway, *I* wasn't there. You didn't need me. I hadn't been there for you. I should have been." Her shoulders shook.

"Ven... *I'm* sorry. I promised you I wouldn't let this happen."

"Ah, yes." Ven swept a sleeve across her face, still deliberately facing away from me, "you should have let Graco fade into nothing, and very possibly die, because you promised you'd look after yourself. I remember. Very important. I should never have made you promise that stupid bullshit."

I stretched out a hand but couldn't quite reach her. I closed my eyes. "Ven, no. It wasn't bullshit. You were right."

Ven rounded on me. "Did you miss my exemplary sarcasm just now?"

"No... I just..."

Her expression melted. She traced a finger across my cheek, before kicking off her shoes and lying down, facing me. She reached out a hand. I took her hand.

Her gaze was the only thing in the room that wasn't still. Something in her was still thrashing.

"I need to slow down, don't I?" I said, my voice breaking.

The fire in Ven's eyes settled a little. "For a while. Hopefully not forever, but yes. I think you need to slow down."

"I'm the only one who sees them, V. The wild magic keeps drawing me back in..."

Ven sighed. "Laceco, when you fled to the mountains, what did you do?"

"Nothing."

"Oh, so you *found* that shack, the fire pit, the moonshine still and all the other gubbins I saw there?"

"Well, no, I made those..."

"Right. So... since being discharged from hospital, have you had a day – one, single day – when you've not been either busy working on something, or in recovery from all the things you've been working on?"

"But the wild magic drew you to me. It wouldn't let me rest."

"The Wild Magic brought you to the Ember Cavalcade. You could have rested there... and you had someone who could have worked on the manifestations in your place. You had me. And I'm sorry I didn't see that in time, but you have *so* many people who can work on the manifestations now. It doesn't always have to be you. You've done enough. Slow down. Rest. Please."

She shifted, withdrawing from the bed. Her sudden absence felt like frostbite – I wanted to scream. She padded to the door. My mouth moved, my mind raced, trying to think of the words that could persuade her to stay. She opened the door and fished about in her pocket. She drew out a piece of paper and crumpled it into a ball. She threw it.

"Ow," said Rikolta.

Ven jerked her head, then padded back to my bedside. "'scuse me," she said. She clambered onto my bed, stepped over me, and settled down on the far side, sandwiched in between me and the wall. Moments later, Rikolta followed, slipping into the bed next to me. Both of them turned to face me, both rested an arm on my chest. Their fingers danced playfully, meeting and parting.

"We're going to have to have The Conversation about this," said Rikolta, his fingers sending sparks through me in harmony with the sparks from Ven's dance.

"Yay," said Ven, "relationship admin."

I laughed, and the laugh spread to them. I sighed, and closed my eyes. A hand brushed my hip. A soft kiss brushed my lips. Slowly, slowly, I let the pace of my breathing decrease. Slowly, slowly, I let my breath match pace with theirs. I reached out, drawing them closer. I breathed, and, in that moment, I knew that everything was going to be alright.

Printed in Great Britain
by Amazon

58690890R00139